-ROM

ESCAPE!

By the same author

Burning Moon (with Ed O'Leary)

ESCAPE!

ARON SPILKIN

NAL BOOKS
NEW AMERICAN LIBRARY
TIMES MIRROR
NEW YORK AND SCARBOROUGH, ONTARIO

NAL BOOKS TRADEMARK REG. U.S. PAT. OFF. AND FOREIGN COUNTRIES
REGISTERED TRADEMARK—MARCA REGISTRADA
HECHO EN HARRISONBURG, VA., U.S.A.

SIGNET, SIGNET CLASSICS, MENTOR, PLUME, MERIDIAN and NAL BOOKS are published *in the United States* by The New American Library, Inc., 1633 Broadway, New York, New York 10019, *in Canada* by The New American Library of Canada Limited, 81 Mack Avenue, Scarborough, Ontario M1L 1M8

LIBRARY OF CONGRESS CATALOGING IN PUBLICATION DATA

Spilken, Aron, 1939-
    Escape!

    I. Title.
PS3569.P54E7   1983   813'.54   82-22576
ISBN 0-453-00433-4 (pbk.)

Designed by Sherry Brown

First Printing, June, 1983

1 2 3 4 5 6 7 8 9

PRINTED IN THE UNITED STATES OF AMERICA

Publisher's Note

The events and individuals described by Aron Spilken in *Escape!* are real and are factually accurate as a composite based upon extensive interviews with the participants. The real names of the survivors have been replaced with fictitious names.

This book is dedicated to peace in Central America

ACKNOWLEDGMENTS

This is a complex story and it could not have been told in such detail without the generous help of many individuals. Those who contributed to the basic structure included Bob Lough and Oscar Miranda, homicide detectives; Hector Ochoa and Jerry Scott, border-patrol agents; Dr. Joseph Halka, chief medical examiner of Pima County; Carolyn Cowan, records supervisor at the sheriff's department; Father Maurice Roy; and Paul Thompson, chief of Visitor Protection at Organ Pipe Cactus National Monument. Rick Gonzales and Mary Lou Harris, lawyers for the Salvadorans, provided background detail and endless logistical support. Gary MacEoin clarified the lessons of Salvadoran history. Sensitive help with translation was provided by Sal Aguirre, Nardi Ramírez, Anna Mercedes, Estuardo Asturias, and Carol Romeo. Much effort was contributed to the preparation of the manuscript by three friends who are skillful critics because they are excellent writers: Terry Kime, Ann Marie Yezzi, and Stan Koehler. Among the many others who also supported this project are Shoshana Ravivi, Father Robert Drinan, Judy Hillison, Rachael García, Norma Aguirre, Barbara and Martha Ruske, Jo-Anne Rosen, Grace Mateu, Ron Saver, Jen and Kurt Kitselman, Gioconda Barillas, Ed O'Leary, my mother and father, and of course, the Salvadorans, who were so enthusiastic and alive that it was a pleasure to work with them.

CONTENTS

ESCAPE!

PREFACE

The great heat wave of 1980 was terrible. Newspapers throughout the land followed its impact on the front page. By Thursday, July 3, it was into its tenth day and had already claimed 119 lives. In Stilwell, Oklahoma, 450,000 chickens scorched to death in a hen house a few minutes after the fans failed. Dallas, Texas, had already endured the longest, hottest period of any major American city in history. And in central Arkansas, the pavement repeatedly blew up. "It sounds like a stick of dynamite," a newspaper reported. They didn't tell us that the heat was building toward a spectacular climax.

It wasn't until Monday, July 7 (the heat and the fatalities still running high), that the story broke about the Salvadorans. ILLEGAL ALIENS DESERT HORROR the front page of the *San Francisco Chronicle* said. "The survivors were stuck by every cactus known in the desert. They had been drinking their urine, after-shave lotion, and even deodorant."

A large number had died, and the rest were barely alive. The women reported rapes and robberies. They said they had been lost, abandoned by their guides, but they refused to give information against them. Quickly scanning the article, I felt that this was just one more tale of pain in a world already drowning in senseless suffering. I decided not to read the story. I turned instead to news I was already involved with: the Russians had invaded Afghanistan and we were boycotting the Summer Olympics; and on the 246th day of captivity the Iranian students announced they had just moved the hiding place of their American hostages.

The Salvadoran story continued on the front page for most

1

of the week. I ignored it. By Thursday it had slipped to page two (the Soviets were busy shelling primitive bands of Afghan rebels), and by Friday, to page four. But on Sunday there it was again, with several pictures. I couldn't understand why they got all that coverage. Because of my head-in-the-sand attitude I was not able to appreciate the tremendous interest they had aroused around the world, until the following year.

In the spring of 1981 an old friend called and urged me to send my recently published novel to someone in Arizona. A woman she knew in Tucson told her the Salvadorans were seeking an offer to tell their complete story. (They had tried to avoid publicity at the time of their arrest and had never released most of the details to the newspapers or corrected the erroneous reports.) My novel, *Burning Moon*, was the story of two middle-class San Francisco women who decided to rob a resort and hike out at night across the Teton Mountains. I saw no connection with the Salvadorans and their troubles. And I didn't want to write about people who had experienced nothing but despair and death.

But my friend was persuasive. First of all, she said, the Salvadorans were mostly ordinary middle-class people, like the ones I wrote about. Even though *Burning Moon* had been about mountains and snow, and the Salvadorans had crossed the desert, both were about city people involved in wilderness odysseys; the theme needed a similar understanding. And there was a great deal more to these people and their experience than just despair. Not only had they shown courage and endured, but they were some of the sweetest and most lively people imaginable. Finally, above all, they deserved sensitive treatment from a writer who would not be inclined to sensationalize their suffering. With many doubts I sent off my book and a brief note, and so came to know Mary Lou Harris.

I've met many people who had some of her strengths, but no one who had them all together. She is an idealistic young lawyer who worked for the Tucson Legal Aid office, representing the Salvadorans in immigration matters. A tall woman with dark blond hair and hazel eyes, who had once sung in nightclubs, she is one of those eloquent speakers who can pull every fact from memory the instant it is needed. She is also fiercely protective. She fought a prolonged battle on many fronts to guard the Salvadorans. When they needed shelter, she brought several of them to live in her home, fed and clothed them, and ferried them about the city to meet their needs. They arrived here indigent and politically at risk, and vulnerable to continued press sensationalism. Mary Lou recognized the need to present their experiences as a collective work. So she set about learning everything necessary to make it possible for them to put it in book form and get it published. *Burning Moon* arrived in her mail at nine in the morning. By eleven o'clock she had finished reading it and was on the phone asking me to take the assignment. When I said I still had doubts, she insisted I fly to Tucson to meet some of the Salvadorans. "Their story is an epic," she assured me. "It covers everything, the full range of feeling, a dangerous journey, triumph, and tragedy. Come and see. There is no way you can avoid being fascinated." She was right, and it is due to her inspiration and tenacity that this book exists.

It was inevitable that while writing their story, I should also learn about their homeland. I had already traveled a number of times in Guatemala and Mexico, but all I knew about El Salvador was that horrible things were happening there. As Mary Lou put me in contact with various experts on Central American history and politics, I began to see that the stories of these people had much broader implications than I first suspected. The forces that caused this group of more than forty to flee their homes and seek haven in the United States are operating throughout the world and shaping our age. The specifics may be particular to each region (as the assassination of their beloved archbishop was uniquely their own), but the struggles over land and diminishing resources, and the interplay of the great powers, are universal.

One of the luxuries of this kind of work is the amount of travel that can be justified for the sake of gathering authentic detail. Naturally I visited the survivors, most of them a number of times, not only to hear their stories but also to get to know them. They were scattered in the areas around Tucson, Los Angeles, and San Francisco, and were, as Mary Lou and her friend had predicted, fascinating people. I was also determined to duplicate their trip by bus from San Salvador to the U.S. border, gathering notes for the book. I ignored friends who warned me not to go, but when the Salvadorans themselves told me I was crazy, I realized it was a senseless risk. Instead, I booked a flight to Guatamala, the next country to the north. On the day I went to pick up my tickets, I read in the paper that rebel activity had increased alarmingly. The road I needed to travel to Mexico had just been blown up, and I would arrive in the midst of Guatamalan national elections, a traditional time of bloodshed. I changed my flight to the southern border of Mexico and was content to ride north from that point, giving up only one day of their five-day trip.

I also talked intensively with both the homicide investigators working on the case, and the primary border-patrol officers. Several friends who were kind enough to read portions of the manuscript critically remarked that the border patrol, as described, seemed a bit too good to be true. Actually, I had gone to their office in the town of Why, informed by a recent movie, expecting the worst. People who did such work must be harsh and insensitive, it seemed, and it would be interesting to describe them in contrast to the Salvadorans. What I found instead were public-spirited people with a difficult job. Hector Ochoa and Jerry Scott each generously allowed the recording of hours of highly detailed interviews, and it is difficult to imagine that they could have seriously distorted their stories and still agreed so closely with each other. In addition, there were the accounts of the Salvadorans to check them against, and the Salvadorans are still grateful for the treatment they received. Of course, it is impossible to generalize about the border patrol as a whole from such limited experience, but certainly the desperate energy that this office invested in saving the Salvadorans' lives could only have come from a certain nobility of spirit.

While it's gratifying that this story speaks well of our

officials, it's unfortunate that it shows the desert in such an ugly light. *Time* magazine called it "an infernal place of Gila monsters, scorching earth, mesquite and giant cactus," and in the Salvadorans' eyes, it was truly hideous. But the area is also a magnificent example of a particular type of wilderness, set aside precisely because of its beauty. If one goes there prepared for the conditions (and that is the only sane way to go there), the unique vegetation, topography, and solitude offer a fine experience.

There is great peace in the desert. It provides space for all the senses. There is a quiet of magnificent depth—not the smothered silence of soundproofing, but a vast, natural, receding stillness that is given perspective by the occasional glints of distant birdcalls and insects. The air is beautifully clear, with only the faintest and most pastel of scent colorings. The eye can stretch to infinity. And even the mind is eased by the emptiness.

1
THE END

Bursting rockets tinted the upturned faces in patriotic colors. It was the Fourth of July, 1980, in the small Arizona town of Ajo. The evening was hot. A heat wave had been running for a week, and it was still building. This was the summer slump for the border patrol: no one with any sense went into the desert in July. So Agents Hector Ochoa and John Rockhill had a few minutes to watch the fireworks.

They stood with the rest of the town in the traditional place, the field next to the high school. They kept close to their patrol car. The explosions were coming faster and the sighs were louder when the call came. Three aliens were stranded on the highway near milepost 65. The agents went to bring them in.

They climbed into their sedan and headed rapidly southeast. It was a sudden shift from the bright lights and noise to the black silence of the desert. They drove eleven miles to the tiny town of Why, whizzed through, and angled south. From here the Mexican border lay only twenty-eight miles ahead. A few miles out of town they entered Organ Pipe Cactus National Monument. The barren expanse of desert park hid several major routes for smuggling aliens and drugs into the United States. About six miles farther they saw the men.

They appeared in the headlights like three generations of disaster: an old man, a middle-aged man, and a young one. They were filthy and scabbed with dry blood. As the officers advanced, the men raised their hands for a weapons search

7

with a submission that showed total exhaustion. They seemed not to care that there were cactus thorns in their flesh.

"Where're you from?" Ochoa asked in Spanish.

"Mexico," answered the younger two. "Sonoita," specified the old man, referring to the nearest town across the border.

"What do you think?" Rockhill asked in English.

"The old man is Mexican," Ochoa replied, "but not the other two." He shifted his concentration to them. "How did you get here?"

"We took the bus." The voice was hoarse and weary. They had asked to be let out because they were afraid of running into a checkpoint if they went much farther.

"I wonder what bus made them look like that," Rockhill muttered.

Ochoa continued to question them. The answers were groping, but he concentrated mostly on the underlying information: accent and regional vocabulary, clothing (what was left of it), hairstyle, and facial characteristics.

"I think they're Salvadorans," he said to Rockhill. "The local man must be their guide. But he wouldn't come this far just for two of them." Ochoa frowned. "And they don't have their *triques*." He used the old Spanish slang for personal belongings. "There must be more of them, holding their stuff. What a hell of a time to be out there."

"If they sent the strong ones ahead, the others are in pretty bad shape," Rockhill said. "Where are the rest?" he asked in Spanish.

"No others," the old man protested weakly. "I came up to look for a job."

"With these two?"

"I met them on the road. It was safer to travel together."

"Where are you heading?"

"I'm not sure. I just wanted to work a few weeks, make a little money. I have a family. I have to go back to them."

"Sure." Rockhill nodded.

"Look, *señor*," Ochoa said, "if people are stupid enough to be out there, you know what's going to happen . . ."

"I'm just a worker. I don't know a thing."

"I can't buy it," Ochoa told Rockhill. "You hold them here. I'm going to try and backtrack them."

Rockhill herded the men over until they were sitting against the sedan, their hands clasped behind their heads. Ochoa crept off the road with a flashlight, studying the ground. He walked back and forth, then he squatted, and finally he went down on his hands and knees, looking for signs. He was careful about rattlesnakes. They couldn't survive the daytime heat, so they waited for night to come out and hunt. The Sonoran desert rivals Death Valley as the hottest, driest place on the continent. Air temperature in the summer is sometimes over 120 degrees, and the ground surface can approach 200 degrees.

There was no way Ochoa could backtrack them by flashlight. The indications were too subtle to read. He stood up and squinted into the dark, hoping to see a fire or hear a sound. Not one car had passed since they left Why. And only silence came from the darkness ahead.

"Hey!" Rockhill yelled. "We'd better get them to the hospital." The old Mexican had fallen over, his eyes fluttering, his limbs twitching in weak spasms. The two Salvadorans watched, horrified.

They loaded the three as quickly as they could, turned back toward Ajo, and floored it. "Jesus," fretted Ochoa, "and these are the strong ones." It was unsettling that the guide was so bad off. Survival in the desert depends on knowledge more than any other factor, and the old man was the only one who had it. Something was seriously wrong for him to be in this shape, and Ochoa wished he knew what it was.

They reversed their way through the microcommunity of Why again; a few cottages and shacks on the right, some abandoned; a gas station at the fork in the road; and then the trailer park that held their regional office in an oversized trailer at the back. But they didn't stop, because the nearest hospital was in Ajo.

Until recently Why had been called "the Y," because of the fork in the road. A small community had formed, mainly because it was a slight snag in an otherwise featureless desert.

A few drifting souls had caught there, as haphazardly as lint. When a post office finally opened, it complained that it didn't like one-letter names, so the town obligingly started calling itself Why.

Ochoa kept checking the old man. He looked worse. In spite of what he said, he had to be a guide. There was almost no other reason why Salvadorans would be crossing with a local Mexican. And it was easy enough to arrange. An alien could walk into any border town, even Sonoita, which was out in the desert in the middle of nowhere, and find a professional in a few minutes. They waited in the bus stations, or the nearest bars, or walked up to strangers wandering around. They generally had up-to-date information from the grapevine on where the border patrol was concentrating its attention lately. And they often had partners on the other side, people who picked them up in an isolated spot and drove them to the nearest big city.

The refugees were glad to pay. The trip was dangerous and they welcomed any help they could get. In many locations along the way they were considered a regular source of income, a particularly vulnerable clientele, an underworld version of the tourist business. Criminals and public officials bled them at every opportunity.

Salvadorans were particularly vulnerable because, as conditions worsened in their country, everyone knew they were desperate to get away. Ochoa had recently talked with three of them who had been stopped in Mexico by police. They had been told they would be released and given a bus ticket out of town if they paid a thousand-peso "fine." A little farther on, they had been stopped again, taken into a checkpoint office, and made to empty their pockets. The chief had studied the pile and told them he was letting them go. He had picked up everything on his way out. Completely broke, they had hitchhiked without eating to the border, where the U.S. border patrol had caught them and shipped them back to El Salvador.

Coming into Ajo, the first thing they saw was the string of lights along the huge ridge of slag that led from the copper mine. The hospital was built on a shelf of rock alongside the pit where it would be ready for mine accidents. By the time they drove into the parking lot the old man was completely uncoordinated. Ochoa picked him up carefully and carried him in. He pushed through the emergency doors, strode urgently down a bright, sanitized hall, and set him on an examining table in front of the registered nurse on night duty.

He told her what he knew as she worked. When she stripped off the man's shirt to administer an intravenous, Ochoa saw the rope burns on his shoulder. "Damn, I knew he was the guide. He's got marks from carrying the water." He pushed in closer. "I want him to tell me about the others."

"Better let me work first," she warned, "or he won't be talking to anybody."

The old man wasn't delirious, but he kept fading in and out like a distant radio station. It was hard to hold his attention. Ochoa questioned him repeatedly but he was unable to learn anything.

Ochoa took his work seriously. If there were people suffering in the desert, it was his responsibility to find them. And now that he was blocked, he found it impossible to escape the worry that he should be doing more, that there was something terrible left undone.

"Hey! More trouble," Rockhill called from the hall where he had been guarding the other two. The young one, a round-faced boy with wild hair, had suddenly slumped to the floor. Nurses hurried over and Ochoa ran back to shout, "You see?" to the tired old man. "You see what I mean?" But the Mexican was too sick to notice.

Like most people who had grown up in that area, Ochoa liked the desert. But experience had convinced him that as a way of death it was one of the worst, one of the slowest forms of violence. And all the time one was forced to face the fact that they were dying. He had been painfully thirsty in the desert himself. There had been moments when his plans had gone wrong and he had to fight down panic. So he knew what anyone still out in the desert was going through. But what could he do? He talked it over with Rockhill. They agreed that the signs and the hunches all said there were more people out there, but they had no idea where. And it was dark. They would just have to leave it for now.

But they couldn't forget. Although their shift didn't end until after two in the morning, by noon the next day they met at the Why office again, ready to try backtracking a second time. But something significant interrupted their plan. As they walked in, they saw that Agents Waterman and Grey had two more Salvadorans in custody.

The gas-station attendant had called their office to report that a suspicious outsider had come in to buy soda. The people of Why were well aware that their village lay across a major smuggling route. They felt vulnerable. Strangers were immediately obvious, and townspeople often called in tips. Several minutes later agents had backtracked the young man to a nearby shack and found the other one hiding there. She was a woman in her late twenties. Now they both sat in the center of a rather bare room in the oversized trailer that the border patrol used for their office. A circle of agents questioned them. In the background the huge air-conditioner rumbled as it struggled unsuccessfully to turn the July air into something comfortable.

Ochoa immediately took over the interrogation. He put a chair directly in front of them and sat down to take a long, careful look before he began.

Salvadorans are a very small people by American standards, as if designed to fit their tiny country. And these two were further shrunken by dehydration, exhaustion, and fear. In the circle of huge agents—most of them well over six feet—the contrast was even more exaggerated. The woman seemed no more than five feet tall, but she was sturdily built in a squared-off way. Her capable, practical-looking face was badly sunburned and her lips were cracked and bloody. And she was frightened. The man was younger-looking, in his mid-twenties, and had the appearance of an athlete. Once he was cleaned up, he would be handsome, with classic Aztec features. He had a small scar over the bridge of his nose. He sat upright and watched them carefully.

Ochoa decided that the woman would be easier, and he concentrated on her. Hector Ochoa also stood out from the uniformed giants around them. He was only medium height, wiry, and slim, with a dark mustache and his hair parted on one side. His face would have looked boyish if it hadn't been so serious.

"How're you feeling?" he asked. "Have you been treated all right?" They nodded uncertainly. "I know you're Salvadorans," he told them. "I know you've crossed the desert from Mexico, and just by looking at you I can tell you've had a tough time." He paused to let them relax. "But you're safe now. No one is going to hurt you, and if you want political asylum, you can ask for it. But the others aren't as lucky as you." As soon as he mentioned "the others," he had a feeling that this wasn't going to work. The woman looked startled.

"Now if *you* want a drink of water, you can go over to that cooler and get one. They can't. It's hot out there. Do you know that this is the hottest day of the year so far? We're talking about 114 in the shade, and there's no shade." But it was no good. It was like poking an animal in its burrow. Each point he made only drove her back. He dreaded asking her straight out, but he didn't know what else to say: "We want to help them. Won't you tell us where they are?"

The woman shrugged, trying to look ignorant but seeming frightened. Ochoa knew he couldn't promise the one thing she wanted to hear: that there would be no deportation after the rescue.

"Look, I know the coyotes said they would get you if you talked." Coyotes were the professional smugglers of aliens. "Or get your families. But this is a different kind of situation here. They won't punish you for saving these lives. And we've got to do something quickly." The sun was now directly over their heads, starting the hottest hours of the day.

She only stared out at him, but he couldn't stop trying. Agents from passing shifts dropped in and leaned their lanky bodies against the walls to listen, to watch him work and make suggestions. Sometimes there were interruptions from phone messages. Other business brought various groupings together, carrying on their regular work along the fringe of his effort. Ochoa finally got up to stretch his legs and take a break with the men on the side. They lowered their voices when they talked.

"Maybe," someone suggested, "these are the last of them. Maybe these are the ones that last night's group was trying to protect."

"I dunno," Ochoa muttered, running a hand through his dark hair. He tallied his reasons. "The Park Service says there are a bunch of new tracks crossing the line at the Aguajita. And they had a guide, and guides like groups. And Salvadorans like groups. And I just feel it in my gut. It's a bugger and it won't go away." At this point he was no longer sure himself why he was so driven, but the pressure he felt was increasing.

He found himself constantly estimating the position of the sun, and each angle brought to mind a number of terrible images. He began to get upset, and he pushed harder. He told her that if she was lying she could be sent right back to El Salvador and handed over to the government. He asked how she thought God would judge what she was doing. He guessed that she would never be forgiven. He grew more agitated, walking up and down and snapping at her in desperation. "Look at yourself. Just look at the shape you're in and imagine how the others are right now. Imagine what they're feeling . . . if they can still feel."

She started wringing her hands so nervously that he knew she was unaware of the gesture.

"Don't you care about them? Don't you?" he demanded. Her head dropped. "Look at me! Why can't you look at me?" he yelled.

And she burst into tears.

Ochoa went immediately to his knee alongside her. "Tell me now, they're out there, aren't they? Tell me!" he demanded. She finally nodded. Yes.

The others, driven back by the force of his long attack, moved closer again. One man brought a fresh cup of water and slid it into her hand, but she was still sobbing and couldn't drink it.

"How many?"

"About fifteen, more or less."

"Oh, no," he muttered. "Women and men?"

"Yes."

"Do you know where?"

She didn't, but then she had been lost. She did have a vague idea about where she had come out.

"This is very important," Ochoa stressed, looking at his watch. "How long has it been since they ran out of water? It's now three o'clock in the afternoon." (My God, he thought, have we been at this for three hours already?)

"No water since yesterday, early in the day," she said.

Ochoa got up immediately and some of the other men were already in motion. They had a bunch of people who had never seen a desert before, lost out there on the hottest day of the year, and they had been without water for more than twenty-four hours. Ochoa's supervisor, Jerry Scott, had the day off. Ochoa called him at home for clearance of the operation. Then he immediately contacted the sheriff's department.

Ochoa drove rapidly south in a border-patrol four-wheel-drive. The tiny Salvadoran woman sat next to him. They were followed by Agent Waterman and a lieutenant from the sheriff's department. And behind them came a detective in an unmarked car.

The woman had been able to explain only that she had crossed a pole line on the way out. Then she reached the highway at a big wash near a sharp hill. From there, she and the man had hitchhiked to Why and hid. That was all.

There was a telephone-pole line in that vicinity, Ochoa knew, but it was forty miles long. Her description was vague, but it suggested the Alamo Wash. A wash is a dry creek bed, and this was a broad depression that passed under the highway, requiring a bridge to cross it. The bridge provided both a landmark and a shelter, and that made it a frequent pickup point for aliens. It was also the same place where he had found the three men the night before. And where earlier other agents had questioned some men who were waiting suspiciously in two parked trucks.

As they sped south through the bright desert, he tried to get the woman to give him more details, hoping the emotional contact they had established through the prolonged questioning would continue. But the connection had broken. As soon as the woman had seen the sheriff's deputies, and the caravan of uniforms, badges, and guns, she changed her story. When they reached Alamo Wash, he asked her if this was the place and she said no. When he asked about the pole line again, she said they hadn't crossed a pole line.

Everyone got out of the vehicles and stood in the dirt by the side of the road while Ochoa, with desperate patience, drew a map of the area on the ground with a stick: the highway running north and south; the pole line running parallel, a mile to the west; and the wash intersecting them both at right angles. "Now, if you came from this side, like you said, you had to cross this pole line to get to the road," he explained. "Earlier you told me you did cross it. Now, where, and in what direction, did you cross?"

"From this side?" she guessed. "Near here?"

"You can't ask me," he explained, "I wasn't there."

"Maybe down more . . . I don't think I crossed the line."

Ochoa turned away. He had no more time to waste. He didn't know why she had lost trust in them, but they would have to do it all themselves now. A rough dirt road ran along the pole line to provide access for service vehicles. "The best thing we can do is head straight for the pole line and then drive down the road, cutting sign." They agreed.

Cutting sign was their term for tracking. In that area tracking was one of the border patrol's most specialized skills. When the sign was prominent, they could cut it from horseback or from a vehicle—or even from an airplane, if the sun were slanting and threw the proper shadows. But if it were vague, they could only follow it on foot, so they could get down close on their hands and knees when it was hard to read.

They all crowded into Ochoa's four-wheel-drive and turned west, cross country. There was a fair amount of vegetation in this desert and they had to zigzag around large cactus and desert shrubs. When they reached the pole line, they headed south on the dirt road, leaning out the windows and scanning the ground on both sides. The road offered an easier surface to read than the desert itself, and they hoped to spot the place where the couple had crossed. Experienced coyotes knew they worked this way and sometimes used brooms made of branches to wipe out their tracks across a road. But the agents didn't think that these people had either the energy or the knowledge to do that.

The sun was low, and tracking was good for the moment. But that also meant that evening was rapidly approaching and, with it, the end to their effectiveness. He toyed with the idea of calling in a plane, but knew he couldn't. The plane would have to fly all the way down from Tucson, 130 miles away, and still save fuel for the return trip. And the desert was big. Unless they knew where to look, it was pointless.

They had gone a good distance and the sun was near the horizon when they drove out of a branch of the wash and saw something in their path. They couldn't be sure if it was a sign, so everyone got out to check. They locked the woman in the back, so she couldn't run off if they got busy. Then they walked to the west side of the road, looking for a trail back into the desert. While he was twisting to ease his back, Ochoa glanced off in the other direction and saw something like a handkerchief or rag hanging from a branch about four feet off the ground. It was on the wrong side of the road for backtracking, and it could have been of any age, or from any of the thousands of people who came through in a year, but it caught his eye and he studied it.

Suddenly, very near the rag, a head rose unsteadily from behind a bush. It was one of the strangest heads he had ever seen. It was round, chalky white, and streaked with dirt. It looked like a tribal mask. The eyes and mouth were raw, like wounds or burns showing through holes in the white, and wild, dusty hair flared in all directions. The expression was sad and the mouth moved silently.

"There!" Ochoa shouted with relief. "They're over there!"

"Where?" The others peered in the wrong direction.

Ochoa was too excited to explain, so he started running.

As he came closer he saw that the head belonged to a plump, naked little man. The man started crying in hoarse gasps, too dry for tears.

And then, as he could hear the other officers pounding along behind him, Ochoa topped a brush-covered ridge and looked down in the shallow depression below. There were people scattered about, mostly naked except for grimy underpants. Some moved feebly and some looked rigid. The little man was still trying to talk, but his sobbing and his intense excitement made him impossible to understand. An empty tube of Colgate lay on the ground, and Ochoa realized the man had cleverly smeared toothpaste over his face to protect it from the sun.

Thank God it's over, he thought. The nagging clock in his head had finally stopped, just as the sun was sinking and the light was going out.

Ochoa was a professional when it came to emergencies and he knew the drill. He raced around doing a quick triage. The first critical task was to sort out those who needed help most. Men were waking up dazed, reaching out, clutching at his clothing and begging for water. Because they had strength to beg he could ignore them, knowing they still had hours to live. But several were stupefied and unaware. He marked those in his mind for first attention.

It had been very unwise of them to get undressed. Sunburn occurs quickly in the desert, with its pale surface reflecting back more than 80 percent of the radiation from above, and sunburn has the potential of being very dangerous. It impairs the ability of the sweat glands to cool the body, allowing internal temperatures to build to a fatal level.

An older man looked dead even from the distance. His eyes were fixed and open, and he was curled in a fetal position on the bank of the wash, his body fully exposed to the sun. Bloody fluid had run from his nose and mouth and dried on his face. Small animals, realizing they had nothing to fear, had already gotten to him. There were gnaw marks on his arms and legs, but no bleeding, so the damage had occurred after he died.

As he raced from body to body, turning them and ranking

them according to need, the throbbing returned to his head once again. He paused several times to peer around. Something was still wrong. These were all men. The woman had mentioned other women.

One man had found the most primitive of shelters. He had managed to get his head out of the sun by stuffing it into an animal burrow under the roots of a small tree. He lay there like dead, but when Ochoa pulled him out, he woke in amazement at what he saw. But instead of thanking him or pleading for water, the man pointed urgently into the desert and gave a hoarse voice to Ochoa's fears.

"The women," he croaked, "you have to get the women!" And he pointed west, into the setting sun. Out there smooth waves of black shadow thrown by the low ridges were spreading and connecting to cover the desert with darkness.

Leaving first aid to the others, Ochoa began to circle the western perimeter. He was trying to backtrack again, but it was maddening. The light grew constantly weaker and his tracking led him nowhere. In their incoherent wandering, searching for shade and water, they had crossed over themselves a dozen times, leaving trails like tangles of string. A solitary set of tracks that did not return led a long way up the wash, ending in the remains of a pale-skinned, sandy-haired young man. The sign revealed it had been a painful journey. He had fallen many times, and other marks showed where he had dragged himself. He had used his last strength to climb up a little ridge, probably in the hope of seeing something. And perhaps he did, since many people saw a great deal in the final stages of delirium. Before losing consciousness he had done something else that was common. He had shoveled dirt into his mouth, convincing himself that his prayers had been answered, that he was finally surrounded by water. And then he died in convulsions, scarring the ground with kick and claw marks. The man had been dead awhile. His face and neck were already stiff, because rigor mortis sets into the fine upper muscles first. And the animals had gotten to him too.

All the dead people Ochoa had ever felt were cool, or slightly warm, always down the scale from normal. But this young man had been heated by the sun. He was as uncomfortable to the touch as the ground was. It made Ochoa feel sick.

Ochoa continued circling for another few minutes, but there was little light and no indication of anyone else nearby in the desert. He returned to the group and the frantic first aid being administered there.

As he passed the youngest one, the teenage boy suddenly started a seizure. Ochoa restrained him until he was quiet. Then he doused him with water. Dehydration was damaging, not only because it disturbed the blood chemistry and short-circuited many internal functions, but also because it resulted in an absence of perspiration, which stopped the body from cooling itself. The rise in body temperature was as dangerous as a high fever, and if there hadn't been help from the outside, it would certainly have killed the boy.

Before Ochoa could give him anything to drink, he had to clean his mouth out. Either from eating dirt in delirium, or just from a lack of saliva to wash away the ever-present dust, the inside of his mouth was caked, and he could choke. Ochoa wrapped a clean handkerchief around his finger, moistened it with water, and scraped out the inside of the boy's mouth. Hoping all the time that the convulsions wouldn't suddenly return and get him badly bitten, he removed a sticky mass of phlegm and dirt. But when he finally tipped some water into his mouth, the boy turned his head away from the canteen and spit it out.

Ochoa had seen that before. The teenager rejected the water because it was hot. His longing was for cool water, so at first he didn't even recognize what it was. But all their water was now hot, even though they had started out with ice. The agents always put their canteens in the freezer at the office when they ended their shift, and picked them up the next day on the way out. But that was too long ago.

When a little water finally trickled down his throat, some functioning part of his brain recognized it as life, and he turned to the canteen to nurse. He was still delirious, however, and as his strength returned, he looked at Ochoa in fright. "Papa! Papa!" he called, and began thrashing violently.

Again Ochoa had to hold him down to protect both of them. He talked soothingly and poured more water over the boy. It was an exhausting battle in that heat. Once the boy looked up at Ochoa in terror and screamed, "But you're dead, Papa! Who are you?" and pushed violently again in an attempt to escape.

Slowly they moved past the crisis stage. Someone had called Ajo for medical help and evacuation assistance. And Ochoa decided to radio Tucson for the plane, after all. He told the pilot, "We're out where Alamo Wash crosses the pole line. We found six live Salvadorans, and a couple dead. And we think there may be a bunch more still out there. Women and children. I'd guess they're roughly southwest from here. Can you take a look?"

It was after hours, and it would take longer than usual to check out the plane, but the pilot promised to get there as soon as he could. "You realize it's getting dark," he cautioned. "I don't think I'm going to be able to do much tonight."

"Yeah, I know," Ochoa replied, "but what else can we do?"

He had questioned the men who could talk and they had all confirmed that the women were out there. But when he asked, "Where?" they pointed in different directions. The ground was rocky and hard and tracking would be difficult. And he couldn't count on their having walked in the usual straight line. The tremendous visibility of the desert encourages straight-line travel. There were distant mountain peaks and passes visible in all directions to sight on. So usually, if he lost a trail he was following, he would just continue in the same direction until he came to better ground, and there he would probably find it again. But these people had been disoriented and their trail was confused.

The agents had brought in about five gallons of water and had used it all. The crisis was over, but now *they* were getting thirsty. Ochoa saw a gallon-size plastic milk jug on the ground and looked into it. It contained about two inches of dark-brown foul-smelling liquid. "What's this?" he asked one of the survivors.

"That's our urine," a man with a low, serious voice explained. "It's all we've had to drink for more than a day."

It was a pittance. There had been eight of them, and normal desert walking required at least a quart for each of them every hour. The fluid had become concentrated from passing through them many times. They had urinated only in the jug, when they could, which grew less and less often. And when they felt thirsty they drank from it. The man showed no sign of revulsion and in fact treated the jug with a certain reverence. It had probably saved his life. "This was so precious," he explained, "that we gave it to the strongest one to guard. So when someone drank from it, he couldn't take it all." Many times they had only moistened a rag with it and put that in their mouths for the relief of the damp cloth against their dry membranes.

By the time the emergency medical team arrived from Ajo and started IVs on the worst of them, it was much too late for tracking. Then the plane passed over. It circled the desert for a while before the pilot radioed down that there was nothing he could see in the dark. From the ground he was visible only as distant lights.

Ochoa sighed as he watched the lights turn and head back. It was after nine o'clock.

The news drew a big crowd to help with the search and evacuation. When he heard there was still a group out there, Jerry Scott, the supervisor, came down on horseback to cut sign. But the lack of light also frustrated his attempts at tracking.

Ambulances had been brought down the road, but they couldn't make it all the way. Ochoa carried out a teenager who was too weak to walk. The boy had consumed a whole bottle of musk-oil after-shave lotion. The alcohol and chemicals had probably been terrible for him. Because he was lacking in normal fluids, the scent had saturated his system. It came out of pores all over his body and it was thick on his breath. Ochoa felt so stifled by the smell in that hot air that he acquired a permanent aversion to musk.

They took the survivors to the hospital, the dead to the morgue. Then the border patrol met to finish their paperwork and decide on a plan for the next day. There was still a possibility that it wouldn't be too late; that a rapid rescue might be important. Scott called Tucson for reinforcements. He was promised planes and trail bikes, all that could be spared. They coordinated their plans.

Ochoa had hardly slept the night before. He had put out extra high energy all day, and still his private dread of death in the desert wouldn't let him relax. He went home to talk it out with his wife, an attractive woman with long brown hair and hazel eyes. But there was little to say. Two men had already died and the survivors had suffered horribly. The children would be more vulnerable to start with, and they and the women would be out there much longer. The outlook for them was grim; if they had started to panic, they might have scattered, and then there would be almost no chance of finding them in time. She gave him encouragement, sympathy, a neck rub, and something to eat. Then he lay down to get some rest. But he couldn't stop thinking and he couldn't go to sleep.

An hour later he decided it would be better to get up. He took a shower, put on a clean uniform, and drove to the office in Why. He began to get ready. He set up the four-wheel-drive and hitched on the horse trailer. He took the horses out of their corrals and loaded them and their tack. He set out emergency supplies and radios. Then he had nothing else to do but sit and wait. It was still dark.

At five o'clock Jerry Scott came and they headed down Highway 85 again. They weren't the only ones out. The sheriff's office had set up a special command post at the visitors' center in the park, and a number of groups had come to join the rescue operation that morning. Scott and Ochoa had been invited to take part, but had declined. The two agents felt it would add an unnecessary delay to attend another meeting, have coffee and doughnuts, and make more plans. They had made their plans the night before, just to save time, and they felt the need to start out as soon as they could. When they explained that to the sheriff's deputy who contacted them, he was annoyed with their independent attitude. "Well, you do what you want," he concluded irritably.

They planned to go back to where they had found the

men, and then cut the horses due west. Last night Ochoa had asked the men how long they had walked since they left the others. About three hours, most of them had said. One can walk only so far in three hours, so they had a maximum distance from that point. And they knew in a general way where the Salvadorans had crossed the border and what route they took. So they had a direction and a distance, and that gave them a search area shaped like a piece of pie.

Tucson sent down three agents, each with a Honda 120. They were excellent dirt bikes for the job, faster and more reliable than horses. The border patrol used them for tracking aliens. They would start nearby and work intersecting patterns.

At six o'clock, when the light first became clear enough for sign cutting, they were already at the site of the men's group and ready to begin. The northern tip of the Sonoran desert is in no way like the Sahara, a smooth sea of sand that holds clear lines of footprints until the wind blows them away. This land is a hard shell of rock, baked earth, and cactus. Sign is usually ambiguous, and it takes a great deal of judgment, and therefore a great deal of local experience, to read it. They didn't see footprints; they saw movement. Their task was to decide if the earth had been shifted in any significant way, if stones had been overturned or pushed aside. They couldn't necessarily distinguish whether an animal or a person had done it. Often the sign was nothing more than a rock that seemed to be pushed into the ground and forward a little bit. That left a small gap of dirt behind it, and the gap might be of a slightly different color because it had been less exposed to the sun and held a fractional amount more moisture. The gap area dried and bleached at a certain rate, depending on temperature, humidity, and wind conditions. So sometimes they could also get a rough idea of how long ago it had been made.

Before they went very far, Scott and Ochoa, both skilled sign cutters and confident in their own judgment, disagreed about some sign they saw. Since either one of them might be right, they decided it would be most effective if they split and each followed his own instincts. Their trails separated and merged and separated again. Most of the time they were alone, walking bent over and leading their horses through the constantly burgeoning sunlight. Silent desert rolled away on all sides in bleached-out yellows and reds, broken by some sort of tough vegetation every five or ten yards.

They would much rather have been leapfrogging. If only the sign had been clear, they would have put one man on the tracks and sent the other ahead to cut across the line of travel. If he could intercept it, then the back man could pass him at a dead run and try to pick it up ahead again. It was one of the only ways they could catch up. Otherwise, they couldn't usually track as fast as a person could walk.

In the meantime, the fixed-wing aircraft Scott requested the night before had arrived. There were two Cessnas, specially modified for tracking, so they could fly slowly and quite low. But to save weight, the planes weren't air-conditioned, and in hot weather, flying through the choppy air near the ground was both uncomfortable and dangerous. For several hours the pilots flew skillful search patterns in near-stall conditions without spotting a thing.

But a Customs helicopter had searched the full length of the pole line and found a body several miles south of the men's group. Rangers on horseback went in to get him. It was a young man, sitting up, dead. He had taken off all his clothing. They notified Scott on the radio. The freshness of the body and the fact that he looked like a Salvadoran suggested he was a member of their group. But no one knew what to make of his location, and it gave them no clues in their search.

They assumed that the Salvadorans had crossed the border somewhere in the vicinity of Quitobaquito Springs, headed generally north, and climbed the low mountains by passing as much as possible between the Puerto Blanco Mountains and the Cipriano Hills. When they reached the Valley of the Ajo, they had probably angled east to hit the road near Alamo Wash. The fact that two separate groups had come out at the same point, and a third had been found in a direct line with it, suggested that Alamo Wash had been the rendezvous point for the pickup. That projected a westerly or southwesterly search corridor leading from the wash back to the mountains. The planes were flying patterns over it, while Scott and Ochoa moved down the corridor, steadily closing up the ends and giving the planes a more concentrated area to search.

Gerald Carico was in the near plane, and he and Scott discussed strategy each time there was a new development. The body that Customs had found was outside the pattern, and it made them wonder about their analysis. "What's the chance they came through Kino Pass? Or up the Ajo on the east side of the Puerto Blanco Mountains?" Carico asked.

"All we know for sure is that they're out there some-where . . ." Scott replied.

Scott was experienced, and he had seen this before. A summer never passed without their finding at least one body, and usually several. He was a tall, powerful-looking man, generally relaxed, and a good storyteller. But this situation had gotten under his skin too. It was the extreme heat, the large number of victims, their obvious vulnerability, and the prolonged, escalating nature of the crisis, all combined. And he couldn't remember when he had seen so many other hardened professionals so deeply involved.

There had already been two other groups abandoned that year, also Salvadorans. But it had been springtime, and con-siderably cooler, and none of them had died. As a matter of fact, Scott had said then, "I sure hope this doesn't happen in the summertime, because if it does, we're going to lose some people." One of the groups had also been found in Alamo Wash, but on the other side of the highway. The other spent two leaderless days, frightened and without any idea of what to do, hiding in a culvert along the road. They had no water or food, but they didn't want to come out. Somebody finally spotted them and agents went down and picked them up. They were the lucky ones.

There were always stories about robberies and rapes. And in Yuma, about three years before, he heard some people had been abandoned in a panel truck left out in the sun. They died in the heat, of course. The drivers might have run off thinking they were in some kind of danger. And years before that, when he worked with the police department in San Antonio, someone had done the same thing with a U-Haul moving truck. There must have been thirty or forty, but only two died that time. A passerby just happened to see urine dripping out the back of it, and then noticed the faint calling and the weak banging from the inside. Otherwise, they all would have died. Scott always said, "There are no humanitarians in the smuggling business." And now this looked like a similar situation. The Salvadorans they were getting, the ones who could afford to pay their way out, were mostly middle-class city people. They were naïve about the coyotes they had to deal with, and helpless in this totally foreign environment. Once out in the desert, the coyotes could do anything they wanted with them.

Ochoa didn't have a radio, and from the time he and Scott split up, he had had no information about the discovery of the body or any other aspect of the search. But at mid-morning he started to scan the sky as well as the ground. There would be plenty of bodies by now, and the buzzards were likely to find them before he did. What he saw instead, however, was that the near plane had broken off its grid pattern and was making tight turns. The only time a search plane makes really high, banked turns is when it has spotted something. Ochoa immediately jumped on his horse.

John Rockhill had come in that morning on foot from the north, and when that area didn't look promising, he had crossed the corridor and started a parallel pattern to the south. He too saw the plane, and when he got an excited message on his radio, he ran an amazing four miles flat out through the desert.

What happened was that Carico had banked wide on a turn and flew a mile or so off course, to the southeast of their corridor. He radioed immediately to Scott that he had spotted quantities of abandoned clothing. "A whole lot of junk spread out in a wide path. It's nearer to the road than we thought." The pattern of abandoned belongings was typical of people in crisis in the desert. Scott headed immediately in the new direction.

"I see some bodies," Carico radioed seconds later, his voice rising. "There are a bunch of them, all laying out down there. Oh, my God, can you get in there quick? Some of them are moving. Some of them are moving. Can you get in there?" He sounded like he was crying. After hours of tense searching the pilot could finally see them but not help them. And whatever he saw was very disturbing.

Scott galloped ahead at full speed. As he reached the rim of the Cessna's frantic circle a trail bike passed him and pulled ahead. Ochoa was right behind. As Ochoa charged into the scene, his horse staggered sideways and almost fell over. Ochoa leaped off to save the animal from collapsing. Horses were fragile in the heat and he had never before abused one that way.

A small army of people began to converge on that spot. In addition to the border-patrol agents on horseback, foot, motor bike, and in 4x4s, there were also Customs patrol mounted units and National Park rangers on horseback. There was the search-and-rescue team from the Pima County sheriff's office. The two border-patrol Cessnas were circling overhead and the Customs patrol helicopter was on the way. Someone had already radioed for an Air-Vac helicopter and a team of paramedics to help evacuate survivors. And even the press helicopters being dispatched from Phoenix at that moment were utilized to carry extra water and equipment. The area churned with engine noise and swirling dust, stamping horses and shouting men.

The first thought in each of their minds was that it was much worse than anything they had imagined. It looked like human violence had been even more terrible than the desert, and the possibilities suddenly escalated in an entirely new direction. Dead bodies of naked women and girls were scattered everywhere. There was a dead man with a club lying near him. Many, including the man, had their faces bizarrely covered with makeup and their lips painted with lipstick. A badly beaten woman was crawling about in her panties, waving to attract help and crying. The first thing they heard was, "Those rotten coyotes . . . they ran off and left us!" She was delirious. She couldn't see them and she was

crawling in the wrong direction. And then she started screaming hysterically. "My babies! Where are my babies?"

Their suitcases had been ripped open and searched. Piles of
belongings were heaped everywhere. Ochoa, ignoring the
dead and dying scattered about him, ran frantically from
pile to pile, searching feverishly for babies who might have
been hidden from the violence by a protective mother or
left under a mound of clothing to get shelter from the sun.
The shrill voice went on and on. Large black buzzards were
now collecting in overhead circles. And no matter how he
searched, he couldn't find the babies. He had a feeling that
reality was slipping, and he wondered briefly if this could
actually be a nightmare. My God, he wondered, isn't this
ever going to end?

Meanwhile, the heat in Tucson had been stifling. To escape
for the Fourth of July weekend, Mary Lou Harris drove to
a primitive vacation cabin she owned on nearby Mount
Lemmon. It was celebration time on the mountain, not only
because of Independence Day, but because the tiny town of
Mount Lemmon was honoring its centennial with the purchase of a new fire engine and the dedication of a new
garage for its volunteer fire department. There were plenty
of fireworks and the parade was the biggest ever.

Mary Lou was one of only two lawyers in the Tucson
Legal Aid office who were familiar with immigration law,
and she had recently handled the most celebrated Salvadoran
political-asylum case the area had known. She was just thirty-
two at the time, a tall woman dressed in jeans, with green
eyes and ginger-colored hair tied up in a blue bandanna. At
the moment she had spots of pitch smeared on her arms and
face from making repairs with uncured lumber, and she was
looking forward to getting home and taking a real bath.

It was not until Sunday evening, just before driving back
to the swelter of the city, that she turned on the portable TV
she had brought with her. She stretched out to relax for a few
minutes and catch up on the world's events before leaving.
But instead of relaxation, she felt a personal jolt as she

watched the images on the screen. When the camera zoomed in on a leafless paloverde tree with six dead bodies spread under it like a miniature Jonestown, she sighed. "I bet I'm going to be drawn right into the middle of this one." And sure enough, when she got back to her tiny office on Monday, her desk was heaped with telephone message slips from every source imaginable. There had been calls from the *Los Angeles Times*, the *Washington Post*, *Time* magazine, various religious and human rights groups, National Public Radio, all the local TV stations and newspapers, and two from *The New York Times*. Overnight she had become a celebrity of sorts. It was too much to deal with, so she didn't call anyone back.

2
THE BEGINNING:
El Salvador in the Spring of 1980

Once things started slipping, it was amazing how quickly it all went. Over the last year the guerrillas had stepped up their resistance and the government increased its counter-measures. Suddenly assassinations and street killings, kidnappings and disappearances were common. There were rumors of torture. The army began shooting anyone out after curfew. They heard automatic weapons in the streets at night, but no one opened their shutters to look. They began to speak of their problems as *la situación*, and soon "the situation" became the center of their conversation.

Fear choked off business. The thread factory of Boulder Industries closed, and Ileana Campos' husband went from supervising three hundred employees to being out of work. He was halfway through an engineering course in night school, but the government closed the university. The students were suspected of being leftists. Then the downward spiral closed Ileana's little shop, which manufactured baby clothes. Suddenly all they had was a house in the suburbs and four children, and no way to support them. They were living on savings and help from their parents, and the future could be only worse.

They were practical people, and they knew that the life they had loved in El Salvador was finished. The best place for educated people to start over was in the United States. There was no possibility of immigrating, but fortunately they still had enough money to hire one of the new services that had sprung up to satisfy that need. They were not yet trapped there, like some they knew.

31

Her husband went first to establish a base for them. The crossing went well, but the only work he could get was as a hospital orderly in Los Angeles. While she was waiting, Ileana had her parents move in with her. She was afraid in the big house, alone with the children. She waited four months before her husband called and told her to make arrangements to join him. Their young son would live with her parents, to whom she gave their house. Their three daughters went to her husband's parents. It seemed too dangerous to bring the children; they would have to send for them later. Through a newspaper ad in the travel section of the classifieds, she found Jorge Dávila. She paid him a thousand dollars to take her to Los Angeles.

Dávila was a dark, heavyset, oily-skinned young man with shoulder-length black hair and a leering nature. From the start he irritated her, but she didn't feel she had the luxury of indulging her tastes. And he was completely confident about the trip. "The details have all been arranged," he assured her. "You're practically there."

She phoned her husband to tell him she was on her way. She promised her children she would send for them as soon as she found a job and saved the money. It would cost another five thousand dollars to have them brought up by a friend. With her parents, she only cried. She didn't know if she would ever see them again.

But she was back home within a week. The U.S. border patrol had seized them in an amateurish and poorly managed attempt to cross the border in the desert outside of Yuma, Arizona. Then she learned that, despite all his blustering, this actually had been Jorge Dávila's first trip. He was as inexperienced as she was.

The chief risk of their capture was financial. Of course there was some rough handling and a great deal of disappointment, but it was the loss of the escape money that would be catastrophic. Jorge, as part of his guarantee, had promised that anyone who was returned from one of his trips would get the next trip free. So the day after they arrived back in El Salvador, Ileana went to his office, determined to collect on that promise. She was not used to dealing with men like him, and ever since she had, everything had gone wrong. If she were to obey her instincts, she would never see him again. But he had her money.

Jorge was slumped in his swivel chair, his feet on the desk, smoking and talking with Esteban Alvarado, another coyote who worked for him. Jorge didn't look pleased to see her. The small office had only two chairs, and neither of the men offered to get up, so she stood between them and talked to a three-quarter view of Jorge's round face. "I came to find out when you can take me to the United States again," she said.

"In a little while," he answered tiredly.

Nothing was easy with him, she thought, everything was a game. "Please don't play with me. I have to meet my husband!" Ileana snapped.

It was not the way to talk to Jorge Dávila. He and Ileana had grated on each other right from the start, and even though he had made certain allowances at first because he found her attractive, he was beginning to get tired of her. "Well, maybe you can go with me, and maybe you can't," he said.

Ileana took a minute to control her temper. Then she begged, "Please, Jorge, you promised."

That mollified him. "O.K. I haven't scheduled the next trip yet. But if you want to go, you should leave me five hundred colones." That was another two hundred dollars.

"You said if anything went wrong I could have the next trip free."

"I'm sorry, but I have too many expenses. I have to make a living too, you know." He wouldn't budge. Finally, rather than abandon the thousand dollars she had already given him, she left a check. "I'll let you know as soon as there is something definite," he promised her.

Ileana walked out quietly, keeping her anger under control. How am I ever going to be able to stand traveling with that man? she wondered.

What Jorge didn't explain was that he could afford to be choosy. The situation in El Salvador continued to worsen, and during the failed trip his office had been swamped with people pleading for help. They didn't know, or didn't care, that his first try had been a total loss. So Jorge raised the price for the second trip.

But that was only Ileana's first unpleasant surprise that day. When she visited her husband's parents to tell them about this latest development, she ran into her sister-in-law, Luisa. Because the tightly interwoven fabric of Salvadoran family life brought them into frequent contact, the women pretended to be friends, but they had never gotten along. They were contrasts in almost every way. Ileana was tall, fair-skinned, and fashionable. Luisa was heavy, moody, and frequently in trouble. She also liked telling stories about Ileana behind her back. So Ileana was not pleased when Luisa announced, "Hey, I've decided to go too."

Luisa had been struggling with the decision for months. Her fiancé had gone ahead to the United States, and then sent her money for her trip. But Luisa had become involved with another man. She lingered and wondered what to do. Ileana thought Luisa was finally doing the right thing, but was secretly sorry she had picked this particular trip.

"We're going by bus to Mexico," Luisa said knowingly. "Then we're going to fly over the border to Los Angeles, in his friend's private plane."

"He didn't say anything to me about an airplane." Ileana was puzzled. "Last time we went the whole way by bus."

Luisa shrugged. "That was your tough luck."

Ileana went immediately to tell her mother. "I don't believe it," her mother exclaimed.

"It's true. I think she did it to aggravate me."

"You'd better be careful of that one," her mother warned.

"Of her," Ileana agreed, "and everyone, and everything."

Two long, anxious months passed without Ileana hearing a word from Jorge. She was impatient (six months had elapsed since she had last seen her husband), but she hated to involve herself unnecessarily with the coyote. Finally she faced the fact that there was no way to avoid it. One morning, when she had to go to the capital anyway to do some shopping, she decided to check on him.

She ate at McDonald's first, to draw strength from that

image of the United States. Then she went to Cuscatlán Avenue, where Jorge had his office in a business district of San Salvador. There was a pharmacy on the corner, a furniture shop, and then a stairway up to his second-floor office with the sign outside: TV AND RADIO REPAIRS. Jorge had previously done repairwork, but he had moved out all his equipment when he opened his specialized travel agency. Ileana couldn't get up the stairs. A flood of people and luggage was pouring down and across the sidewalk. Esteban Alvarado stood by the curb, trying to cram them into Jorge's microbus.

"Where are you going?" Ileana asked.

"To the motel," Esteban said, "to wait for the bus. Didn't you bring your suitcase?"

"*The* bus?"

"Yes. Didn't Jorge tell you? We're leaving tomorrow. Everyone's waiting together so we can get an early start."

She got the address and went as fast as she could to her in-laws to say good-bye to her girls again. Luisa was there, and in a generous impulse Ileana told her sister-in-law about Jorge's attempt to leave without them. Luisa was furious. Their mutual mistrust of Jorge formed a new bond between them, and they packed together sympathetically. They went to say good-bye to Ileana's parents and son, and then to the motel. They were the very last to arrive. Jorge was there with all the people. He gave them a hearty welcome.

The motel was cheap and filthy. There were two tiers of rooms opening onto a concrete courtyard with a small garden in the middle. Garbage lay scattered across the yard. A group of Jorge's clients had gathered downstairs. They had already gotten to know each other and were sitting in the patio, drinking beer and amusing themselves with horseplay and name-calling. They looked intimidating to Ileana and she was relieved to have Luisa with her. There was some snickering and someone made loud kissing noises as they walked past.

They went immediately to their room. It had a hammock and a bed, and since neither liked the hammock, they decided to share the bed. They sat down on it and looked around at

the bare walls. Luisa had never been out of the country
before, and she wasn't certain she wanted to leave this time.
She was depressed.

Ileana was anxious. "I have to wash," she said after a
minute.

"So wash."

"Come with me," Ileana insisted. "I don't want to go in
front of all those men alone." So in their new togetherness
they went to search for the bathroom. There was only a
single toilet for the entire group, a small, predictably dirty
room on the far side of the courtyard. As soon as they
appeared, someone shouted, "Oh, my, look at what I see! So
stuck up. Must be *very* fine ladies."

"Don't answer them," Ileana told her sister-in-law.

The bathroom was an uncomfortable refuge, so they
freshened up and braced themselves to face the taunting
again. Again there was hooting and lip-smacking, but this
time a tall, thin man interrupted it. "All right, that's enough,
settle down," he said, waving his arms. It was Julio Espinoza,
Jorge's partner on this trip. Espinoza was an experienced
coyote, and after his initial failure, perhaps Jorge felt he
needed the guidance of someone who knew what he was
doing. But if bringing in Espinoza was an admission of weakness, Jorge never showed it, and by force of personality he
remained dominant.

"Everybody come downstairs. It's time for a talk," Espinoza
hollered up to the balcony. Now Ileana saw that she hadn't
been the only one hiding in her room. It was a much larger
group than she had realized. There were some older people.
And although it was hard to count them in the confusion,
there were at least four or five mothers and seven or eight
children and babies. The hecklers were only young boys
traveling without supervision and a little out of control. She
was relieved that there were some responsible-looking people
going along, because Jorge certainly was not.

After Espinoza called the group together, it was Jorge who
got up to talk. "O.K., I know you don't like the rooms here,
but let me remind you that this is not a vacation. The important thing is that we all help one another. Then we'll have

a good trip and everything will go right. If one of us"—he pointed to himself, Julio Espinoza, and Esteban Alvarado— "tells you to do something, do it. There must be a good reason. . . . There's just one more thing to understand, but it's very important. There are *no* coyotes on this trip. Just friends. I'm your friend and you're my friend. Same goes for them." He pointed at the other two. "That means if anything does go wrong, and Immigration asks you, 'Who is the coyote on this trip?' you say, 'There's no coyote here. We're just friends.' Understand?"

"No problem," someone assured him. Someone else cheered, "Let's go, we're ready." Many of the men admired Jorge. The work of a coyote was important in El Salvador.

But Ileana wished she were going with anyone else. Jorge liked to drink when he should be sober. He liked to play when he should be serious. He was temperamental. And he didn't keep his word. She couldn't imagine a worse person to travel with, and she hoped the trip would be mercifully brief.

And something else made her uneasy. There were so many people. Usually these groups were kept to less than twenty, to be more manageable and less noticeable. It was important, because they could become helpless victims of almost anyone who spotted them along the way. But Jorge's greed had swelled them to double a healthy size and made them more vulnerable.

Then someone called her name. A short, pretty young woman with honey-colored skin and a heart-shaped face came over and hugged her. "Well, we try again, eh?" she beamed up at Ileana. Flora had also been on the first trip. They talked for several minutes and then Flora asked, "Have you seen my uncle? He should be here, but I can't find him."

"No, I'm sorry. So he's coming again too?" But Ileana was distracted and looked around her with annoyance. The Last Night in El Salvador Fiesta was picking up steam. "This is too noisy for me," she told Flora. "I'm going up to my room. Would you like to come?" But Flora decided to stay and celebrate with the others.

Upstairs the mood was quieter. People were visiting one

another and introducing themselves. In one room three young sisters were joined by a few older women who enjoyed the girls' company. Across the hall a lonely young man listened to the sound of their voices. His name was Francisco. He was tall and thin, with a tentative mustache and a hesitant, gentle manner. This would be his first separation from his family, and he was feeling sad. If things had been normal, at that moment he would have been sitting with his relatives at his aunt's house, watching *The Fugitive* on her TV. But the situation wasn't normal, and now Francisco was the fugitive.

It was nearly dark on March 21, a Friday, when he first learned that they were hunting him. Francisco and his friends were coming home after a soccer game. As they walked the familiar cobblestone streets of Quezaltepeque, they laughed and slapped one another on the back. The March evening was warm and sweet, and the purple and gold on their team jerseys glowed in the dusk.

Francisco was the quiet one in his group. He lived in a pleasant house with a vegetable garden, along with his mother, his sister, and his brother. They kept some chickens, for eggs, and a black dog named Toto. They had quiet, rural lives, which suited them. Since he left school at fourteen to help the family, Francisco had done only seasonal work in a coffee factory, gone to dances on weekends, and played soccer with his friends.

They stopped briefly in front of his home, still talking happily, reluctant to end a good day. It was not until he left them and went to his door that he became frightened. A voice from the bushes whispered his name and asked, "Is anyone there?"

"Everyone's gone to dinner," he replied.

"Get inside," demanded the dark, muscular young man who squeezed from behind the red hibiscus plant. He pushed Francisco through the door in his panic to leave the street. It was Ramón, a close friend.

"They're looking for us."

"Francisco?" his mother called from the kitchen. "Is that you?" They hardly heard her.

Ramón, unable to find the words, stared rigidly into his face. "Orejas have named us," he finally hissed. "We're on a death list."

Orejas means "ears" in Spanish. It is a slang term for spies and informers. There are people in most villages who will report disloyalty to the secret execution squads. Ads in newspapers even ask for anonymous condemnations, so the practice of informing not only provides an outlet for patriotic fervor, but also allows some to settle grudges or remove competitors.

"But we haven't done anything."

"It was at the dance, a month ago. Remember the people who were singing?" The local church ran dances to raise money for their building fund. They were not political, but several times small groups had used them to express their feelings by singing protest songs. Francisco and his friends had moved away from them immediately. Francisco was nonpolitical. He wanted to live. Singing or talking against the government was suicidal.

"Oh, no." He rubbed his forehead in misery. "How did you find out?"

"My grandmother told me. I was away last night. When I got home today, my whole family was waiting. I came right away to warn you."

About an hour after dark on the preceding night, five strange men pushed into Ramón's house without knocking and demanded to see him. Luckily he was spending the night at his brother's. Only his godmother was there at the time. The men showed her a list of people they wanted. Ramón and Francisco were on it. They had been denounced for singing protest songs at the dance and for belonging to antigovernment organizations.

Francisco would no sooner sing protest songs than he would pour gasoline over himself . . . and for the same reason. But there was no way to explain that there had been a mistake. *Everyone* claimed to be innocent when the death squads came for him. And everyone was ignored. If they were caught, they would find out what kind of acts angry men were capable of committing when there was absolutely no restraint on them.

Francisco's mother started screaming. She had been rolling chilies in batter when she heard the unusual tone in their voices. She came in, holding her sticky hands away from herself. But when she realized what was happening, she clutched her face and moaned in pain.

Francisco went to comfort her. "It will be all right," he insisted, hugging her and patting her on the back. "We'll think of something . . ." But he didn't know what. He was terrified himself, and suddenly he noticed that he was no longer soothing his mother as much as clinging to her.

"We have to go away," said Ramón. "Immediately."

It was true. There was no choice. "I have to leave, Mama," he told the tall, plump woman. "If they find me here they could do things to everybody."

"I'm going," said Ramón nervously. Francisco let go of his mother to thank the friend who had risked his life to warn him. But Ramón, too tense for formalities, was already at the window, peering through the curtains to check the street. When he turned back, he looked at Francisco, squeezed his hand tightly, and ran out. The death squads didn't like to be seen. They came after dark, and night was falling rapidly.

Francisco had to decide. People who fled to neighboring Central American countries had been followed or sent back, so that was not safe. He would go to the United States. He had heard that a refugee could have a difficult life there, but at least he wouldn't have to worry about torture and execution in the middle of the night. And he did know one person.

He ran to his dresser and began searching for a letter with his friend's address. His mother was sobbing and he was throwing papers in every direction when the door burst open and his cousin's wife ran in, looking terrified. There were ORDEN men in the street. They were asking for Francisco. They wanted to know where he lived. So far the neighbors had pretended they didn't know him.

ORDEN was an acronym that stood for "order." It was

one of several secret police groups that handled unpleasant business in unofficial ways. He had been frightened before, but with this news Francisco was overcome by a feeling of weakness. The danger was so near, and he didn't even have the strength to run. They'll catch me and drag me out, he thought helplessly, before I make a gesture to save myself.

"Run, Francisco! Run and hide from them!" his mother shouted at him. He just looked at her. She stepped over and shook him until she woke him.

Francisco kissed her. "Good-bye, Mama!" he called, and then ran with the same desperation as Ramón, taking the back door into the night.

As if they had heard him, shouts and police whistles shrilled. But now his fear had turned into energy. He bounded through the garden, glad that he knew the way in the dark. Anyone trying to follow him would stumble into fences and vegetable rows. He dodged across the field where he practiced soccer and up another street. The commotion multiplied behind him. He wondered if it could be the sound of triumph, as he remembered that Ramón had tried to escape in that direction. He flailed his arms and legs, trying to control his gasping as he cut through yards and alleyways. Finally he came to Ramón's brother's house.

It stood dark and silent on a dark, quiet block. When he tapped softly on the back door, there was no response. Where can I go if no one is here? Francisco wondered. He searched his mind for another safe hiding place. Who would take that kind of a chance for him? Without any warning, the door opened, and an arm reached out and yanked him in. It was Ramón's brother. Ramón was there too, safe but terrified.

They searched for anything they could use against the automatic weapons of the ORDEN men. They found a hammer and a kitchen knife. The brother stood guard at the door with the hammer. Ramón took the knife. Francisco, who knew he couldn't bring himself to kill anyone, crouched in a corner and waited. They heard men's voices approach and pass close by. They held their breath and stared at the dim shapes of one another's faces. Again they heard whistles and shouting. There was no way to know if that group was searching for them, or if it was another on a similar mission. It made no difference. They were trapped now. It was curfew time and anyone found on the street would be shot. They waited in darkness the entire night. They did not sleep.

Weary but relieved, they saw the sun rise. Francisco slipped home in the early hours before anyone was up. His mother and his cousin's wife were sitting there, waiting for him. His mother gave him $150, so he could go to the capital and make immediate plans to leave the country.

The money was the last of their savings. They had heard there were people in San Salvador who could get documents. He and Ramón went immediately to the Zacamil District, because that crowded and dangerous slum was the center of many illegal activities. The two wandered for days through back alleys looking for the necessary contacts. But it proved more difficult than Francisco had imagined. The people were cautious about talking to outsiders and he made no progress. Then history pushed him a step backward.

On March 23, 1980, Archbishop Oscar Arnulfo Romero spoke out in his sermon to the soldiers of El Salvador. He told them that God's law forbade them to continue killing their countryfolk. The next day, while he was saying Mass at a hospital for cancer patients, men with automatic weapons rushed in and shot him to death on the altar, like a modern Thomas à Becket.

Archbishop Romero had a huge following. The Sunday broadcasts of his sermons over the Church's radio station had perhaps the largest audience in the country. The common people of El Salvador saw him not only as their leader, but also as their protector, and the loss was a catastrophe for them. Only a month before, he had talked to a Mexican reporter about the death threats he had received for advocating peace. He had said that he felt obliged by divine law to give his life for those he loved, and that as a Christian, he didn't believe in death without resurrection; so if they killed him, he would rise again in the Salvadoran people.

The people did rise. Their reaction went beyond grief and they erupted in rage. There were huge protests and bombings. The government fired into crowds at his funeral, killing many. It was a national crisis, and it was no longer safe to stay in the capital.

There was no hope that Francisco and Ramón could buy illegal documents in the midst of that upheaval. For the time being, they were trapped in El Salvador.

They reluctantly returned to Quezaltepeque, and Francisco moved into his cousin's house to hide until he could make other arrangements. He didn't like the danger he brought to his cousin and himself, but he couldn't think of another thing to do.

Ramón moved to another part of the country, where his parents had a ranch and where hopefully he would not be on any wanted list. Francisco never went out of the house to take a walk or enjoy himself. He never went to another dance. He never spent another night in his mother's home. And he avoided everyone he knew because he was afraid Orejas might find his hiding place and report him to the ORDEN enforcers again. Much of the time he struggled to accept that his youth had ended in an instant and that from now on his life would be different. This went on for three months.

In the meantime, several more of his friends received night visits from ORDEN, but all were lucky enough to avoid them. And each of them took it as a warning to run and hide. With so many in hiding, Francisco wondered, how can there still be any hiding places left?

In May, a fourth friend was also visited at night, but his luck had run out. His name was Alfredo, and he had previously served a term in the National Guard. The protests following the archbishop's death made the government feel threatened, and Alfredo had been ordered to report for an additional term of duty. When he didn't show up, it was taken as a sign that he had become a political enemy of the state. In fact, he was only yielding to simple fear for his life. Policework was becoming increasingly dangerous, and he felt he had already served his time. He didn't run; he just hoped they would understand and leave him alone.

He was not arrested by the government. Instead, the familiar "unknown men" came to his house in darkness and took him away. The next morning his body was found at La Lava, a volcanic crater used as the town dump. He had been tortured at length, even though no one could have supposed he knew anything of interest. It had been done more as a lesson for others. His teeth had been broken off at the gums and his lips sewn together. His fingers had been crushed when they rolled a pickup truck back and forth over them. Then they inched the truck over his body until blood burst from his mouth and he died. His killers were recognized as belonging to ORDEN. He was twenty-two years old, and in that place, at that time, there was nothing remarkable about his death.

Francisco had begun to relax in the lull, but now he couldn't forget for a minute that out there were people impatient to do similar things to him. He was afraid to attend Alfredo's funeral. The only relief from this monotonous terror occurred when a neighbor came to tell him that she had learned of someone who might be able to help. It was a man who operated a TV repair shop and travel agency in San Salvador. Word was spreading that this man was a coyote. For a large fee he could arrange travel and illegal border crossings to the United States. Francisco was desperate. He didn't have the $1,200 required, but he went to the man anyway, gave him what little he had, and promised to get the rest from his friend in the United States when they arrived. The man finally agreed to the terms, on condition that they would both go immediately to the friend's house and collect all that was owed.

"It would be a terrible mistake to even think of trying not to pay me," the man warned.

Francisco believed him, but to escape, he was willing to make any bargain that was necessary.

Most of them were up and packed early the next morning, but they did not leave the run-down motel as promised. After several hours Jorge finally arrived and explained that there were serious problems at the border, but he was working on them and should soon have them straightened out. (More cynical souls, such as Antonio, Francisco's new roommate, muttered that there was a chronic shortage of buses in the country and that Jorge was probably just having trouble finding transportation.) "By the way," Jorge mentioned as an afterthought, "there's a little problem about the documents, but nothing to worry about."

The young men who had been joking and drinking until late in the night got up with headaches, considerably subdued. But the women upstairs had gone to sleep early and woke up cheerful. The evening before, some of them had formed a sympathetic little group, sharing their predicament and generating a great deal of quiet warmth for one another. Now they got together again.

Berta was a shrewd little woman who had worked in a factory until "the situation" closed it down. Her husband was caring for their two children, she explained, while she went ahead to look for work. They had sold their TV and Subaru truck to pay for her trip, and now they owned nothing. Berta was a person who carefully assessed the people around her, weighing their good and bad points. She found the company of the three Lugo sisters very comfortable, especially Alicia, the oldest. Alicia Lugo was eighteen, with very white skin, very dark eyes, and black hair that was short and curly. She was slim, with a pretty little body. Alicia and Berta shared a passion for snack foods.

Berta gained weight easily, and sometimes avoided sweets, but at the motel there was a good excuse. It was dangerous to walk the streets shopping for food. No one wanted to be recognized as a fugitive the day before they left. And no one wanted to get caught in a confrontation between soldiers and guerrillas, and catch a bullet. So they dashed to the nearest store and bought what little was available. Then they brought it back, to picnic with the others, perched like little birds, sitting together in the huge hammocks.

Berta and Alicia lived happily for almost two days on sodas, juices, candy, cookies, and toasted melon seeds. They had *charamuscas*, a Kool-Aid-like mix that was frozen to slush in a plastic bag and sucked out through a hole in the corner. And *pupusas*, a Salvadoran specialty made of tortillas stuffed with cheese, meat, or *chicharrones*, which are fried pork skins. Salvadoran food is generally quite mild, and made without chilies, although there is a highly spiced cole-slaw relish for those who want a touch of fire with their meal. There were also the much-loved *churros*, long, extruded tubes of doughnut dough that are fried in hot oil and rolled in sugar.

Juanita Lugo, the twelve-year-old sister, was worried because she still didn't have her passport. She was afraid that she was the problem that Jorge was having with the documents, and although she was normally quite cheerful, the tension of leaving and the uncertainty about her papers made her fretful. She and her sisters had not seen their mother in a long time, and although they were excited about being reunited, the separation also created some uncertainties. It was almost five years ago that their mother had gone to Los Angeles to work to bring them to the States. But stories about the "land of opportunity" had not prepared her for the fact that the only work she would find was as a cleaning woman. After she had sent money home for the girls' support, there was only enough left to survive on and nothing to save toward their trip. They had hung on like that for years, hoping for something better. But the situation turned dramatically worse instead. Frightened that it might soon be too late to get them out safely, their mother borrowed $3,600 and gave it to a coyote who guaranteed a safe and well-supervised trip for the girls.

Berta dubbed young Juanita "the American," because of her blond hair, blue eyes, fair skin, and red lips. She was a beautiful child, and to Berta she fit the image that American advertising gave of its country. Juanita was thin, but Inés, the fourteen-year-old, was fat, "Like me," Berta added in her evaluation. And like Berta, her hair was short and curly. Inés had a dark spot under her nose, with hair growing out of it. And a scar on her lower lip, which she hated. It wasn't a bad scar, but she wasn't at an age when she could tolerate any form of disfigurement. "A dog bit me," she explained. "It's very ugly, but my mother promised me when I got there I could have plastic surgery to fix it."

There were three other regular members of their group. A

plump and kindly middle-aged woman had made herself available for mothering, when needed, and to keep an eye out to make sure no one was tempted to take advantage of the naïve girls. Like many, she had mixed feelings about the trip. She was sad she was leaving her young child behind with her parents, but happy that she would finally be reunited with her husband after two years of separation. Happy, but also anxious. She wanted to be sure everything went right between them after their time apart, so each morning she carefully put her hair up in rollers, practicing at looking her best. In fact, it was her anxious concern with her looks that stabilized the little group. They would get together every day, at least once a day, to spend hours fixing one another's hair and experimenting seriously with makeup. Berta was particularly pleased when, the first day, they gathered around her, brushing and combing, and painting all twenty of her nails a bright, glossy shade of red.

The last two were a very short (under five feet) middle-aged woman named Guadalupe, and her nineteen-year-old niece. Guadalupe was quiet but agreeable. Felícita, her niece, was attractive but timid, and existed, by choice, on the fringe of the group. She was tall and slender, with very pale skin and long, thick chestnut-colored hair. She had never been away from home before, and being forced into contact with a large number of strangers had started her headaches.

Guadalupe hoped that Felícita and Alicia Lugo would become friends, since they were almost the same age. But they were too different. Felícita sat to one side, distracted by her thoughts and still as a flower, while Alicia took an active part in the long hours of grooming and conversation. In the absence of a conventional society to structure and protect their world, they had formed their own and returned instinctively to the comforting ways of a small tribe. And if at times these people showed the warmth, color, and simplicity of a Brueghel peasant scene, perhaps it was because they had remained connected to their village roots long after moving to the cities.

Across the hall Antonio was reading. Francisco listened to guitar music on the radio and daydreamed. If he were home now, he would be working in the vegetable garden, he thought. But he would not see it ever again. Even if something terrible happened to his mother, he couldn't go back. He looked sadly into the distance, sometimes catching a glimpse of Felícita through the doorway.

They woke the next morning when Jorge Dávila pounded on each door with his heavy hand. "Everybody up! Let's go!" he shouted.

It was five-thirty. Tired people rushed to get ready and they felt out of sorts. The more ambitious dressed quickly and ran down the block to get coffee in the small shop. It was closed. There would be nothing to eat until they stopped for lunch, except cookies and beer from the night before. Outside the motel a huge Guatemalan bus throbbed, souring the air with diesel smoke. But overhead, as it usually was in El Salvador, the early-morning light was beautifully clear and fresh.

People ran back and forth washing, packing, and loading. As they hurried to take their seats, Jorge gave each of them a hundred colones, the equivalent of forty U.S. dollars, to show to the Guatemala Immigration officials at their first border. "Nobody talks about going to the United States," he warned. "You're tourists. You're only going to visit Guatemala. And I want every cent of this back right after we cross."

As Juanita Lugo got on the bus Jorge handed her a passport. "Oh, thank you," she said with relief, until she opened it and saw that it didn't have her name and that the photo was of a fat middle-aged woman with dark hair. "But it's not mine. It doesn't even look like me," the blond twelve-year-old wailed.

"This is better than yours," Jorge assured her. "Believe me. Yours wasn't ready yet, and I knew you didn't want to stay behind, so I got you this one instead. Now don't worry about a thing." And he helped her onto the bus.

"Have you seen my uncle?" Flora ran up and asked. No one had. "He would never miss this. Jorge, I'm afraid."

Jorge shrugged helplessly, but Espinoza was nervous enough to run around the motel one last time, checking rooms to be certain no one would be left asleep. Flora ran to the manager and asked if there had been any messages, then she came back and stood in the street, looking in one direction and then the other. Finally everyone else was aboard, except Jorge, who stood at the door and waited for her.

"I'm sorry, but we have to go, Flora," he said sympathetically. "Do you want to come with us or do you want to go search for him?"

She stood on her toes and looked as far as she could see. Finally, with painfully mixed feelings, she got on the bus and they closed the door. It was six o'clock sharp when they rumbled off.

It was six-thirty and the city was just beginning to stir when a cab pulled up in front of the motel. Peasant women from the countryside were climbing off the first buses with armloads of cut flowers to sell on the street. Shopowners were hosing down their sidewalks. A slender, intense thirty-year-old man literally jumped from the cab. He was followed more slowly by a long-legged, well-dressed woman, already fully made up. "Damn!" exploded the man. There was no bus, and many of the motel doors hung open. He ran to the office, where his knocking brought the manager from her breakfast. She stood in the doorway with a rolled tortilla in her hand, sleepily munching as they talked.

"They can't have gone already," he insisted.

"But of course."

"They weren't supposed to leave until six. And it's only six-thirty now. They never leave on time."

"But this time they left at six." She sighed. He did have a point. They never left on time.

"What a fine day to start being punctual," he complained to his attractive friend.

"Well," she said, not at all upset, "we might as well go back to my place, then."

"Ricardo never called. Flora could at least have called me. How could I know they were going to leave on time?"

Until the very moment he arrived at the motel, Flora's uncle, Robles, had been enjoying himself marvelously. His woman friend had decided to cater to him totally on his last day. They had spent it on a beautiful beach outside the capital, bathing in the warm ocean, lying under the sun until their skin became fragrant and hot. Then they sipped cold beers under rented umbrellas and talked sadly of how they would miss each other. When they returned to her apartment, she cooked him a lovely dinner. They kept drinking, and soon they were in the mood to go to bed, where they played until early in the morning. Despite an intense desire to spend the next day with her, he had behaved with the utmost sense of responsibility. As soon as the alarm went off, he jumped up, dressed, and rushed to the motel. But his second trip had already ended in disaster, just like the first one.

Flora had initiated the first trip. She had written to relatives in Los Angeles who sent her money for her fare. She hoped to continue her education, but that was almost impossible in El Salvador with all the schools closing. A young man she was in love with was going, and she wanted to be with him. Finally, there was her father. He had gone illegally to the United States more than five years before. He had intended to send money to help the family, but once he left, they had never heard from him again. There were people who said he had forgotten them, but Flora didn't believe it. He might be hurt, or in serious trouble, and she was determined to find him.

When Robles heard she planned to go, he decided to go with her. His life in El Salvador was good, but he felt ready for a change. And his friends told him that a man with his cleverness could make a fortune in the fertile economy of the United States. Robles bought and sold cattle. He made decent money and had his own truck. He stayed out of politics and, so far, everyone had let him alone. Even his family life had finally straightened out. He and his wife had fought a lot.

There were rumors that he had caught her with other men. One time she took their daughter, Isabel, and ran off. Robles followed her. His wife had never liked their daughter, he felt, and she had taken her only to punish him. When he found his wife, she was working as a belly dancer in a circus. Robles took Isabel home with him and never heard from his wife again. Then Robles lived with Consuelo, who became the new mother of Isabel, who was six. Consuelo could go legally to the United States, so it was decided that she would leave right after they did, and meet them in Los Angeles.

Robles discovered Jorge Dávila's ad in the newspaper. He had to read between the lines to understand it. It said that the agency would be booking vacation trips to the United States, with all border crossings arranged. They were a small group, that first time. There were only fifteen in all, including two coyotes (Jorge Dávila and Esteban Alvarado), Flora, Robles, Isabel, Ileana, and a woman named Josefa, who were all to be on the second trip.

There were no complex arrangements. In fact, there seemed to be no arrangements at all. They took local buses to wherever they wanted to go. They bought tickets like anyone else, got on, and hoped for the best. Flora volunteered to take care of Isabel, and the two spent most of their time together. Isabel was a pretty little six-year-old, with large brown eyes and dark-blond hair. She was at a stage where she liked to wear patent-leather shoes and frilly dresses, but on most of the trip she had been confined to sandals and slacks. And she liked to repeat things. She asked over and over where they were going, just to hear Flora explain that they were going to the United States to see her mother (Consuelo). Several times she gave people in the group great frights because of this innocent pastime. When they were in Mexico, for instance, where their accents easily identified them, she walked up to a group of strangers in a Mexico City bus station and announced loudly and proudly, "I'm the little girl who comes from El Salvador and is going to the United States to see my mother!" It was only what people on the bus had been saying to her, and she didn't understand the commotion that followed. After that, someone always watched her closely when she was in public, ready to cover her mouth the instant she began an announcement.

Isabel became good friends with Esteban Alvarado. He had had a beard on the first trip and Isabel liked to sit on his lap and pull it. It was a bond between them. He liked to tease her, and since she didn't have the words to respond, that was her reply. Alvarado had also become friends with Ileana. In Hermosillo, in northern Mexico, he bought her a pair of red shoes.

Benjamin Hill, just north of Hermosillo, is a bottleneck. Everyone headed for the United States goes through there, so it is a natural place for Immigration officials to concentrate their efforts. The group stopped on the outskirts of town, before they got to the inspection station, and Jorge put them in a hotel. "Right now it's too hot here," he told them. "Too many Migra. We have to wait until it cools down." But the fact was, he had no idea of how to get them through the area. So they were stuck for days in the cheap hotel. They were forbidden to go out because the coyotes were afraid that someone would recognize their accents or that one of the children would give them away. They had to eat whatever Jorge and Alvarado brought back from the market for them. And most of that time Jorge stayed in the local bars looking for contacts. He drank too much because he was nervous about being caught with all those people.

Locked in without anything to do, Isabel became cranky and cried often for her mother. "We'll see your mother," Flora promised her, "just as soon as we get to the United States. In the meantime we have to be good and wait patiently." Finally, on the fourth day, a van came for them before sunrise. They drove along a dirt road into the desert and got out. They walked for four hours to circumvent the inspection station. Then the van picked them up again and took them to San Luis, on the border near Yuma, Arizona.

In San Luis the pattern was repeated. They waited in the hotel while Jorge struggled to make arrangements to move them the rest of the way. It was still dark on the fourth day when three small cars came to get them. They went to a spot in the desert where a little river flowed. They got out on a hill and hid under a low tree, so they would be concealed from people who lived a short distance away. Josefa asked Alvarado if he had any food for them to take on the crossing. He said he could get some, got back into one of the cars, and drove off with the driver. Without any explanation, Ileana went away with them. The other two cars also left, and the people waited.

There were five children, including Isabel, in the little group. They couldn't play or make noise of any kind. They had to stay under the tree so they wouldn't be seen. There was no food or water for them. There were no blankets, and they sat on the ground. The stream looked pretty, only a short distance away, but no one was willing to take the risk of going to it, not after they had come all that way. When the children started crying, the adults tried in every way to keep them quiet. They were constantly afraid someone would hear and report them. Everyone was thoroughly wretched by the time Ileana, Alvarado, and the Mexican coyotes returned. It was seven in the evening, and they had waited for eleven hours.

"I know why you went with them," Robles said angrily when he saw Ileana. "I know what you were doing. When I get to the United States, I'm going to tell your husband."

Ileana looked shocked. She tried to explain. "We only went to look at the border," she told the group. "They wanted to make sure there was a good place to cross. On the way back we stopped to buy food and blankets. That's all that happened."

"No, you can't expect us to believe that," Robles taunted. "They told you they would take you across the easy way if you had sex with them." They all knew that coyotes were notorious for such propositions, but Robles was ignoring the fact that Ileana was still very much in Mexico.

Ileana started crying, but she was furious. "That's not true," she insisted, but Robles continued goading her. She turned to him in a rage. "When we get to Los Angeles, I'm going to tell my husband to kill you for saying that," she promised fiercely.

Robles laughed in her face. "I don't care. I'm not afraid of your husband."

Then it was time to start for the border. It was dusk. The wind was blowing strongly, picking up sand and dust. The coyotes made them a makeshift bridge over the little stream with two planks they had hidden along the bank. The people crossed over, carrying the children. Isabel was tired from the long wait and she didn't want to walk. Robles had to carry her the first part of the way. But there was a mother and an infant who were having a much more difficult time. The other children could walk part of the way and would let others carry them occasionally to give their parents a rest. But this little girl was too frightened and their situation was much too strange for her to be able to allow that. Her mother was the only familiar person there, and she had to carry her every step of the way. If anyone else touched the child, she would scream wildly.

The Mexican coyotes told them the walk would take four or five hours. They had gone that far a few days before, when they circled around the inspection station at Benjamin Hill. But the wind had not been blowing then and the land had not been as difficult. They crossed a long series of hills first, and then the ground became flat and soft. It was dry, but their feet would sink in and trip them and there was a feeling of wading. When they fell, the sand blew into their eyes and they coughed on the dust. The little girl cried the entire way. Finally they came to a swampy area and stopped. It was as if a river had died there. The Mexican coyote told them, "We're less than a mile from the border now. And after that it's only a few hundred feet more to the highway." The same three cars were supposed to cross over and pick them up for a quick trip to Los Angeles. "But we have to be quiet when we cross," he warned. "They have electronic listening equipment along there." They all looked at the baby.

"What should we do?" asked Jorge Dávila.

"We usually use sleeping pills," the man said. "It's safe, we do it often." He handed Jorge a capsule, and Jorge gave it to the child's mother. She looked at the drug, and everyone looked at her. The child continued to squirm and scream. It was a struggle, but she made her child take the pill.

Then they started across the mud flat. It smelled alkaline, and it stuck to them when they fell in it. Everyone felt the tension of an impending crisis, and the child continued to howl. Her mother was more exhausted than the others because she had to carry her all the way. As the woman lost more strength, she fell more. They were both bruised and scraped. Ahead of them was a small hill that hid the border on the other side. As they dragged themselves up the slope, the child rested more comfortably in her mother's arms, slowed her screaming, and finally became quiet.

As they crested the hill they could see the lights of the highway a short distance beyond. The cars were already there, waiting for them. Between them and the road was a ten-foot storm fence with sharp points on top. The coyotes climbed to the top and covered the points with the blankets they had bought. The others began to scramble over. The woman with the baby was unable to climb, so she held her child while the men on the bottom handed her up, the men on the top pulled her over. They spoke in whispers and worked as quickly and quietly as they could.

After the fence there was still one more obstacle. Ten feet farther was a concrete culvert. It was five feet across. The sides were vertical and far below water rushed through with great velocity. If someone fell in, it would be impossible to get out. They would die. There was a bridge across the culvert. It was for the border patrol, and it connected with a gate in the fence to give them access to the other side. There was also a gate in the middle of the bridge, but it was pad-locked and surrounded by barbed wire. They couldn't take the time to struggle with it. They had to jump across.

The first man to try looked frightened. But they gained confidence as they saw each other do it. And it became a relatively safe procedure once there were people on both sides of the gap to catch those who barely made it. Finally most of them were over and the only problem remaining was the woman with the baby. Her arms had become so tired that there was no possibility that she could jump holding her child. A small group of them stood by the edge of the churning water and tried to decide what to do. Finally Robles said, "If you want, I'll try to take her for you. Someone will have to jump with her."

The woman looked at Robles carefully. Then she studied the water. It clearly frightened her. Finally she turned back and handed him the child. None of the choices suited her, but she didn't know what else to do. Standing on the very edge of the channel, she took several deep breaths and then threw herself out into the dark gap. She made it only to the far edge and slipped back, but strong hands grabbed her and pulled her over.

When she saw her mother disappear, the little girl immediately began to scream. There was a brief pause, and then floodlights were turned on them. Two four-wheel-drive vans appeared and came charging down, cutting them off from the highway.

One of the Mexican coyotes was still on top of the fence. He climbed down immediately on the Mexican side and ran into the desert. Alvarado was standing with Robles by the culvert. "C'mon," he urged. "Quick, come with me!"

"No," Robles replied. "I'm with my daughter. I have to look after her."

Alvarado ran to the fence and climbed frantically. The 4x4s pulled up on the opposite side of the channel. They had their headlights on the group and their spotlights on him. Agents jumped out and ran toward him, waving their guns and yelling for him to stop. But when Alvarado reached the top, he let go and dropped over. The impact sprawled him out on his face and he lay there stunned. One of the officers ran out on the bridge, but he couldn't find the key to the gate. Alvarado got up and ran with all his might. Because it was night and they were surrounded by bright lights, he quickly disappeared in the contrasting darkness.

Flora was shocked at being caught. For the first time she felt she was doing something wrong, and her reaction surprised her. She was ashamed at being seen like this, sneaking across the border at night. But that feeling was quickly washed away by a massive wave of disappointment. We almost made it, she thought unhappily. Behind the uniformed men she could see the highway. Two of the cars were already gone, and the third pulled into traffic and disappeared as she watched. While they were being rounded up, she thought about all she had gone through for nothing. But she found the feeling oppressive, so she began the process of shaking it off.

For the entire trip Robles had stayed close to Isabel, but now the Migra put them in different vans. Several Mexican men had joined their little group at the last minute, for the crossing, and Isabel and Flora were put in with them. "Are we in America now?" Isabel asked plaintively. "Will we see my mother soon?" Flora's attempt to explain that they were, and she wouldn't, only confused her more.

The agents finally opened the gate and drove through into Mexico. They used their spotlights as they zigzagged rapidly through the desert searching for Esteban Alvarado. They drove over bushes and all kinds of natural hiding places. If Alvarado had been concealed underneath, they would have crushed him. They searched for twenty minutes but found no sign of him.

While this was happening, the Mexicans in the back of the van were talking with Flora. "They're going to interrogate us next," they whispered to her. "We three are all brothers. If you want, you can say you're a relative of ours. We'll vouch for you. Then they'll release you in Mexico and you can come right back here and try again."

To Flora it sounded like an unexpected opportunity to salvage her wrecked plans. When the Migra questioned the people in the van, Flora told them she was Mexican.

"No, you're not. You're from Nicaragua, I think," the agent replied uncertainly.

"No, I'm his sister." She pointed to one of the men.

"Who was the president last year?" he asked her. "What are the colors of the Mexican flag?" She told him correctly. The Mexicans had coached her earlier. Her accent wasn't anything like the men's, but he begrudgingly accepted her claim.

When they unloaded at the department's office, Robles was reunited with his daughter and Flora. They huddled together and Flora whispered, "Don't say anything, but I told them I was Mexican, and they believed me. They're going to let me go in Mexico, and I don't have to go all the way back to El Salvador again."

"Are you crazy?" Robles asked her. "That's not safe. And when I go back and the family sees me, they're going to ask, 'Where's Flora?' They're going to tell me that I'm your uncle and that I was responsible for making sure that you were all right. What will I tell them?" He walked over to one of the officials. "She's crazy," he told the man. "She's really my niece. We're both Salvadoran."

From the Yuma office they went almost immediately to Los Angeles in a bus that was like a jail. In Los Angeles they were questioned for biographical data. They stayed in jail until midafternoon. Their lunch looked like dog food. Isabel and Robles were apart again because the men and women were kept separate.

They were taken to the airport and flown to the Federal District of Mexico, where they landed about nine that same night. They went to a holding facility built right at the edge of the runway. In Los Angeles they had been treated fairly well, but that changed now. They were shoved roughly wherever they went, and the guards cursed at them. They called them Guanacos, which is an insulting name for Salvadorans. "You fuckin' Salvadorans give us more trouble than anyone esle," they said angrily. They seemed to take the presence of these outsiders as a personal insult.

Men went to the second floor and women stayed on the first. There was an international gathering there—Salvadorans, Guatemalans, Dominicans, even people from South America. They made the best of the situation, introducing themselves, chatting, and comparing notes.

The guards told them they could take a shower if they wanted. Flora was filthy from falling in the mud, but she felt too tired to bother. It had been a very long day. They slept in rows of folding cots with dirty blankets, and Flora fell into hers. Isabel asked about her mother again. "This is not the United States, right," she wanted to know, "but we're going back there?"

Flora tried, with the last of her energy, to explain that they were not going to the United States anymore; they were now on their way back to El Salvador and they would see her mother there. In the middle of the night she woke with a start, her heart pounding in her chest. The cot of the woman next to her had collapsed on the floor.

In the morning they were bused to a plane and flown to El Salvador. They were poised for danger, for brutality, for jail, but nothing happened. U.S. Immigration had given each of them a card with basic biographical information, and they surrendered these to a Salvadoran official who met them at the plane. Then they were free. It was anticlimactic. The relief collapsed quickly into depression. Flora felt ashamed by her failure and didn't want to go back to Santa Ana to face her family. So she went with Robles to Usulafter. where Consuelo and he had lived. Consuelo was gone. While they were under way, she had left for the United States.

They contacted Jorge Dávila's office and were told another trip would be leaving in a few days. Flora waited, but soon it became clear that every time they called the agency, there was a different story, a new departure date, and everyone seemed totally disorganized. Flora missed her mother, so Robles drove her home.

Dávila said that Isabel couldn't come again unless she paid a full adult fare, in addition to what Robles had already paid for her. Dávila had soured on children because of their experience. It was probably for the best, Robles agreed. The trip was too hard for a little girl. And now Isabel was terribly confused. They had gone to America, and her mother wasn't there because she was still back in El Salvador. They had come back to El Salvador and her mother wasn't there because she had gone to the United States. Robles tried to avoid talking about Consuelo because it only seemed to make his daughter more upset. He decided to try again, by himself. He would get himself established, with a secure job and a home, and then he would send for her legally somehow. It was over two months before Dávila was ready to go again, but it took them all that long to recover from the first trip.

The mood on the bus was quiet and serious. Everyone had thoughts about leaving. The more religious ones used the moment for Bible study. An old man, respectfully referred to as "Don" Cruz, was reading scripture to himself with pleasure. And a few seats behind him, two young men also had their Bibles open.

No one seemed to know exactly, but there were at least forty adults on the bus, and seven or eight children. Every seat was taken, and infants were forced to ride on their mother's laps.

They took the new, divided highway out of the capital, and headed northwest. They passed through Santa Tecla, turned southwest through Armenia, and then connected with Central American Route 8, to the border after Ahuachapán. The bus was labeled "air-conditioned," as they uniformly were, but as usual, it was not working. Not that they needed it. This was the dry season, and so early in the day the air was clear and sweet. Everyone had his window cracked to enjoy the breeze while it was still cool.

Most of the route took them past coffee plantations, their tiny country being one of the main suppliers in the world. But the red berries of ripe coffee would not be visible until November and December. Now the low trees with the shiny leaves were spattered with hundreds of tiny fragrant white blossoms. They also saw cattle ranches. And fruit plantations with huge, droopy mango trees; silver-green rows of olives; coconuts; and the *zapote*, which has a papery brown hull outside, and inside the color of wet brick and the taste of sweet squash.

People rested, or read, or chatted lightly with their seat partners. They still felt too dislocated to do much socializing. By nine they had reached their first border.

They descended through the small hills and emerged on a riverbank by a row of government buildings and barracks. Armed soldiers guarded the concrete bridge ahead. The bus was waved off into a parking area. None of El Salvador's borders were comfortable places, and several uniformed men held automatic weapons tensely across their chests and stood watchfully. Another came on board and walked slowly down the aisle, collecting their passports. Then he ordered them to take their luggage and get off.

The travelers lined up along the side of the bus with their bags in front of them. A soldier went down the line, searching every suitcase thoroughly, while two others stood guard. Their first concern was to detect guerrillas or other political undesirables, and the movement of arms or explosives. After that, they had a casual concern for the usual smuggling and immigration offenses.

After the search, passports were given back one at a time, as the guard called out the names and matched the faces to the photos. Those called took passport and luggage and got back on the bus with relief. As the group dwindled, Juanita Lugo began to swallow and blink in the sunlight. Halfway through the list the soldier called out, "María Ramírez," and no one moved. "María Ramírez!" he barked again. The guards gave each other quick warning looks, the people shifted uneasily, and Juanita shut her eyes in fear. But no one came forward. The soldier put the unclaimed passport carefully under his arm and moved to the next one. Jorge Dávila cleared his throat to attract his attention. "Pardon, but . . ." he mumbled, and came forward to talk to the official. He was waved away with a curt, backhand gesture. He returned to the line, where he rocked his weight from one foot to the other as if he would like to walk somewhere.

The soldier continued to call names and return passports. The last few in line turned to give sympathetic looks to the twelve-year-old as they left. Her sisters hung out the bus window, not even whispering to each other. Finally there was only the single passport he took from under his arm, and the child standing in front of the bus. The officer slapped the passbook on his palm reflectively while he decided what to do.

"Please, sir," Jorge tried again in his most humble voice. "There is no problem, I assure you. If only I could have a minute to explain . . ."

The man gave him a glaring look, but this time he was permitted to approach. They whispered together for a moment, and then, after a slight suggesting gesture from Jorge, they walked out of sight around the front of the bus. The guards, faced only with the frightened blond child, finally relaxed. One even snorted, his way of acknowledging some humor in the situation.

The two men returned, and now Jorge held the passport. "Come along, dear," he said kindly, but he had to walk over to her, put his arm around her, and physically help her get started. She was awkward from fear, and stumbled getting back on the bus, but Jorge caught her and helped her up. He handed back her passport and said, "I told you there wouldn't be any problem." But it was more than half an hour before she could stop trembling. Just the same, there was greater respect for Jorge Dávila, for the fact that he had handled the crisis. The barrier was raised, and with more relief than sadness they left their homeland of El Salvador and crossed the bridge to the new problems of Guatemala.

The bus climbed winding roads up to Guatemala's central plateau, which shelters most of the country from the heat and diseases of the lowland tropical swamps. Jorge remembered to collect the money he had given out. It became cooler now, and they squeezed their windows forward to cut down on the air. It was 140 kilometers to the capital, and several perpetually smoking volcanoes became visible as they neared it. (Guatemala had recently threatened to invade their tiny neighbor, Belize, and Belize responded by promising to bomb Guatemala's many volcanoes and flood the country with lava.) The bus drove to the middle of Guatemala City and stopped at the edge of the huge market.

The area is an anthill. In its center is a civic market building, several blocks across. And surrounding that, for blocks in every direction, are ramshackle booths made of scrap tin, old lumber, and cardboard. The aisles are bright displays of produce and dark tunnels of goods. Handmade wares bulge from shelves and racks, hang from wires overhead, and spread out along the floor. Shops that serve similar needs tend to group together. There are whole aisles where leatherworkers haggle over boots, shoes, and wallets, with a few fancy saddles here and there. Elsewhere are multicolor hammocks and net bags, native clothing, great mounds of candy, kitchen utensils, and fresh flowers. Miniature doll furniture and masks. And the diversity of fruits and vegetables surpasses anything available in the United States.

Some of the cheapest and best meals in the city can be had at the little restaurants tucked into the market, and after the long bus ride, the change was a tonic. They were ready to enjoy their break. Francisco stopped worrying about his home, and Flora decided that her uncle was probably all right and would just have to make the best of his situation. They fanned out to several small eating places and had their rice and beans, enchiladas or stewed beef, at counters and benches in the midst of the bustle. The food was hotter than they were used to, but not bad. Guatemalans use some chili, but it was Mexico that was legendary for its consumption of hot peppers.

Back in the bus, full and logy, they zigzagged down to a lower elevation, into the humid heat again. "Guatemala has so many rivers," Berta remarked to Alicia Lugo, watching the deep-green countryside. They had bought bubble gum at the market, and now they passed the time blowing bubbles. When dusk came, they saw tiny red snake tongues of lava flicking from the top of one of the huge gray cones on the horizon.

It was late evening when they got out in Tecunumán, on the Guatemalan side of the Mexican border. The bus left them directly across the tracks from the train station, not a scenic location. A short distance ahead, a large river flowing out to the Pacific formed the boundary line. The jungle humidity was tolerable only because a breeze from the sea stirred it continually.

Directly in front of them was a crumbling hotel. They could guess from experience that it must be theirs. Jorge directed them through an arch, stopped briefly at the manager's office, and then started to distribute rooms. They were in a long, single-story row, with a yard of sorts opposite. People were more crowded here than in San

Salvador; three were assigned to most rooms. Berta was put with Guadalupe and her niece, Felícita. "This place would have flopped a long time ago if it weren't for people like us," was Berta's shrewd assessment. This was a clear sign of what it was going to be like to travel with Jorge, she decided. Now that they were away from home and had little choice in the matter, he would pack them into the cheapest hotels he could find to save all the money possible. So much for his promise of a deluxe, all-expenses-paid tour. The place was falling down. The rough board walls sagged with such large chinks that she decided to put out the lights before getting undressed.

Finally Jorge led Ileana and her sister-in-law, Luisa, down the long row to the last room at the end of the yard. He opened the door, snapped on the bare bulb, then turned and walked away without a comment. Ileana followed him immediately. "No, Jorge," she said, "I won't sleep there."

"Why not?" he asked irritably.

"Because I don't want to," she insisted.

"Yes, but why, why, WHY?" he exploded with impatience.

But Ileana was just as impatient. "Because it's dirty! That's why! And it's dark. And it's far away from everybody. And do you smell that? The toilet is right next door, and it stinks! First, you try to leave me behind, and then you try to give me the worst room. What are you going to do next? I'm a decent person and I want a decent room!" When she started to raise her voice, people poked their heads out of their doorways. There was soon a considerable audience in what had been a dark and isolated spot only a minute before. Their interest was vaguely menacing to Jorge. By continuing to persecute her he might be picking a fight with them all, and he didn't want that.

"What exactly would please you?" he asked sarcastically.

"I want a nicer room, up there." Ileana pointed toward the front. And when they looked, Jorge found there was indeed a vacant room that was cleaner, brighter, and near where she wanted to be. Ileana and Luisa took possession of it triumphantly.

Jorge had been wise to retreat from a weak position. There was unanimous dissatisfaction with the rooms, and everyone agreed that the toilet was one of the most foul they had seen. Again there was only one for them all, and only cold water. But now there wasn't even a shower. There was only a cement tub, a bit like a birdbath, which was used for washing clothes. It was filled with a bucket from a well in the yard. In order to wash, they had to carry several buckets to the small, waist-high tub, and then ladle it over themselves from the tub with a scoop. The water ran across the slanted floor, along the wall used as a urinal, and out a drain hole into the yard. But they felt sticky after a day of sitting in the bus, and one by one they hurried to wash. They had to be quick because so many were waiting.

While this was going on, there were two mysterious events. Jorge scurried from person to person, whispering. He was careful to hide this from Pablo, a short plump man with an excitable temperament. And then they noticed that someone had cracked the door of one of the front rooms, a room not taken by one of them. From behind the slit a single bright eye made them uneasy as it watched everything they did.

Pablo discovered his secret first. After he washed, Jorge asked him for some help. He had been looking at a guitar one of the border guards had for sale, he said, and he wanted Pablo's advice on it. Was it worth anywhere near the $150 the man wanted? "That's a lot to pay like this, on the road," Pablo cautioned. But he took up the instrument and strummed it experimentally. Then he played a succession of chords and did some finger picking. His look was appreciative, and he handed back the guitar with reluctance. "That's O.K.," he approved. "You know, it's not really such a bad price."

"Well, that's good." Jorge sighed with relief. "Because that's what we just paid for it. It's yours now." And he handed it back.

"No! Really?"

"Yes, we all chipped in to get it for you. The bus was like a funeral today. We need some music, and you sing like a bird." It was a brilliant stroke, and it wiped out all the resentment that Jorge accumulated when he had tried to put Ileana in her place. The irony was that the forty-some adults who chipped in two dollars or less apiece had not covered half of the $150, and Jorge had had to make up the rest from the money he had saved on the cheap rooms.

Pablo, a Latin leprechaun, started dancing about, strumming and singing in a high sweet voice. Passing Flora, who had already adopted him as one of her uncles, he gave her a kiss on the cheek and a flourishing chord, and made her laugh. The door opened behind them. A man stepped out quickly and grabbed Flora by the shoulder.

"So, this is where you are," he said. "I've been looking for you."

"Robles!" Flora screamed when she saw her uncle. "What are you doing here?"

"What are *you* doing here?" he asked. "Why didn't you wait for me?"

"Jorge said you had called the office. You knew when we were leaving."

"I did! But how was I to know you were going to leave on time?" They laughed at him, and even Flora, who had been hurt by his tone, now forgave him. "Why didn't you call me?" Robles tried to go on, but they were still laughing and it was difficult to be so serious.

"Sure, who knew where you were?" Flora scolded him. "You have women all over the country. How should I know what bed you were in that night? You crazy thing, you had me so worried." She gave him a shake and then a big hug.

They followed Pablo to the front porch in a party mood. "How did you ever get here?" Flora wanted to know.

"I went to the motel, and you were gone. I was desperate. I ran around in the street like a crazy man until I found a taxi that would take me to Guatemala City. It cost over four hundred colones. Jorge Dávila was getting my passport, so I didn't have that, but fortunately I could cross the Guatemalan border with my identity card. From Guatemala City I caught the express bus to the frontier and got here before you did. I just counted on Dávila staying in the same hotel as the last trip. I knew if it hadn't fallen down yet, you would all be here, because Dávila could never find another place this cheap." They laughed in agreement. "And sure enough, the manager said you had reservations for tonight, so I hid to surprise you."

They thought Pablo was "perfect" on the guitar. When he sang, his normally excited and squeaky voice straightened out and became extraordinarily sweet. He sang some sentimental songs from home, and then, after some of them went to a store for beer, lively songs. "The Song of the Gang with the Red Car." The raunchy, "El Caimán" (The Lizard), which was just a string of sex jokes. They sang with him. And then Pablo sang one of his own, about wanting so much from life and searching so long.

Ileana liked the singing now, but she was tired. She and Luisa went in to sleep. The two young men who had been reading their Bibles on the bus came out for a few minutes to see what was happening. But this only made them feel more cut off from the others. They didn't see any reason to be happy.

One of them asked Jorge Dávila if he could change some money into Guatemalan quetzals. Jorge said he could do it the first thing the next day and took twenty-five dollars. Antonio overheard the transaction and gave Jorge a hundred dollars to change.

At about eleven, the breeze stopped and the air became heavy with moisture from the river and jungle. The mosquitoes liked the still air and now appeared from wherever they had been hiding. They were a breed that was new to the Salvadorans, tiny and silent, whose bites didn't last long but smarted painfully the first few minutes. But no one minded terribly. The trip was finally under way and everything was going well. They were happy.

They decided to take a stroll with their minstrel, men and women arm in arm. They walked about in the warm night streets, singing and talking, telling little jokes on each other, for about an hour. When they returned to the hotel again, many drifted away. The mothers had clothing and diapers to take care of, and they had waited until the bathroom was free. Now they washed in companionable groups and hung their wet laundry on ropes strung between trees in the yard.

The other women went to bed and found a pleasant surprise. The rope lacing on the bed frames, which had been supplied instead of real mattresses, was right for the hot climate, and actually quite comfortable. But most of the men stayed up with Pablo and his guitar, enjoying the beer and singing until dawn. No trains came and there was only the sound of their voices in the streets.

Jorge and Pablo had once been friends. That was how Jorge knew about Pablo's singing, and perhaps some past fondness also played a part in the gift of the guitar. But they were no longer close. In Pablo's opinion, Jorge had changed.

Jorge had been born poor, but had bettered himself. By his early twenties he had a wife, two children, and a shop in the capital where he made his living repairing TVs and radios. He was a decent man who didn't drink or smoke. He had his moods, but he was still considered a friendly person, someone who would share what he had when others needed it more. That was the custom in their community, where the people all had roots in peasant villages, and traditions of life-long relationships, mutual respect, and aid.

When he tried to explain why Jorge had changed, Pablo came up with various theories. "He became ambitious," he decided one time. "Success ruined him," he said on another occasion, "easy money." In fact, he really had no idea why success or ambition had taken hold and distorted him. Perhaps something had happened to disillusion the man, but that, too, was theory.

It did seem to be connected with his new desire to be a coyote. Once he felt he had discovered the formula for easy money, it changed every aspect of his life. He started neglecting his home. He disappeared for days with women he met in bars. He bragged about the money he would make. He acted proud.

His role as coyote, smuggler of people, gave him power, but so did his body. He was only of medium height, but he was built thick and heavy, the extra bulk divided equally between muscle and fat. A mustache and longish black hair fringed his round and oily face. Women were especially uncomfortable with him. Pablo, who did not have to suffer him in that regard, was inclined to excuse it. "He's like all young men," Pablo said. "The majority of young men, when they see a bunch of women, they go crazy." But the women had a different perspective. The way he stared at them was rude and unpermissible in their country, and he had a nasty, smirking way of making his little invitations. The women were afraid to antagonize him, but behind his back they warned each other to stay out of his reach. And they admired Ileana for her ability to stand up to him.

But he must have had another side. There was a sweet, quiet song Pablo had written about unfulfilled longings, and Jorge asked for it often on the trip. "I want . . . I want . . . I want . . ." it pleaded, "I want you to tell me that you love me . . . that everything you say is true . . . Because that way . . . that way . . . that way . . ." It was hardly the sort of song you would think would be Jorge's favorite.

Pablo was thirty-six years old and five feet, two inches tall. With his large bright eyes and round shape, he looked like a bubbling, middle-aged cherub with a mustache. And when he sang, his voice was high and sweet, much higher and sweeter than his speaking voice, and with none of the super-charged, carbonated quality of his speech.

He was a cheerful man, but the situation had finally made his life unbearable. It had started that spring, when he lost the sales job he had had for fifteen years. He had worked for the same distributing company since he was twenty-one, but the company closed, like many others. To support his wife, his four children, and his mother he tried to set up a business modeled after his job. He bought household goods such as soap, beans and rice, sugar, salt, and instant coffee, for resale to local shops. But stores everywhere were closing, and he couldn't find enough customers. By now people in El Salvador hesitated to go out even in the daytime. His wife stopped at every corner and peered around the edge of the building before she crossed the street. Too many people had already blundered into fatal crossfire. And some deaths were not accidental, but an expression of frustration and malice. An old man in the neighborhood had been stopped by some young soldiers and ordered to run. They shot him in the back. Pablo saw the body lying in the street where they left it. They had dug out his heart with a bayonet.

In March his daughter's grammar-school teacher, a personal friend, was tortured, raped, and killed in the middle of the night. An unofficial death squad left a note claiming responsibility. They had hacked her body into chunks with a machete and left it in a plastic bag to be dragged away with the garbage. As with many victims it was not clear why she had been chosen. Now, because of her link to his children, Pablo was afraid for their safety as well.

In April, to his great relief, he completed a large sale. He had 700 colones (about $280) in his pocket, when he was forced from his microbus by six men. They prodded him with pistols and took the money. He felt lucky to be alive, so lucky that he didn't tell the police or even his own wife. He was afraid that if word spread by rumor and some particular person or group were blamed, he might be killed in retaliation.

Later that same month, again in the district of Soyapango, where he had built his own home, he was about to enter the town hall when he saw men with masks chasing the staff through the corridors and shooting them. The mayor and his assistants were executed while trying to escape. Pablo ran away. He didn't want to be a witness. Not everyone else was as lucky, and four passersby were shot.

The little money they had went to feed the children, and they fell three months behind on the car payments. His wife sewed in a factory, but she didn't make enough to support them. And in May she was terrorized when a labor organization seized the plant in a protest and held her and her co-workers captive for three days.

The accumulating strain began to destroy their marriage. They started arguing and sometimes screamed and hit. They began to avoid each other. And finally, although they remained close to the children, they took other lovers for their comfort.

El Salvador is a beautiful country. In many ways it is a fine place to live. The mountains are cool, the lowlands are warm, and there is enough water for crops. Pablo was not looking forward to the dangerous two-thousand-mile journey to a land he had never seen, where he had no friends and didn't understand the language. And he had no desire to drop suddenly to the bottom of the social scale, from a respected business person to an illegal alien. But he sold his VW and went to Jorge to pay for his escape.

To travel safely in Mexico they needed a Mexican bus. Jorge was too hung over the next morning to get it, but instead of admitting that, he claimed there were some last-minute border problems he had to take care of. So Julio Espinoza, his partner, agreed to go, and Flora and Pablo, both still full of energy, went along to keep him company.

They got into a cab and rode the thirty-five kilometers to Tapachula. The countryside was lush and many homes they passed were simple huts with stick walls and roofs of palm thatch. The materials were free and grew everywhere. Tapachula turned out to be a substantial small city with cobblestone streets and a colorful market. The cathedral in the main square rang every quarter-hour with a particularly unmusical chime that sounded exactly like someone hitting a pipe with a wrench.

The bus station was a smallish cobblestone yard; ten or fifteen buses were wedged in along one side with only inches between them. To leave the lot (and there were continuous comings and goings), they had to back out into the middle of a busy street. The drivers couldn't possibly slide into that crowd of vendors, waiting passengers, and passing pedestrians, without help, so a young boy would go to the last seat and look out the rear window. He signaled the driver with loud slaps on the sheet-metal roof, once for stop (for an old woman with a basket of eggs on her head, who couldn't jump aside), and three to keep coming (if there were only a few young men passing who could look out for themselves).

Julio Espinoza went in the office to get the owner. The others waited in the cab until he came out again and suggested that they go to the bar on the corner and have a beer while he did the business. "I'll come and get you when I'm through," he said. In the bar the waitress brought them *tapas*, free appetizers, in this case mussel soup. They each got a cup of spicy broth flavored with tomatoes and garlic, each with a bright-purple mussel with its dab of tangy meat. It took Espinoza half an hour. All the details had to be discussed and agreed upon, but nothing could be written down because the deal was illegal. Espinoza came for them in the bus, and their new drivers took them back to the others.

Back in Tecunumán people were in a good mood. They drifted out in little groups to find breakfast: scrambled eggs, or ranch-style with salsa, or fried "like stars," as sunny-side-ups are called in Spanish.

After breakfast the hair clan met again, in the room shared by the Lugo sisters. They were getting to know each other and were more openly curious. "How come you put your hair up in the morning and take it out at night?" Bertá wanted to know. "Everybody else does it the opposite," she told the woman who always wore rollers.

"I can't stand to sleep on them, so I have to do it that way," she explained. She was getting ready for her husband. No one mentioned that she wouldn't see him for almost a week. The sisters were nervous about seeing their mother again, so they understood. But Inés Lugo thought, I would never walk around in rollers. At night, when the woman was not using her rollers, the others took turns with them. The group would pick one of their number and put her hair up for her.

There was an interesting bit of gossip that morning, about a woman with her five-year-old son. The man traveling with her as her husband was a fake. He was really her husband's best friend. Her husband was waiting for them in New York. The friend had agreed to pretend to be her husband to protect her from the problems single women sometimes had on such trips. They were not sleeping together, the source reported. Later Alicia and Berta went shopping for snacks to bring on the bus.

Jorge Dávila was getting his hair cut in a little shop with a sign that said, Unisex, when Antonio and the young Bible reader found him. They wanted the money he had changed for them. "I didn't actually change it," Jorge confessed. "I was all ready to change it when I thought, In a few hours they'll be in Mexico and they'll just need to change it all over again. So I decided to wait until we crossed the border, and then give it to you in pesos."

The young man wanted his money so he could change it for himself after they crossed, but Jorge insisted he didn't have it with him. Antonio didn't say a thing. He accepted that it had cost him a hundred dollars to find out what kind of man Jorge was, and since he had paid well for the information, he would be sure to use it well. There was always a way to get even, he knew.

They weren't the only ones Jorge didn't want to see that day. Word went out that it was time to cross the border and that they should break into little groups to be less conspicuous. So Flora's uncle Robles came to Jorge Dávila to get his passport.

"I'm sorry, my friend, but we have a little problem," Jorge said, putting his arm soothingly around the other man's shoulders. "But don't worry, I've already found the solution. Come over here with me and I'll show you what you have to do . . ."

The Guatemalan border guards had their own tax on well-dressed tourists who wanted to leave the country. More than fifteen soldiers were waiting expectantly at the entrance to the bridge. They intercepted each little group and led them to one side for private discussions. *Mordida*, the familiar "bite," was taken out of each Salvadoran. But the rates were not uniform. One man had to pay twenty dollars, while Ileana had to pay only five. "Probably because she's cute," he complained.

Little Juanita spent the entire morning trying to get herself emotionally ready for the crossing. The twelve-year-old didn't want to tell anyone how frightened she was, and no one guessed. They had already forgotten the incident on the Salvadoran border. Her hands sweated and she struggled to control her stomach. When she reached the guard, she tried to shove her false document at him confidently, but he refused it. Like the others, he only wanted money, and after he got it, he had no further interest in her. She walked across that long bridge with tremendous relief.

Flora's uncle Robles was furious at Jorge Dávila. He knew Dávila perfectly well from the first trip, so it had been stupid to trust him. But Dávila had insisted over and over that he would take care of everything, that there would be no problems this time, and Robles had more interesting things to do during his last weeks in El Salvador than to chase after pieces of paper. But the minute Jorge mentioned the familiar "problems," Robles knew he had been had again. There was no passport for him.

"How the hell do you expect me to cross into Mexico?" he asked in exasperation.

"Don't worry, no problem," Jorge assured him. "You'll cross by the river, just like most of the people around here," and he outlined a plan he had put together hastily after Robles surprised him by showing up. Robles complained, but he knew it was no use, and he watched forlornly as everyone from the bus disappeared over the bridge into Mexico. Then he turned and trudged out of town in the direction Dávila had pointed.

The path traveled west, toward the Pacific, a few miles away. At first the riverbank was heavily overgrown, and trees and brush blocked a clear view of the water. But half a mile farther on, the bank dropped and the trees receded. A low, rocky shore sloped to the current, and now he could see it was impressive, about two blocks across at that point.

He noticed a woman below him at the edge of the river. She was bent over, washing clothes. Not exactly pretty, but pretty enough, and he was fascinated by her concentration. Somewhere in town there is a very lucky man, he thought. It immediately passed through his mind that he too could be happy if only someone would wash his clothing that way, with such commitment, even reverence. It was ironic that Robles, with his looks and charm and frequent success with women, often felt lonely and acutely deprived. He could enter a romantic idealization of almost any woman he saw on the street, and then feel rejected if she passed by.

Just ahead was the place local people came to swim. And if they didn't care to bother with the formalities of the border, that was where they crossed over. Swimming was all right for a child in a bathing suit, but those with clothing to keep dry and goods to transport used the local ferry system. There were a number of people with large inner tubes from truck tires, with planks over them. A rope around the tube was tied to the waist of the man who pulled it, wading in the shallows, swimming furiously in the deep current. They were less than a kilometer from the government border crossing, but there was not an official in sight.

Robles gave two quetzals to a wiry man with very dark, shiny skin and then climbed on his float with a toothless old farm woman. The woman balanced two big bags of groceries on her plank, as if this were an everyday trip for her. Robles was amazed that the primitive contraption was so well rigged that he could ride with his new boots on and not get them wet. They pushed off, and Robles, his eyes constantly on his goal, noticed immediately when the two Mexican soldiers with black submachine guns stepped out from behind some bushes to watch his progress.

Their ferryman pulled them skillfully through swift channels and over shallow sandbars. Robles wondered if a bribe could help soothe the grim looks from the soldiers' faces. Then he wondered if he should jump into the river while he was still near Guatemalan waters, with people all about. But he wasn't a strong swimmer and he cringed at the thought of ruining his boots and getting his fine clothing wet. He was wearing his favorite metallic-blue shirt, and while he hesitated, it became too late.

"Where are you going?" he asked the peasant woman, grasping at any straws.

"I have to wait for the bus," she rasped.

"I have to go to the bus too. I'll help you with your bags," he offered eagerly.

She studied him carefully. "You're not from Guatemala," she said.

"No, I'm not," he admitted.

"I can tell by the way you speak. Where are you from?

"El Salvador," he said tensely. They were getting close to the shore and the soldiers were strolling down to meet them.

"And you're trying to get across the border?"

"Yes, I am."

"Do you know the way?"

"No, I don't," he said unhappily, watching the soldiers.

"Then come with me. Bring the bags. It will be all right," she assured him in her rusty old voice.

He hoped sincerely that she was right. Everyone else was already across, and he didn't trust Jorge to wait for him. When they reached the bank, the guards were only a few yards away, waiting above the mud line so they wouldn't soil their shiny boots. Robles got out and turned to pick up both bags immediately. They were heavy, but they partly hid him, and even though they wouldn't stop a bullet, they gave him an illusion of protection. Looking down, he could see sugar, rice, beans, and tomatoes. He clutched the bags too tightly, and some of the tomatoes broke and seeped through to wet his shirt and his chest.

The soldiers looked at Robles. "Where are you going?" one of them demanded.

"To my house," the old lady answered for him.

"Where do you live?" She gave the name of a village, not a place Robles had ever heard of.

"And him? Where does he go?" They leaned closer and inspected him carefully.

"The same. He's my son," she explained patiently.

"O.K. Go on."

Robles hurried ahead of her along the path back to town. Only when they were out of sight was he able to slow down and let her lead. He was in Mexico. He was safe. And he felt very happy.

"It's a good thing they didn't make you talk," she told him. "They would have known in a minute."

They followed the path to Ciudad Hidalgo. "I have to stop here," the woman said. "I have to wait for my husband. Thank you for helping me with my bundles."

"Oh, no," exclaimed Robles, "I have to thank you. I really

appreciate what you did for me." He reached into his pocket and gave her five dollars.

"Oh," she exclaimed, "may God bless you!"

"Thanks, I'll need it."

She kissed him on the cheek and they hugged each other before he left to go to the bus station.

In the middle of the hot little town, with its dusty, unpaved streets, the bus station was an oasis, a natural gathering place. It wasn't really a station at all. In the doorway of a private apartment that opened onto the street, someone had placed a small table. Behind it sat a heavy fourteen-year-old girl, her cheek resting on one palm in boredom, her mouth open as she stared out at the street. She had a pad of all-purpose tickets in front of her, and a metal ruler she used to tear them off at the proper price. Behind her, her mother was visible in the shadowy interior of the next room, cutting vegetables at a table.

Just outside, a long tin awning shaded the sidewalk for thirty feet in each direction. The awning reached a row of leafy trees along the street, and they had anchored the tin by overgrowing the outer edge of it. The trees added shade to the enclosure, and the green transparency of leaves in the sun. Rough benches lined the breezeway on both sides, and dogs slept peacefully underneath, enjoying the cool packed earth. Vendors, mostly clusters of children, sold fresh-cut fruit, ice cream from a cooler, and nuts and candies from baskets. The children cared for even smaller babies. Several took turns being bathed in a washtub by the curb. Others were carried about, naked and drooling, pop-eyed with interest, totally absorbed by the life around them. The pace was slow and they sat or played near their goods until someone came over to buy. Next door a liquor store with an ice chest sold clear bottles of Corona Export. It was a very pale and excellent-tasting beer, and reasonably cold, considering the weather. Across the street the buildings facing them were painted in two-tone tropical colors: emerald and rose, gold and blue, lemon and pink.

Robles' companions were waiting there with the townspeople. Few of them realized that he hadn't come over the bridge with them. "What happened to your shirt?" was all anyone said. He had almost died and didn't care to answer the question. Instead, he walked over to a little girl to buy some pineapple. She cut a piece off a large wedge, sliced it freshly into chunks, and put them into a small plastic bag.

"Do you want it hot?" she asked.

"Sure," answered Jorge, who had no idea what she meant. He had been absorbed in watching her thin brown arms as she worked. She sprinkled a generous amount of bright-red powder over the fruit. Although the cayenne burned his throat, he was surprised at how well the hot and sweet tastes complemented each other. He was hungry, so he ate it all, using the distance to observe his group objectively. They stood out clearly from the sleepy townfolk who lounged about in baggy, dusty clothing. His people had freshened themselves up in Tecunumán and were now dressed in their best. Most of the women wore slacks and heels, although Felícita and a few others had on dresses. All the women had their hair fixed, the men's shoes were shined, clearly city people. He approved of them, and relenting, he went over and began telling them about the amazing thing that had just happened to him.

Bus travel in Latin America encourages fatalism. The roads are narrow and mountainous, with steep gorges and no guardrails. Operators try, as a matter of pride, to drive at top speed at all times. Passing on blind curves or blind hills is blandly accepted by those who live there, although outsiders usually find the experience terrifying. As a consequence, every week the headlines report some massive head-on collision or a full bus that dropped into a ravine. Still, it is an exciting means of travel. The countryside is dramatic, and the Salvadorans' purpose (what they fled and what they sought) heightened the experience. They were in good humor and looking forward to their future.

Now began the major effort of the trip, four or five days of constant travel, cut off from the world but inseparable from each other. They stopped only to eat or use the toilet.

Time blurred and most of their normal patterns were disrupted. Perhaps that explains some of the behavior that developed.

This continuous travel was accomplished by a team of two Mexican drivers who worked in relays. One drove all day, and one all night. The off-duty man slept on the shelf above the last row of seats, under the back window. They made beds like rats' nests among the luggage piled there. In the high country at night, when the bus was sometimes chilly, this bed over the diesel was warm and comfortable, although noisy and vibrating.

To pass the time the drivers flirted. "Who's that one over there?" one would call, making eyes into the rearview mirror at full-figured Josefa. "I *like* her. She looks *good!*"

Josefa laughed.

"Hey, that's my sister!" countered Robles from down the aisle.

"O.K., brother-in-law." The driver laughed back.

Behind the driver sat an anonymous Mexican man and woman. They were friends of the drivers and were being brought to Guadalajara as a favor. When the bus had arrived, they were already entrenched, and no one had ever challenged them. Across the aisle, in the front seats on the right, sat Jorge Dávila and Julio Espinoza, the two coyotes in charge. Jorge was the prima donna. He sat on the aisle if he wanted to see through the front window, and against the side if he wanted Espinoza to insulate him from complaints. Behind them sat Pablo with his guitar, and then came a number of rows filled with women with young children. They had babies and baby things to carry, and those seats were given to them to make their lives a little more comfortable.

Farther back sat the three Lugo sisters, Alicia, Inés, and Juanita. Behind them were Guadalupe and her niece, Felícita, and across the aisle an unhappy couple who seemed to be perpetual outsiders, Señor Pagán and his wife. She never used her own name, and was known only as "Señor Pagán's wife." The two quiet-natured Bible students, Emilio and Raúl, and the religious old man, Don Cruz, had the bad luck to take the next seats, in an area totally unsuited to them. Don Cruz, who kept his Bible open on his lap most of the time, sat next to Roberto. Roberto was a student who had left the agricultural university when he was followed one day by a group of armed strangers. He had a lively and outgoing nature, like the people behind him.

Flora and her young cousin, Ricardo, came next, and across from them were Francisco and Antonio. In the last row were several seats used by various people in rotating fashion, and then Ileana and her sister-in-law, Luisa. With the addition of Robles and the two Mexican guests, there weren't enough seats to go around. Robles often sat on the arm of someone's seat, and when he needed to sleep, he lay down in the aisle.

Pablo was now one of the best-known of the group. "Come down here and sing to us," someone from the back would call, and Pablo would obligingly get up and take his guitar. But as soon as he stood up, someone would take his seat. More seats disappeared as mothers used them to diaper in, or to leave a sleeping baby. Sometimes there were squabbles over territory, but Pablo was not one of those who complained. He stood and sang because he wanted to. This was his first holiday in years. He was leaving an unhappy marriage, he was away from the awful pressures of El Salvador, and he was looking forward to a new life. So he sang like a bird escaped from its cage.

They all joined in on favorites. "My Last Disaster" ("It is my destiny to live so . . . in sad agony without you . . ."). The bawdy "El Caimán," which was so outrageous that it never failed to make them howl no matter how many times they sang it. And when he changed to delicate finger picking, they let him sing his "Quiero, quiero, quiero" ("I want . . . I want . . . I want . . .") by himself. It was too pretty to cover up.

There was not a person on the bus who didn't like the music and enjoy his singing. But not everyone wanted it all the time. At this point they began to divide into opposing groups. Some wanted to be left in peace. But the purchase of the guitar, and the arrival of Robles, caused the balance of power to swing against them. Back in the motel in San Salvador the rowdiness had been only the horseplay of a few excited teenagers. Once they were packed into the bus with strange adults, shyness and normal politeness had prevailed again. But Pablo's music united the group and broke down that reserve. He lent a tireless voice to the exuberant mood of the younger people.

And Robles was a powerful catalyst. He hated to be bored; even a squabble was better than dead quiet. Those who preferred to retreat to their rooms now had a very different environment to deal with. The limited space in the bus offered no opportunity to hide.

From the very first night outside the hotel in Guatemala, Raúl and Emilio had not joined in the singing. "This isn't our kind of party," Raúl said to his friend. It seemed strange to joke and sing when they had just left behind everyone they loved. They were serious, religious young men, and their pain only heightened their devotion. Raúl was Evangelical Protestant, and Emilio was Catholic. Their most natural response to a crisis was to concentrate on giving themselves to God. "We'll make it," Raúl would say determinedly. He was quite handsome, with classical Aztec features, a black mustache, and curly black hair. His eyes were golden brown, and he had a small scar on the bridge of his nose from an accident in a pickup truck.

"Of course we'll make it," Emilio would answer. "He'll take care of us." Emilio's eyes were startlingly blue. He was the taller, but they were both well-built athletes, soccer players.

They had been born in the same small town of San Ignacio, and always felt more like brothers than lifelong friends. They had left home together and were roommates in the capital. Despite their apartness, both were well-liked and were always respectful and considerate of the others.

Emilio had been studying engineering in San Salvador. Several times he had come home with stories about the government firing on students. One day soldiers came right into his classroom and shot a number of them. Three died. It was the last day Emilio went to school. "I don't think they were looking for anyone in particular," he said. "To them every student is a leftist." He had lain on the floor under his desk, not moving until they went. "If I had even given a dirty look, they would have killed me right there," he told Raúl. He had relatives in Los Angeles, and when he called and told them what had happened, they offered to help pay for the trip. He set out immediately to find a coyote.

At the same time Raúl was working for the government at an army PX. They sold household goods to the families of soldiers. One day when he got home from work, Raúl found a letter addressed to him, which had been pushed under the door. The name of a revolutionary group he had never heard of was signed at the bottom. They wanted Raúl to help their cause by hiding a bomb somewhere in the army store.

If I don't, they will kill me, he thought. They know where I work and where I live. He had to leave quickly.

Neither of the friends was political. Raúl was only an employee, not an ally, of the government. His first impulse was to open the door and run. But he controlled his panic and planned carefully. The next day he told his supervisor about the letter. He was quitting immediately, he said, and asked for his severance pay. His boss, a captain in the army, was quite sympathetic. "You're right to leave," he said. "The situation is getting worse, and we can't do anything to protect you." His payoff was 1,400 colones, enough for a down payment to Jorge Dávila, the coyote Emilio had just found for himself.

The boys made a last, quick trip home to San Ignacio. Their family life was extremely close and everyone hated the thought of a separation that might last forever. But if they stayed, they might put their families in danger as well. They told no one but relatives what they were doing. Everyone's loyalties were secret now, and even someone who had been a friend might betray them. They lived in pretense and fear right up to the moment they disappeared. And now they were feeling the effects of being so violently uprooted. The laughter they heard was impossibly alien to them, and when the singing started, they turned to their Bibles and began reading.

Felícita was another quiet one. At first, in her pastel dresses, she had been compared to a fresh flower. But she quickly began to look lifeless. The strain of being forced into contact with such a large number of strangers was wearing her out. Her aunt, Guadalupe, worried about her. She knew the girl's headaches had increased, and recently she discovered that Felícita had been secretly vomiting when she went to the toilet.

Roberto and old Don Cruz were poorly matched and seldom paid any attention to each other. But during one of the lulls in the horseplay, Roberto turned to him and asked, "Why are *you* leaving?" Don Cruz just looked at him without answering. Roberto was not discouraged. "Are you married?" he asked. That was a more acceptable question. Don Cruz pulled a photograph out of his wallet and said, "This is my family." There were three children and his wife, standing in front of their home.

"They look quite happy," Roberto commented.

"Yes, we are happy," the man replied proudly. "We are very Catholic people." But Roberto had only a passing concern with Don Cruz. He was more interested in the jokes of Jorge Dávila, Robles, Ricardo, and Flora. The two men were content to ignore each other once again after their little chat.

But those who wanted to be alone were not always permitted that. Their separateness was sometimes seen as stuffy, or taken as a rebuke. And in fact, the rebukes were not totally imaginary, and angry looks escalated steadily toward a fight. It started with teasing. Someone would throw something, a ball of paper or a grape. A few fingers dipped into a cup of water were flicked over the sleeping face of someone considered unfriendly. And afterward there was the safety of anonymity.

Ileana was resented by some for keeping to herself, for talking only with her large, sour sister-in-law, Luisa. "She thinks she's too fine for us," was the complaint.

Señor Pagán was especially irritated by any lack of courtesy in others, although he could be unpleasant himself and became easily upset. He was a man in his forties, but military-straight and in excellent condition. There were rumors that he had been in the National Guard and was now trying to run away from his past. He would get up, turn around, and yell, "Shut up, will you? Can't you see I'm trying to sleep?" No one wanted to confront him, but they made fun of him behind his back and occasionally tormented him with sly little tricks.

But most frictions were submerged, if not dissipated, under the optimism and excitement of the trip and Pablo's music. During one break Robles announced, "Listen, everybody, we're like a big family and we ought to have family names." It is a custom in El Salvador to give nicknames.

"You"—he pointed to the quiet woman who continued to put her hair up each day—"you'll be, 'Rollers.'" They laughed, accepting his choice. Very soon the few who did know her real name would forget it. From then on, people would say, "Have you seen Rollers?" or "Here, would you pass this to Rollers, please." It was practically a rebaptism.

Robles sifted the faces up and down the aisle. He stopped at Emilio, and Emilio waited for the judgment. "Aha! You're 'the Priest.'" Everyone now watched Robles with varying mixtures of amusement and anxiety. He stopped at Antonio, Francisco's new partner. Antonio was quite well-liked. He made little noise, but everyone listened when he spoke. He had good sense and a straight-faced, dry wit. And his voice had an interesting, Humphrey Bogart quality about it. But his upper teeth protruded slightly, and Robles seized on it. "You're 'the Squirrel,'" he announced. "And you"—he shifted to Antonio's constant companion—"'Panda' . . . ?" That was too accurate for Francisco. "No. You're 'the Stone Face.'" He mocked his gentle seriousness, and everyone laughed good-naturedly.

Flora became "the Yo-yo," because of her trips up and down the aisle to chat. Guadalupe was dubbed "Chaparra," or Little Squatty One. Felícita, sitting next to her, became even paler and tenser than usual, but in a rare merciful impulse, Robles skipped over her. The nice young man with fair hair and very white skin became "Chief of the Pale-faced Indians," or "Paleface," for short. And Pablo was "Dog," perhaps for his tail-wagging good nature. (Robles later remarked about the naming process, "Who knows what comes into your head at a time like that, or why.") Jorge Dávila, wanting to play too, named Roberto "the Parrot," but it didn't have the proper snap. Robles returned on a note of triumphant exaggeration when he named voluptuous Josefa "the Seven Butts." Then his eyes rested on the profiles of Pagán and his wife, as he considered the possibilities. Everyone waited expectantly. But in the end he decided to turn to other things.

Perhaps the softness Robles had sensed in Francisco emanated from his feelings about Felícita. From his seat, without moving, he could usually see some corner of her face and her chestnut hair. Antonio noticed his revery, his head back, his eyes lowered to slits, and his gaze fixed. "You like her," he said softly, "eh?" and nudged him. Francisco shrugged. "Go talk to her. Go on. She'll like it." But Francisco smiled painfully and waved him away.

Antonio turned to look out the window and think about his wife. He and his wife had met at the university, years before, when he was in his second year of medical school. She had insisted on leaving for the United States. Antonio found it impossible to continue studying without her, and a short time later he followed her to San Francisco. It was easier in those days. He went alone to Tijuana, paid a coyote $250, and hiked for several hours in a small group. The hardest part was on the other side, when two cars met them and crammed seven into each of their trunks for the ride to Los Angeles. Antonio and his woman got married and had two beautiful children. He became an auto mechanic. He was a thoroughly satisfied man, delighted with his family and happy with his work. He never regretted what he had left behind. But Immigration interrupted his life when he was caught and returned to El Salvador. Now his chief preoccupation was to go back to them as quickly as he could.

Antonio and Francisco weren't the only ones with longing hearts on the bus. Miguel, at seventeen, was the youngest of the young men. And he found Josefa, who was about twenty-seven, fascinating. Miguel was a sleepy, awkward teenager who, as a junior member, took a lot of abuse. When they saw him watching Josefa, he was pushed to talk and visit with her. His romance became public property. But he bore up well and may secretly have welcomed the help. He became a frequent visitor to her seat, where they often talked and drank Cokes together.

Francisco fell asleep. When he woke up, he sensed immediately that something was wrong. And when he touched his breast pocket, he confirmed it. His passport was gone. Jorge Dávila had come down the bus and was sitting on the arm of the seat, watching him. Francisco looked around, and then got up and looked underneath. "Did you see my passport?" he asked Antonio. Antonio hadn't.

Across the aisle Flora was asleep. "Jorge?" The coyote raised his eyebrows. "Did you take my passport?" Jorge said he hadn't. "You did, didn't you?"

Now Jorge was offended. "When I say I didn't, it means I didn't. Be careful who you accuse, or you may find yourself in trouble," he warned.

"Damn, who took it?" It was the first time any of them had ever heard Francisco raise his voice.

He was frantic. They had already crossed the border, but Mexican Immigration was notorious for frequent surprise checks. At any moment they could run into a patrol that would stop the bus and examine everyone. Sometimes a ruinous fine was enough, and sometimes nothing would prevent rough treatment and deportation. Francisco didn't have any money for bribes, and he was terrified at the thought of returning to El Salvador. He kept thinking, My God, what will they do to me if I go back? and trying to blot out the answering images.

He sat in his seat, ashen and fidgeting. After a minute he got up, searched around and under him again, and sat down. It was only because he couldn't sit still that he had gotten up. But he knew the passport was gone.

Francisco's anxiety reminded them all of their vulnerability. Robles didn't have his promised passport either. Juanita Lugo had an obviously fraudulent one. And even with passports, their Mexican visas were good only as far as the capital. At that very moment they were rocketing toward Mexico City. Once past it, they would all be illegal and could be stopped and returned regardless of passports.

"If we pray together, everything will be all right," Don

Cruz promised. And although no one led them, many bowed their heads for a few minutes. But it was not until three hours later that Jorge Dávila came down the aisle, and slapping Francisco heartily on the shoulder, said with a chuckle, "Here, I found your passport. Maybe that will teach you to be more careful with it."

Francisco said nothing to Jorge. He hid the passport to avoid any more jokes.

Antonio, who had earlier lost a hundred dollars to Jorge, now really despised him. "You know, this Jorge is a liar," he announced to the group. "We're never going to fly over the border." Jorge laughed at this, good-naturedly, as if it were a joke and he could take it.

The Lugo sisters laughed too. Antonio made a lot of straight-faced jokes, and they were never quite certain when he was sarcastic. "Then how will we cross into the United States?" they asked him. He pointed at their feet and they laughed again. But they were anxious about the tone in his voice, and they asked him seriously, "Señor Squirrel"—everyone now called him by his nickname, except Francisco—"you're not serious about the airplane, are you?" They laughed again when he said he was. He had to be joking; there was no other possible explanation. The only reason their mother put herself deeply in debt for this trip was because it was guaranteed to be safe. And free from hardship. They would be flown across the border and land near Los Angeles. The coyote had promised.

Ileana complained to Luisa about Jorge. "He's like an animal in heat," she exclaimed. "First he runs after one, and then another." He regularly tried teasing and poking, patting and tickling various women.

One day, inevitably, Jorge came and sat by them. "Ileana, are you tired?" he asked solicitously. She said she was. "And, Luisa, are you tired too?" He couldn't have been more concerned.

"Yes, of course." She sighed. They had been traveling for days and nights, and she wished it were over.

"Then come and sit on my lap, and I'll comfort you both while you rest."

"You must be crazy!" erupted Ileana.

"Get away. We are traveling by ourselves and we want to be left alone," Luisa said.

"Oho! Haughty!" he snapped.

"I don't want you to stay here. Please!" Ileana insisted.

Jorge went, and after that he talked to them only when business required it.

There were other squabbles. Pablo grew tired of playing his guitar and of losing his seat. One afternoon, when someone gave him a place, he immediately stretched out his legs and went to sleep. Unfortunately he was near the rear of the bus, near Robles, who took a can of shaving cream from his kit and carefully covered the face of the sleeping Pablo with it, leaving him just enough room to breathe. Pablo didn't wake, so the work continued. By building in rings, Robles slowly piled a large crown of lather on top of Pablo's head. Then, for a finishing touch, he took the bag of mango strips he had bought at the last stop, and placed the sticky fruit as decorations in the crown. But now he had overreached himself structurally, and the crown collapsed over Pablo's nose and mouth. Pablo woke up, sputtering, to their laughter.

Robles jumped away, in case of a violent reaction.

"Don't worry," Pablo assured him, scraping off handfuls of foam. "I won't get mad. But one of these days I'm going to play a little joke on *you*."

Robles was in a great mood. The prank tickled him and he continued to laugh over it. Eventually he sat down across the aisle from Pablo, to talk with someone. His arm was hanging loosely over the side of his seat. On impulse, Pablo reached out and, with his fingernail, dug a long furrow down the conveniently vulnerable arm. It bloodied immediately. Robles jumped up in shock while everyone laughed at him.

"Just a joke," Pablo assured him. "Just a joke." But as he sat there, smiling with satisfaction, he admitted to himself that perhaps he had been a little bit angry.

Young Miguel was another one who liked to play but didn't care for jokes on himself. One time, when he got up to say something to Josefa, Pablo jumped into his seat. Miguel was mad, but Pablo refused to move. There was no way he could haul him out, so Miguel just sat on him. But Pablo only laughed, called him "sweetheart," and kissed the back of his head, until Miguel fled.

The scene made Flora laugh. She liked to laugh, her voice squeaking when she got so excited that her vocal cords couldn't carry the overload. Because she was small and pretty, at first everyone expected her to be delicate, but she wasn't. She walloped her thigh after a good one. And she was a reliable audience. A good old joke was just as satisfying as a new one, and once she had a favorite, she would howl every time she heard it, no matter how often it was told.

On one occasion Robles decided that Raúl's and Emilio's pious silence would have to be corrected. He stood in the aisle and announced, "Ladies and gentlemen, we are now going to listen to the word of God. And we're going to start with a little religious song."

This time Flora thought her uncle was both heavy-handed and sacrilegious. "Apologize and sit down," she commanded.

But Robles was under way and it was impossible to turn him. You had to either strike him down or let him through. He led them in a parody of a popular hymn, which he made up on the spot. The two young men sat without moving or speaking. Their faces reddened and they looked deeply offended. The group continued to sing and clap their hands, ending with a vulgar chorus. And then a tense silence.

Suddenly the boys started laughing together. "This son of a bitch Robles really knows how to cause trouble," said Emilio appreciatively. And everyone laughed with them. Afterward, although they continued to be quiet and prayerful, the two were no longer outsiders.

A few seats forward sat Pagán and his wife. Pagán was often critical of Robles and his band. And Robles, in turn, found that everything about the couple bothered him. The wife was too ugly, and he didn't like her potbelly. And he didn't like the way Pagán was so protective of her. She never talked with anyone but her husband. He seemed terribly jealous and didn't like it when others even looked at her.

It was an hour after lunch. People were full and sleepy. Pagán and his wife were napping with the rest, and Robles decided that the time had come to play with them. The fact that the man might have been with the National Guard didn't intimidate him. As he told Ricardo, "They're just a lot of talk when they don't have their guns."

He began calling to them, making rude puns on their names. It didn't take long. Pagán jumped up, pulled off his watch, and started to climb over his wife's knees to get at Robles. Robles looked surprised, but he pushed forward to show he was just as ready to fight. Pagán's wife, usually meek and obedient, grabbed her husband around the waist and hung on with all her might. Pagán struggled to get away, but she held him too tightly. Robles took care not to provoke him by moving any closer, and finally Pagán wore out his rage struggling with his wife and slumped sourly back in his seat.

They stopped on the outskirts of a village to let a train cross, and watched a circle of seven large black vultures being plagued by a yellow dog. The vultures wanted a carcass that lay on the side of the road. By the size of it, it might have been a goat, but it was unrecognizable now, dried in the weather to the thickness and texture of old carpet. The dog charged across the ring, snarling and snapping at the birds. The birds leaped high into the air, popped their wings open like great black umbrellas, and glided across to the opposite side. It was as regular as a mechanical toy, and they might have been at it all day. They were still there when the bus left.

Late that afternoon Robles went up the aisle to visit with a woman he found attractive. She had three small children with her and the trip was exhausting. Most people were asleep, but she had two in the seat next to her and a heavy little child on her lap. She felt too cramped to relax. Robles spread his jacket gallantly on the floor and said to her, "If you give him to me, I can put him down and you can get some sleep. Don't worry, I'll watch him for you." The grateful woman passed the baby and his bottle to Robles, and Robles made him comfortable in the aisle.

But they were only one seat in front of Pagán, who woke

up and saw Robles there, straddling the baby protectively. The thought of Robles standing in the aisle next to his chair for another hour or two made Pagán crazy.

"You'd better get out of here," he shouted, immediately out of control.

"Go to hell, you old fart," Robles countered. He felt it was unfair to be attacked when he was doing something useful. Babies all over the bus were startled and began screaming. Pagán jumped up for the second time that day, but this time he was on the aisle and his wife couldn't stop him. And he didn't bother to take off his wristwatch. Instead he reached into his pocket and pulled out a large switchblade. It opened with a snap.

Robles was frightened. He looked for something he could use to defend himself. There was nothing. The only thing within reach was the baby bottle. He bent low, so he wouldn't shower the infant with glass splinters, and smashed the end off against the base of one of the seats. Then he raised it toward Pagán's face in a counterthreat.

Everyone shrieked at once. Some wanted to see them fight. Pagán's wife cursed at Robles. Flora screamed for her uncle to stop, or he would be hurt. Most of them realized that any serious violence would endanger them all. And Jorge Dávila was desperate to protect his business. A murder or even a bad fight in Mexico, and there was no way to know what could happen to any of them. He struggled down the aisle, pushing aside people who leaned out or stood up to see. Progress was agonizingly slow. But the intensity of the moment drained the combatants, and then they became intimidated by all the shouting against them. By the time Dávila got there, the stalemate was evident. He merely had to pull Robles away from the battle scene, push Pagán back into his seat, and it was over.

Pagán continued to grumble for several minutes, but no one paid much attention. Robles, however, had finally burned out. He had had to stand for much of the trip, and he was constantly entertaining others and himself, singing, taunting, and now almost fighting for his life. It finally had exhausted him. He sat on the floor, heavy-eyed, and within a few minutes he and the baby were curled up together, sound asleep in the aisle.

The scenery around them changed constantly. In the countryside they often passed small groups of peasants who had walked down from their villages. They stood along the highway in their freshly ironed dresses and crisp white shirts, bags and baskets of produce at their feet, while they tried vainly to flag down the Salvadorans' bus for a trip to market.

As they drove through the small towns, certain patterns repeated themselves. There were always churches, and in the center, always a park and a bandstand. Usually a few huge gray sows roamed the streets freely, looking for garbage and fallen fruit. Their eyes were pink and their elongated teats swung while they walked. They were intelligent beings, and they had a jaded look from seeing life at street level.

Because of the heat, the homes were open at front and back for ventilation. In the smaller villages most front doors were permanently open. They were covered with a sheet or curtain for privacy, but unless the family left for an extended period, there was no need to lock up against one's neighbors. Life looked orderly and the peace seemed complete.

They crossed many small rivers over simple concrete bridges. Often women were bathing children and doing laundry below. Once they saw two pickups that had been driven into the river up to their hubcaps, so they could be washed.

Once two men on horseback flagged the bus to stop with a red bandanna. They were trying to herd seven or eight Brahman cattle across the road. But the cows doubled back on them, using the bus as a blockade, and scattered into the brush again. The men rode after them, cursing.

They entered a flat coastal plain. The continental divide, a range of razor-sharp mountains, lay near to their right. Ferocious winds caromed down the slopes, across the land, and out to sea, where they were legendary for knocking down sailboats in the Gulf of Tehuantepec. In the gusts the grass lay flat and frantic, rippling and flashing in the bright sun. For miles all the people they saw walked with their heads down and their arms raised to shield their eyes. In this land of perpetual wind the birds couldn't fly, the billboards were shattered, and the trees all bowed subserviently in the same direction.

Driving was dangerous here, the bus catching the wind like a great sail and jibing across the highway into the lane of oncoming traffic. That was too much for even the fatalism of their drivers, and they cut their speed almost by half.

The wind finally eased when they turned inland and climbed toward Oaxaca. The only farming on these steep and barren hills was the rows of silver-green agave, or century plant, the basis for several kinds of liquor. The area was considered distinctive, like the wine regions of France. Only mescal from this state was permitted to include a single small yellow agave worm in each bottle, as a mark of its origin. The barrenness reminded them that Mexico was foreign to them, and far from home.

They began to develop permanent feelings of ache and fatigue from so much time on the bus. When they made a lunch stop, everyone eagerly got off, except Pagán and his wife. Several times Flora asked politely if they wouldn't care to join them. "Thank you, but we're not hungry," Señor Pagán replied for both of them. Not everyone had taken sides in the "Big Fight," as they mockingly called it. But to Pagán it seemed that way. Robles remained as irrepressible as ever, joking as if nothing had happened (although he and Pagán took care to avoid each other). Pagán remained cranky, and since he usually talked to no one anyway, it looked as if he had been isolated.

Berta was bored with the ride and had only the meals to look forward to. Not that Mexican food was generally so pleasing to her, but there was always some snack available if you looked for it. They stopped for lunch that day at a little restaurant with tables in front. Everyone sat in the bright sunshine, tanning and relaxing in the heat.

It was a surprisingly good meal. Berta got chicken enchiladas and chocolate milk, and ate them with Alicia. The enchiladas were hot, but tasty nonetheless. Then Alicia made her a present of a grape Jell-O in a plastic cup. Berta returned the favor by buying them each a flan (egg custard), also in plastic. Then she gave the girl a can of strawberry juice and got one for herself. They were relaxed and happy for the minute, but the driver climbed back into the bus and started the motor, so they followed obediently, obliged to eat their desserts on the road.

There was no toilet in the bus, so there were frequent stops in the countryside. Late one evening everyone wanted to stop, so the driver pulled over and they got off. Privacy was a problem with more than forty adults in a fairly barren area. But the women went to one side of the road, and the men to the other, and there was enough shrubbery to serve. As they were gathering by the bus again a few minutes later, Josefa ran up, crying.

"What's the matter?" Flora asked.

"Something bit me." But it was not a bite they found on her leg, but a patch of cactus spines. She had brushed against something in the dusk without realizing the danger, and it had stuck her painfully. Flora worked on her for several difficult minutes. The thorns gripped her flesh, and Josefa groaned miserably each time one was torn out. "We don't have this problem in El Salvador," Josefa said nostalgically. In a strange land the dangers were mysterious and unexpected.

"Take your pants down, so we can see what happened," Robles suggested helpfully, but Flora shooed him away with impatience.

The next morning, high in the mountains on the way to Mexico City, they had a very different experience. They stopped for the same reason, but there were no cactuses here. In fact, each species seemed to live in a very narrow zone. A short distance up or down any of the mountains they now crossed would change the plant population entirely. When they got out into the cold morning air, they found themselves surrounded by snow-white fields of flowers. They had never seen this kind before. They had long stems, a faint sweet smell, and grew abundantly.

When they had finished with their toilet, most got back on the bus. But some were just too enchanted by the flowers, and too desperate to refresh their spirits. Felícita, Flora, the three Lugo sisters, and Berta all went down into the fields. For once no one yelled at them or honked the horn. On the bus everyone waited patiently, enjoying the sight of them wandering among the flowers.

They each gathered an armful, brought them back on the bus, and handed them out. Babies had flowers to play with and people stuck them into cracks between the seats, or hanging down from the luggage racks overhead, or just held them and sniffed the blooms. Francisco, who thought Felícita's hair looked especially beautiful with the white blossoms gathered against it, hoped she would give him some of hers. But she never came that far back. It was Flora who gave Francisco some as she passed by.

The bus was full of sweet-smelling white flowers; everyone was getting along; and the feeling was brighter and more peaceful than at any time before. The mood coincided with the altitude; it was the high point of the trip.

They were still several hours from Mexico City, just rounding the eastern shoulder of the great volcano Popocatepetl, when they drove under the edge of the capital's smog. The view faded in the haze as the bus labored up to the high valley. The cactuses had disappeared and they were surrounded now by pine trees, a great forest looming through the sooty gloom. Mexico City, one of the most populated cities in the world, was perhaps the most polluted of all. Life there went on as if underwater, the sky visible only as various shades of gray. An article in a local paper said the heavens were bending under the 10,300 tons of pollutants added to their air each day.

They skirted along the edge of the city as much as possible. Jorge told them it was very dangerous in the capital. "Lots of Immigration in there," he said. From this point on they were "illegal," their visas invalid and their documents worthless.

Suddenly everyone became serious. The gray light fostered dark thoughts. It was time to stop celebrating what they had escaped and to start preparing for what still faced them. Mexico was one long trap, and ahead lay the border like a guillotine.

But there were also countercurrents to this underlying

mood. Typically, Robles was not worried about future problems; he was nostalgic. For him the trip had been a rich and exciting experience, full of what he liked best: closeness with many people, and varied, intense interactions. The fact that there had been fighting and bad feelings was not significant to him. In his mind they were all friends who had endured much together and were therefore bonded forever by their experience. And he, for one, was very sad that it would end. Some of the others, however, were bitter, exhausted, and sick of the bus. Their only thought was to have it over as soon as possible. It was to them that Robles addressed his feelings in sweet sincerity.

"Well, it's almost done, my friends," he said sadly. "It's been a wonderful trip, a trip like no other. Pretty soon we'll be across the border and it will be over forever. I hope when we get to Los Angeles we won't forget each other. That would be a shame. I hope we can meet for dinner. I hope we can take walks together. Let's all exchange addresses and meet regularly for reunions . . ."

From there the talk turned back to El Salvador. Now, through the filter of memory, the sun had always been shining, the fruit had always been sweet, and the life full. "The women," Robles eulogized, "are like no others in the world. I know of at least four in the capital alone whose beauty would make you weep. My last weeks were so bittersweet, I will never forget them. The time I spent saying good-bye broke my heart."

The mountain road from Mexico City to Guadalajara was long and tortuous, and they made progress slowly. But even so, soon they would be at their destination, board the airplane, and within a few hours, be reunited with families, lovers, and friends in Los Angeles. The anticipation was intense. When they passed a tiny airstrip with only a two-seat Piper parked there, Antonio called out to the bus driver, "Stop! Please, our plane is waiting for us. Go back at once!" Everyone laughed, as much because they were tense as for the silliness he intended. But the drivers were also tired from the trip. They had stopped joking and stuck grimly to their work. So

Antonio replied to the silence, "O.K., then, so we won't go by plane. But it's your fault for not paying attention."

They started getting ready. Rollers took back her hair curlers from Inés and put her hair up for the last time. The Lugo girls took all their things out of their bags, folded them carefully, and repacked. The mood was contagious and soon all the women were combing hair and putting on makeup they hadn't used in their everyday travels.

They stopped to eat in a small bus terminal. Everyone went into the cafeteria, and when they saw *quesadillas*, they ordered that. But Mexican *quesadillas* were quite different from the Salvadoran favorite, and they laughed about not getting what they had ordered. They had only a half hour, so they ate quickly and climbed back into the bus, eager to finish. Now everyone was full and tired. They lazed in post-dinner relaxation as they looked out the window and day-dreamed about the life ahead.

They entered a large city. The bus wound its way through crowded streets for the longest time. Gradually the buildings began to thin again, the countryside appeared, and they headed off into it. "Hey, Jorge! That was Guadalajara!" someone called.

"So?" he replied innocently.

"Well, we went right by it. Where is the airplane?"

"Oh, the airplane," he said sadly. "I'm sorry, but there are problems. We can't cross in the airplane." They were stunned. Antonio gave a cynical snort. "It's not my fault," Jorge protested. There's no airport for us in the United States anymore. The man doesn't want any trouble, so he won't let us land on his ranch. But don't worry, we've taken care of everything. It won't make any difference, I promise you."

"I told you he was a liar," Antonio said softly to Francisco, but the silence was so complete that the words carried throughout the bus.

"Shut up!" Jorge snapped from the front. "Don't be a troublemaker, or I'll fix you."

But Antonio was not worried. Jorge was powerful, but he would never touch him or he would have problems with everyone. In this matter it was the people versus the coyotes, and they would help one another if they needed to. They whispered that Antonio had been right, Jorge was a liar, and they wondered what else he had lied about.

"What do you think?" Emilio asked his friend Raúl. "What should we do?"

"What can we do?" Raúl replied. "We can't go back. We have to keep going any way we can."

They were on Highway 15 now, running along Mexico's west coast. Several times they saw the Pacific in the distance, sparkling in the powerful sunlight, deep turquoise with a sudden bright white line of surf. They felt grubby from so much riding, and the sight of the water refreshed them. But basically they were exhausted now, and instead of observing the scenery, they put their energy into enduring. So they didn't notice at first how the land changed around them. It became steadily more barren and dry. And hotter. The nearness of the Gulf of California provided some sense of balance and reassured them. But when they turned away from the slanting coast and its sea breezes at Guaymas, and headed inland, they realized at once that they were in a very different place.

Guaymas is an ugly little commercial fishing port, and perhaps it was the fish that brought all the flies that pestered them now. The U.S. border was less than a day away, and there were large numbers of gringo tourists, pale-skinned and sunburned, driving expensive-looking campers. Guaymas was also a terminal for the lovely ferry ride across the gulf to Baja, California.

When they turned due north and headed directly into the Sonoran desert, which smothers northern Mexico and southern Arizona, Francisco was amazed. He had never seen such a landscape before, except in cowboy movies, where it had no more impact than a stage set. It was very different to actually be there. This land was not a passive backdrop, but an aggressive presence. It projected a hostile, coiled energy, like the rattlesnakes that lived there. There were dips and ridges that made the surface difficult for walking, and mountains in the distance, but basically sand, gravel, cactus, and short, dead-looking brush stretched away to the horizon in every direction. Just waste.

Instead of turning away to avoid it, they were carried deeper in, against their basic instincts, on a search for the most barren, difficult, and unpleasant places. Because that was where the fewest people would be . . . and the best possibility of crossing unseen.

Neither had Francisco ever experienced heat like this before, heat that seemed to burst up from the harsh land rather than flow soothingly from the sun. And despite the impossible temperature, all the windows had to be kept closed so dust wouldn't blow continually into their faces. Even so, a fine silt filtered in and coated everything—skin, hair, clothing, and food—with a layer of yellow grit.

Death shrines appeared regularly along this stretch of road, usually crosses about a foot high, with vases for votive candles and a few plastic flowers. They had been placed there by the families of people who had died in accidents at that spot. The fact that the road was straight and flat, and visibility excellent, made them mysterious.

A little farther on, they were slowed by an accident. A semitrailer coming toward them had crossed the road earlier and overturned, crushing itself with its own weight and speed. The cab was flattened and there was no sign of the driver. The trailer had burst, and cartons of unidentified bottles were smeared along the pavement, a total loss. There was no sign of any cause for the crash, a disaster as mysterious as the shrines. But their driver was not impressed, and as soon as he passed the wreck, he returned to full speed.

Rollers didn't like the desert. As soon as she felt that hot, dry air, she knew it was an antagonist. From then on, every time she tried to brush her hair, it became charged with electricity and crackled in all directions. The harder she worked, the wilder she looked. "I'll be glad when we're done with this place," she said to Guadalupe.

Coming into Hermosillo, they passed huge stockyards on the right, with acres of cattle waiting in the sun for slaughter. A truck pulled out in front of them, loaded with piles of freshly skinned cowhides stacked in the back. They were folded as soft and neat as blankets, but blood oozed from their corners.

At one point Jorge had the bus driver pull off onto the paved area of a small gas station and wait. His announcement that there was a "small problem" was met with silence and suspicion. Jorge and Espinoza got off and walked up the highway, out of sight. In fifteen minutes Espinoza came back and told them, "We're only a little way from the checkpoint at Benjamin Hill. We thought there might be a problem, but there isn't any. We only wanted to be sure that the right people were there to pass us through. So please, everybody be quiet, stay in your seats, and don't open the windows. It won't be long." They were reassured. They believed Espinoza when he spoke because he was direct and considerate. And sure enough, it was only five minutes before Jorge came walking back.

The driver continued for half a mile to a roadblock with armed guards standing by a little office. A soldier got on, but he didn't ask anyone for a passport or visa. He merely walked down the aisle, counting heads. His only concern was that the bribe had been calculated honestly and he wasn't being cheated. When the tally checked, he got off the bus without a word and they continued on.

They stopped in a small desert town to eat, but no one had an appetite. There was a grocery store, though, and while wandering through, Raúl found a shelf with bottles of water. He bought one for himself, one for Emilio, and took them back to the bus. When they saw the water, the others wanted some too, and by the time they pulled into the desert again, everyone had a bottle. They were thirsty and drank some, but when they were full, they enjoyed the rest by pouring it over themselves. They wet their hair and soaked their shirts, and some of the men took off their tops and rubbed it over their glistening bodies. But it dried quickly and it didn't last nearly long enough.

The heat sapped what little energy they had left. They flopped limply in their seats. Flora did no more visiting and Pablo's guitar was silent. The view discouraged them and the temperature in the bus collapsed everyone under its pressure.

Finally, early in the afternoon, with the sun still high, the bus came to an unexpected stop.

The driver turned off the motor and it was suddenly quiet. They peeled their damp backs from the seats as they leaned forward to look out through the dusty windows. As a destination, this was the most minimal place imaginable. Three small houses of a single room each were scattered over several miles. Nearby was an abandoned one-room school of concrete block. Nothing else as far as they could see in any direction. Not a single tree. Nothing. This was the end of the line.

3
THE DESERT

They called this place Ejido, but that only meant "public land" and told them nothing. They pulled off Highway 2 and parked behind the school. The bus driver was ready to return south, but Jorge asked him to please wait. Alvarado, his assistant, got out and looked around. Another man who sometimes helped the coyotes (they called him "the Hawk") got off also. The two walked back to the road and stood hitchhiking in the sun. It was after eleven, and getting hot.

"This place is an oven," grumbled Robles as he walked down the aisle toward the door.

Jorge got up to block him. "Go back and sit down," he said. "This isn't the time to take chances. See that house over there?" He pointed to a primitive shelter of wooden poles, corrugated iron, and cardboard several hundred yards away. "Anyone could see us and report us. An old woman, a child, anyone. So sit down and keep quiet."

No one had any energy in that heat, and even Robles, who would normally have argued, went back to his seat.

Jorge sat watching the two men through the window. Every few minutes a car would pass. No one even slowed down. There was no water left on the bus. Guadalupe began to swallow anxiously. She felt she was suffocating. "It's too hot, Jorge," she called.

Felícita looked at her in surprise. Her aunt never complained.

"Too dangerous to get off," Jorge repeated tiredly. "Only a little longer." He pointed to the two men hitchhiking in the dust. "They have to go into town and set things up. When

103

they come back with the trucks to take us to the border, then you can get off, and the bus can go back."

Now everyone watched the men. They were beginning to droop in the sun. The cars still passed in complete disinterest. "He's crazy," snapped Ileana. "We could be here for hours like this. Come on, Luisa, we don't have to stay here."

That was enough for Guadalupe, who found the bus claustrophobic. She too moved purposefully toward the door.

"No, we have to be careful," pleaded Jorge.

"You should have made better plans," said Ileana as they all followed Guadalupe out into the open air. "These are your problems, not ours. That's what we paid you for." She felt no satisfaction from this revolt. She was too disgusted. The realization had finally hit her that Jorge was no better prepared this time than he had been the last. God help us, she thought.

When the two men saw everyone getting off the bus, they came back. They wanted help, and they knew someone who could be counted on. They went to Flora and explained their need. She laughed and slapped her leg and shook her head, and each time they pleaded with her she started laughing again. But finally they wore her down, as they had hoped to. She was still giggling when she got back onto the bus. When she got off a few minutes later, she had changed into her shortest pair of white shorts and her briefest top, a scarlet halter. "O.K., boys, let's go," she said cheerily, and took each by an arm and led them back to the road. The men sat with their backs to her, while she thumbed about fifteen feet away, giving the impression that they were not together. The very next car stopped. Josefa asked the driver if he would mind giving her friends a lift, and when they drove off together, she walked back, dusting off her hands for a job well done.

The school was a long building painted dull red. It looked abandoned. The door was broken open and they went in. It was a single bare room, but the concrete walls and preformed roof made it much cooler than the bus.

Jorge made no move to direct them. He was angry that they had not followed his orders and didn't feel like having anything to do with them. He pulled a rolled-up boxing magazine from his back pocket, carefully flattened it, and sat in a corner reading.

"I can't stay here any longer," announced the bus driver. "I have to go back to Tapachula." So they all tramped out and carried their luggage into the school. Then they watched as the bus swung in a wide turn, climbed back onto the highway, and rapidly shrank to a point on the horizon. It was impossible to tell when it disappeared because the dust it raised hung in the air behind it.

They were cut off now, with no way back. Then Alicia Lugo murmured a warning from the rear, and they turned to look in the opposite direction. Someone was walking toward them from the little house.

He was a boy of about seven. He wore an old T-shirt and shorts. His skin was dark and he walked barefoot. He came slowly because he carried a heavy bucket that banged against his legs with each step. "I brought you water," he said. "There's no water in the school, and you can't stay here without water."

There was a dipper in the bucket and they took polite turns with it. The water was cool and delicious and it went quickly. The boy just stood silently and watched them.

"I didn't realize I was so thirsty," said Ileana. Luisa felt the heat more than many, perhaps because of her weight. She used her share to wash her face and cool her neck.

"Look, if you'll bring us another one I'll pay you well," Robles promised. "Can you do that for us?" The boy nodded and ran back to his house, swinging the pail.

"We're just lucky he came with water," Luisa said, lighting a cigarette. "Or what would we have done?"

The jab was aimed at Jorge Dávila, and he answered it. "Sure you're lucky. And you'll also be lucky if you don't end up in jail. These ones who live by the border make their money from turning people like you in."

"That little boy?" snorted Ileana, joining the battle.

Jorge ignored her. "We'd better have a good story," he warned the group. "We need some explanation of why so many strangers are out here in the desert." They agreed, it was better to be safe. "We should say we're here to visit a church. We can say we're a bunch of Mormons."

Ileana was a Mormon. She didn't know if this was an attempt to insult her or just some idea of his that Mormons traveled around visiting churches. There were many Mormons in El Salvador.

"Is there a big Mormon church anywhere near here?" someone asked Ileana. She shrugged. Like the rest of them, she hardly knew where she was.

"We can say it's in San Luis, and we're just waiting for our Mormon friends in town to come and pick us up," Jorge said. He was pleased with the idea because it would explain the arrival of the coyotes later.

"No!" exclaimed Don Cruz. "That's a terrible thing to do."

Jorge looked at him. Wasn't there anyone left who wouldn't defy him?

"God is God," Cruz told them. "About God you don't tell stories or play games."

But Espinoza assured him, "It's only a little story. And it's for you, for all of us."

Everyone agreed. It was a good idea to be careful.

Don Cruz could see he was outvoted. "But it's still a lie," he muttered, retreating. He felt strongly that such things were not done just to get a little water.

But when the boy came back, he didn't have any water. And he didn't come alone. He was with his two sisters. One was about sixteen and plumply pretty. The other was closer to twenty, slender, olive-skinned, with striking features and lovely dark eyes. She walked straight to Robles, who stood hypnotized by her. "Did you want water?" she asked.

"I told the little boy I would pay for some," Robles said, his voice unnaturally soft.

"It's no problem. You can drink all you want. And if you want to rest, you can come over to our house." She pointed to their shelter. As they walked along, Robles stayed close, amazed that such a flower could bloom in the desert. Although the home was quite poor, the girls wore nice dresses and new tennis shoes. The bus travelers also looked fresh from the front, but along their backs, where they had sweated against the seats, their fine clothing was bunched and creased.

A short, round woman with gray hair came out to meet them. "This is our mother," the girl said. The younger one got another bucket of water and passed it around again.

"What brings you all here?" the woman asked.

"We're church brethren, on a trip," Jorge said piously.

"What church?" she wanted to know.

"Mormon," he said.

"Oh, how fine! We're Mormons too! Come, let's everybody sing some hymns."

"I'm *not* Mormon," Don Cruz muttered, and they looked at him nervously. He had decided not to lie, no matter what the cost.

"Well, what is your church?" she asked. He was Catholic, he told her. "I hope you will also sing us one of your hymns," she said, and started them off, her voice enthusiastic, waving to Pablo to pick up the tune on his guitar. Her family and Ileana did most of the singing, although Robles struggled mightily to look like he was with them. The others tried anticipating lyrics they did not know, mouthing words silently, and humming mildly to produce a very lame version of the hymn. No one suggested they sing another.

The bucket was dry again and the younger sister went off to refill it. Now, in addition to drinking, they had all started washing their faces with the water.

"Come in, you can rest with us awhile," the mother urged. It was clear there wasn't enough room for them all. A few accepted the invitation, but most were too shy or fearful of exposing themselves to strangers just before the crossing, so they sat in the shade outside or went back to the schoolhouse to wait.

Surprisingly Felícita was one of those who went in, letting Guadalupe return to the school without her. This was the first time she had gone off by herself. Francisco followed her. In one corner of the home was a bed with a shelf of Mexican novels above it. She sat down and started reading.

There was only one room, with a kitchen on one side and

beds and hammocks on the other. There were also two chairs and a bench. The floor was dirt. Berta decided that it was very poor, but beautifully clean and orderly.

"Now, this is your house," the mother offered the traditional welcome, "so please make yourself comfortable here."

Berta looked around, assessing the situation, and noticed there were little animals, sniffing and watching the newcomers from several corners of the room. They were like hamsters, but with tails, and when anyone came near, they would pop down holes in the floor. She didn't think it would be polite to mention them, but Robles felt no such compunction.

"Look, rats!" he exclaimed, pointing them out to everyone.

"They're not rats," the slender girl said patiently, "they're *guanajitos*. They live in the desert here, and they're like pets." And when he looked closer, Robles saw that they were pretty little things. They were quite used to people and didn't hide unless someone came very close. Sometimes one would stand on its hind legs and drum rapidly on the wall with its front paws. "We have one outside that we keep in a cage. Would you like to see it?" she asked Robles.

Robles was only mildly interested in the little animal, but he had been hoping to go off somewhere more private with the lovely girl. "We'd better go now," she said. "You'll be leaving any minute. They're very quick." She was referring to the coyotes, and evidently knew all about their mission. He wondered what she and her mother thought about their Mormon story.

Out behind the house they stood together under a sheet-metal awning and looked at the cage. Or at least she did. Robles was more aware of how close she was to him. Her dress was short-sleeved, and he admired her long smooth arms and her fine hands.

"Do you have any children?" he asked her.

"No, I didn't get married yet," she answered innocently.

"Well, I like you," Robles told her. "You have such nice ways. They please me."

"What a shame you're leaving now," she said. "But you're only passing by. You would never stay here."

Other people came, interrupting their privacy, and they went to the front, where Pablo was singing and playing. But the heat, and standing in the direct sunlight, gave Robles a headache. He asked her if she had any pills that might help him. She took his hand sympathetically and led him in to her mother.

"We have something, I think," the mother said. "Go and look." The daughter got the medicine and presented it proudly to Robles. "Now get him some water, so he can take it," the mother scolded, seeing them standing there just looking at each other. The girl brought the bucket, but it was empty again.

"There is no more, Mama," she said.

"Yes, there's a little in the barrel. Go get it for him."

"Tell me, where are the water pipes?" Robles asked.

"We don't have faucets here."

"Don't you have wells?"

"No, we don't have wells either."

"Then where do you get your water?"

"There is a truck with a tank that comes every week. We buy it from them." She showed him where they stored it. The water tasted cool and delicious because they kept it in a barrel sunk deep in the earth. When Robles realized they had drunk all the family's water, he felt embarrassed. The family had been generous, and the travelers had been insensitive, accepting gifts without thinking what they were costing the givers. Something had to be done. He looked around for inspiration. There were several large sombreros hanging on the wall.

"May I borrow one of those?" he asked. "The sun is so hot and I don't want to get another headache."

Outside, he went to the group around Pablo. "Do you know what these people did?" he asked them. "They gave us all their water," and he explained the problem. Then he turned the hat upside down and put a hundred pesos into it. The others followed his example, throwing more money into the hat. Robles ran over to the school and told his story again. Then he ran back to the home, pleased with his efforts.

Inside, Felícita was still reading on the bed, and several others lay in the hammocks, dozing comfortably. They had truly made themselves at home. Robles came in with Antonio, Pablo, and Flora. He walked up to the mother and handed her the hat full of money. "For your great kindness," he said. "I'm sorry we can't give you more."

The woman was delighted. "God is going to bless you," she told them. "There has never been a group here as good as you people. I hope my husband comes home before you have to leave. He'd want to meet you."

When the excitement had settled, the older girl asked him, "Do you want to play something?" She took a volleyball and a net and they set it up on a smooth space outside. They made two large teams, with Robles making certain he was on her side. It was late in the afternoon and the sun was no longer as strong. They played enthusiastically for several hours, relieved to be active after all the days they had spent trapped in the bus.

Earlier, when Antonio had urged Francisco to talk to Felícita, Francisco had said he would wait. He wasn't shy, he insisted, he only wanted the right moment. But the trip was almost over and the moment hadn't come. When he followed Felícita inside, he hoped something would happen to throw them together, but he had remained too far away. Finally he took a deep breath, walked over, and sat down next to her.

"Your name is Felícita?"

"And you're Francisco," she answered calmly, not looking up. Francisco was still young enough to be amazed that she knew who he was even though she had never paid him any attention. He had not been that close to her before. She wore no makeup and her skin was sweet and fresh-looking. He asked her about her plans for the United States.

She was on her way to San Francisco, with her aunt, she told him. She had an excellent future. She had two certificates, one as a hairdresser-beautician and another as a bookkeeper. She had finally begun to look at him. She was serious, almost stern, and at times she seemed to be lecturing. Her voice had the distinctness he associated with schoolteachers, but it was still whisper-soft, and he found himself bending close to her to hear it. He felt wonderful. And suddenly, on a wild impulse, he teased her, repeating in a funny voice something she had said. She giggled, her composure gone, and put her hands up to hide the blush.

Two trucks drove up and stopped outside. Esteban Alvarado got out and went to talk to Jorge. The drivers, who both looked quite hard and not at all like one might imagine pious Mormons, waited behind their wheels. The ball game broke up and everyone came to hear the plan.

Jorge didn't look happy. "More problems," he announced. "Mexican Immigration up ahead won't let us through unless we pay too much money. We have to find some other way." He hadn't done all that work to leave most of his profits in the pocket of some cop.

"Not here," Ileana spoke up. "It was no good here last time, and it won't be any better now. I don't want to go through that again."

"Calm yourself, Ileana. We have another idea. We're going back the way we came, and we'll cross the border at a place these people know." The drivers were local coyotes, part of a large gang with the eerie name of Los Muñecos, The Dolls.

Robles took the arm of the Mexican girl and led her behind the house where they could be alone. "I have to say good-bye to you," he said. "It's too bad, I really like you."

"I like you too," she told him.

He asked for her address and wrote it on an old envelope. He promised he would come back and see her soon. Then he looked at her unhappily again. Suddenly the girl leaned forward and kissed him on the cheek.

"May I kiss your cheek too?" he asked. She nodded. He took her face gently in his hands. She leaned toward him again, presenting her cheek. But he turned her face and gave her a quick kiss on the lips, and when she didn't pull away, another one, more slowly and with more feeling. "Are you going to be mad at me for that?" he asked her.

She shook her head. "I'm going to save it." She smiled.

Back in the house her mother was blessing and hugging everyone within reach. "Have a good journey, and God bless you," she told them. "Ah, Papa!" she exclaimed as a large man in work clothing came in and looked around in amusement. "We have company, very nice people."

"You have a big family now," Pablo told him. "We've all come to live with you."

"That's wonderful," he said, "and in a minute I'm going to put you all to work."

They stood joking together while Jorge yelled fruitlessly for them to come out and get into the trucks. By the time they finally went back to the school to pick up their luggage, Jorge had turned surly with resentment. "I want all the men to go out and get into the red truck," he snapped. The mood was suddenly serious. This was it. The men left obediently.

Then Jorge sorted the women. "You, you, you . . ." Jorge pointed at each face and then flicked his finger at the door. The ones he chose went out and got into another truck. There were only two trucks, and Alvarado remained behind with the mothers and children who had not been chosen.

Pagán had expected to ride with his wife, as usual, but they were pushed apart in the anxiety of loading. And besides, the new drivers were intimidating. So they each got into their separate trucks as ordered, and everyone settled down on the hard wooden floors for a jouncing two-hour trip back through the desert.

Sitting in the women's truck, bent over to duck the hot wind, Felícita confided to her aunt, "Francisco wants to be my friend. He talked to me today." Guadalupe already knew that Felícita liked him. He was the gentlest of the men on the bus, the only one she could imagine her niece feeling comfortable with. That afternoon she had seen them walking in the desert near the house, holding hands.

"He's nice for you," Guadalupe told her.

"Maybe, but it's silly. There's no time. And in the United States we'll never see each other again."

"Those things can be fixed, if you both want to."

"No, I told him I had a fiancé waiting for me."

"But why?" Felícita's mother was in El Salvador and her

father was dead. Except for Guadalupe, she was alone, and Guadalupe wanted her to take this opportunity.

But Felícita had the last word. "This way is better," she said, stern again.

It was almost dark when the trucks stopped. And it wasn't at the border. It was at an isolated old restaurant outside Sonoita, in the desert, where they were going to spend the night. There was a patio in front and in back there was an outhouse. Nearby were some trees, and beyond, the usual brush. The lights were on inside and they could see people at their dinners. The trucks stopped several hundred feet away so they wouldn't be noticed. Jorge jumped out to caution everyone to keep quiet, but the women from the first truck ran back to question him.

"Where are the others?" they wanted to know. There was no sign of the women with the children.

"They stayed back there," he told them. "They're going another way, with Esteban Alvarado."

The women looked at each other. Part of their group had just disappeared, without even the chance of saying good-bye. "Why?" they wanted to know.

"They're going an easier way. It's better for mothers with babies." That explained the disappearance, so it removed one anxiety. But if that group was taking the easiest route, then this group must be taking a harder one. Jorge, however, was in no mood for discussions. "Be quiet now. We're near the border and there could be a lot of Immigration here. I want you to go into the restaurant a few at a time," he said.

Pagán had heard Jorge's words, but he was too angry to care about the danger. During the entire trip he and his wife had gone everywhere together, earning them the sarcastic title of Los Matrimonios, The Married Ones. Pagán saw this separation as an interference with his private life. And perhaps it had been a bit malicious of Jorge to have insisted they ride apart, even though he claimed righteously that the same rules applied to everyone.

Pagán ran to the women's truck and grabbed his wife. "Come here," he said, and pulled her over to where Jorge was watching the unloading. "I've had enough of this," he told Jorge. "You guaranteed a good trip, good hotels, private planes, everything. And we got nothing. Now we're in this godforsaken hole."

"Lower your voice," Jorge commanded.

"If I lower my voice, you won't hear me. You're a little deaf when it comes to complaints."

"Well, I hear you now, so be quiet. We're here because it's too dangerous to cross over there. Stop worrying, it will be all right."

"That's what you always say. I paid a lot of money to avoid problems, but it's been one problem after another. Enough. I want our money back. We're leaving the group."

Jorge didn't answer. He just stared at him poisonously.

"I mean it," Pagán insisted. "Better give it to me right now, or I'll go to Immigration." They continued to glare at each other until Jorge turned and walked away. "Jorge!" Pagán shouted.

"Go ahead," Jorge answered over his shoulder. "Go to Immigration. Tell them anything you want. I'm not giving you a cent. You're just a pain in the ass to me." He walked into the restaurant. The Salvadorans who had gathered stood there silently, watching Pagán struggle with his decision.

"Come on," Pagán said. They picked up their suitcases and he led his wife down the road toward the town of Sonoita, several miles away. The group went in to get their dinner and to tell the others what had happened.

"What do you think?" Francisco asked. "Are we in danger?"

"We'll have to wait and see," Antonio answered wearily. There was no end to the complications on this trip.

The restaurant was a poor one, with rough benches and uncovered tables, but the food was good, traditional Mexican cooking. Rice and beans, salad, enchiladas, chicken, and beef were all available, and they ate big meals. Halfway through dinner they saw Pagán and his wife come in and sit near the door, as far from the rest of them as possible. Even Jorge left them alone this time.

The food soothed them. Whatever anxieties they had had

about Immigration disappeared as they ate and drank and talked. They were, after all, on the threshold of their goal. They felt a natural urge to celebrate. Most were drinking beer, but Jorge switched to brandy, a label called Viejo Vergel. It was moderately priced, and the aftertaste had the roughness of turpentine about it, but that was why he liked it. A man's drink shouldn't slide down submissively, he thought, it should fight back.

Francisco sat off with Felícita and Guadalupe, and Antonio left them alone in case they wanted to talk. Across the room Pablo played and sang, and Antonio went over by him. The Lugo sisters were there too, all drinking. Even the little one sipped a beer and talked animatedly. Next, Flora came, and then Espinoza and Jorge. Pablo and his guitar were almost always the nucleus of a party. Jorge, already heavy-lidded, watched the little girls with interest. Then he saw Antonio watching him.

"Hey, Squirrel," he called, "why do you bug me so much? Why don't you shut up?"

"Because you're a liar," Antonio said.

Jorge laughed. It implied that Antonio was a great joker. "Look, let me explain something to you." He leaned over confidentially. "My business is my business," Jorge intoned a syllable at a time. "Not your business."

"Oh, it's your business all right. Just don't tell me lies."

Jorge laughed again and turned to Flora. She made people feel good, and everyone talked to her.

This was the most primitive stop they had made yet. There were no rooms at all this time. Several men who tired of the party went out to sleep in their clothing on the ground. They clustered under a tree, only for the sense of enclosure it gave them, since there was no chance of rain for months. Raúl and Emilio went first, and old Don Cruz. They talked quietly of spiritual strength and guidance until others came to join them. Then they put rolled-up towels under their heads and stared thoughtfully up at the clear patterns of infinity until sleep came.

Accommodations for the women were slightly more refined. So they wouldn't have to sleep directly on the ground, they were offered the wooden bed of the owner's old truck, or the inside of an old Datsun, where they could sleep sitting up. Pagán refused to sleep apart from his wife, so he climbed into the truck with her, the only man with a large group of women. No one challenged him.

Ileana chose the car. It seemed to offer the most protection. She took her sister-in-law with her. They crowded into the small space, Ileana and Luisa in front with another woman, and three more in back. Ileana didn't like the loose look of the drinking and wanted to be somewhere that was less accessible. But the men, it turned out, were willing to put out the extra effort necessary to get to the women.

Sitting up in a crowded car, they had difficulty falling asleep. Luisa kept lighting cigarettes. "You shouldn't be smoking, the way you are," Ileana said. But Luisa ignored her. The truce was breaking down and they were beginning to get on each other's nerves.

And then Jorge and his partner, Espinoza, came out drunk. With much laughing and cursing they forced their way into the car and onto the laps of the three women in back. They wrestled and tickled and laughed. The women screamed, "Get out of here, get out, right now." But they were laughing too. The three were married, but they were far from home and in the middle of an adventure. They had been drinking and it all seemed like a little harmless fun. Until Jorge said, "Come on, this is no place to sleep. You can't even lie down. Come with us and we'll find a more comfortable place." He and Espinoza pulled two of the women out with them. They didn't go far. Those in the car could still hear their voices as they continued drinking from Jorge's bottle of brandy.

"Will you please put that cigarette out and go to sleep," Ileana said peevishly.

"I am sick and tired of this trip," Luisa replied, continuing to smoke.

"You should have thought of that before you came," Ileana countered.

"I did, but you were always lecturing me about doing the right thing. Well, it was a big mistake. I never should have come. There are people in El Salvador that I want to be with. So if I see any Migra, I'm not going to run away and hide. I'm going to walk right up to him and say, 'Here I am. Please take me back to El Salvador. I want to go home.' "

"Don't be stupid."

"I mean it."

"You don't understand the problems you could have. You want to go back, but you're not thinking about everything else that would happen. For instance, what about your fiancé in Los Angeles?"

"Shut up. You don't know how I feel."

"I know how you feel, but you also have to think about what he feels. He had to pay a lot of money to bring you here. You owe it to him not to waste that."

Ana, Josefa's companion, joined in from the back, "Please, Luisa, don't do it. Not after we came all this way."

"But I don't want to go to the United States." Luisa started crying bitterly. "I really don't want to."

"Listen," Ana suggested, "wait until we're safely in the U.S. Then you can go to Immigration and tell them anything you want. But if you do it now, you risk all of us. We can't let you."

Ileana had dealt with Immigration on the last trip. "They'll ask you how you got here and who was with you. And they won't leave you alone until you tell them. Even if you don't tell them, they'll come and look for us anyway."

"It's true," said Ana. "It's not right to hurt all of us just so you can get your way."

"And forget your friend in El Salvador," Ileana told her. "He doesn't love you. It would be stupid to go back for him."

"Be quiet, you don't know. My mother told me you don't care about my problems."

"That's right. Your problems are *your* problems," Ileana said. "I have my own problems." Luisa sat with a frozen face, smoking furiously and not replying. "That's O.K. if you don't want to talk to me," Ileana told her. "I don't care. But if you feel lonely, don't come looking for me."

Their conversation had taken place on a number of levels.

The problem was a complex one, and Ileana was not even supposed to know about it, although she gave enough hints to make it clear she did.

Luisa was engaged to a young writer who had gone to the United States to find freedom to write. He got a job and sent Luisa the money to join him. But she had found a lover. Her fiancé wrote constantly, pleading with her to join him, asking what the problem was. She didn't know what to tell him. All of this passed to Ileana through the grapevine.

Then Luisa began to act strangely, weeping without reason, becoming more temperamental than usual. It was stress, Ileana thought, and it was Luisa's own fault for putting herself in such an impossible position. But one day during a squabble Luisa blurted out that she was pregnant. Ileana could still remember the exact day because they had been talking in an upstairs room at a family gathering. "Are you sure?" Ileana had asked. She suspected her sister-in-law of histrionics. "Have you seen a doctor?"

She had, and the doctor said they needed more tests, but Luisa thought she was.

Ileana, on the other hand, thought she wasn't. Luisa's gynecologist was an old friend of Ileana's and she went there immediately to check. "It's possible," the doctor had admitted, "but I can't be sure yet."

Ileana insisted. "Just how possible is it?"

"Ninety-nine percent," the doctor confessed under pressure, "by this man in El Salvador. But I want you to promise me you won't say anything to Luisa. I told her she needs more tests." The doctor knew Luisa didn't want the baby. She thought that, as a doctor, it was her duty not only to protect Luisa from the risk of an illegal abortion, but also to protect the fetus. She planned to stall with more tests, and when it was too late to interrupt the pregnancy, she would tell Luisa the truth. Then she planned to stay by Luisa's side and help her through the pregnancy.

Ileana kept the secret, so it was a double shock when Luisa told her a few days later that she had decided to leave immediately for the United States. Everything suddenly became more complicated than Ileana and the doctor had anticipated. Now Luisa would be taking a difficult journey while pregnant, and perhaps not realizing it. She would join her fiancé while carrying another man's child. And the gynecologist would have no chance to explain why she had lied, or to help resolve the situation she had protected. The trip started only two days later and Luisa never saw her doctor again. Perhaps Ileana's willingness to be friendly to Luisa was influenced by her secret knowledge of her sister-in-law's condition.

After their argument in the car Ileana turned away and went to sleep. Luisa sat up smoking, feeling very depressed. Although she had mentioned the possible pregnancy to Ileana, she herself still didn't believe it. After all, even the doctor had not seemed sure. So she continued to ignore the physical signs she saw in her own body, or to explain them away. But the closer they came to Los Angeles, the harder it became. Now they were only a day away, and the strain of so much wishing was wearing her out.

She was too unhappy to sleep, and to make things worse, she could hear Jorge and the others who had camped behind the car. The giggling had changed to moaning. "I want to touch your breasts," she heard a voice murmur, and other voices said, "I want to kiss you there," and "I want to suck you." Luisa began to sob.

Ileana stirred in her sleep and put an arm around her. "It's all right," Ileana told her. "Everything will be all right, you'll see."

"Oh, Ileana," Luisa cried, "I'm so sorry about how I acted. Forgive me. I don't know what to do. Sometimes it drives me crazy."

"Shhh," Ileana soothed her. "When we get to the United States, everything will work out. Now go to sleep. You need your rest."

But Luisa couldn't sleep, and in the morning, when the women returned to the car, explaining, "I just came from the river," and "I just came from the toilet," Luisa whispered that they were lying and told Ileana what she had heard during the night.

There was a river, but it was unlikely anyone had gone to

it in the middle of the night, for it was several miles away through the desert. Now everyone wanted to wash, and there were no restrooms, so the owner offered to take them to the river in his old truck. It took two trips to carry them all over the rutted path he used regularly for that purpose.

Almost everyone felt wonderful that morning. They smiled at each other and laughed freely over little jokes. It was an exuberant drive to the river, jouncing about on the floor of the open truck. And when Robles offered to hold the women's behinds in his hands so they wouldn't bruise themselves, no one was offended.

At the river they separated, the women going a bit upstream and the men a short way down. The water was very shallow, only knee-high in its deepest places, and the countryside was open. Perhaps it was the looseness of the mood, but the groups stayed within view and peeked discreetly at one another while they were undressing. The women took off their bras and stripped to their panties. Most men took off everything. Ileana had white underwear, but that would become transparent when wet, so she borrowed a darker pair from Berta to bathe in.

Pagán and his wife broke off from the group, as usual. They went far upstream from the women, as much removed from the men as possible. Pagán didn't want anyone looking at his wife, and they withdrew until they lost definition in the distance.

First they had to wash the clothing they were wearing and the dirty things in their bags. The air was so arid and the sun so hot that the clothes would dry while they were bathing. They spread the wash on rocks and low bushes. Then they washed themselves slowly and pleasurably. The Lugo sisters were already playing in the water. When Rollers finished, the girls clustered around her and put up her hair.

They had sweet, young bodies, Robles noticed, but it was out of the question. By now they had become like a big family and he thought of them as sisters. Out of a certain fastidiousness, Robles decided not to take off his pants in front of the women. He washed with his trousers on. Some of the men started playing. They splashed each other, and

Robles escalated the battle by throwing sand. Suddenly the group focused on him. "Let's get that little whore," Jorge Dávila shouted. Espinoza, Antonio, and several others joined him. They chased Robles through the water, but he broke for the bank and ran to the women for protection. But instead of helping him, the women screamed at him to get away. They splashed him when he tried to hide among them.

"Since he's such a little *puta*," Jorge yelled, "let's catch him and do it to him. Come here, you *puta*, we want you." And the men descended on him and dragged him to the side. They held him down, and while he struggled, they pulled off his pants. The women screamed, covered their eyes with their hands, and looked between their fingers to see the most famous lover on the bus.

"Oh, how small his little 'dove' is," one woman hooted.

The men picked him up by his wrists and ankles, swung him several times, and threw him into the river among the women. The women promptly began to splash him again.

Robles tried to escape, but the men caught him and threw him in one more time. This time he landed on a sandbar and hurt his back.

"It serves you right," Jorge said without pity. "We're just paying you back for some of what you did on the bus."

Robles carried his clothing discreetly to the other side of the river to dry out.

By now they were getting hungry and thirsty. The river water looked too dirty to drink, even before it became their bathwater. They got dressed and started walking back. Robles put on all his dry clothing before he realized he would have to cross the river again to get to the restaurant. He called to a tall, attractive woman who had changed into shorts and a blouse and was rinsing her feet before putting on her shoes. "Hey, Chalatenango"— he used her nickname, which was the name of the province she came from—"come and take me across, please. Otherwise, I'll have to take off all my clothes, and you wouldn't want that."

"No, that's one thing we don't want," she said, and she waded good-naturedly across to get him.

Robles climbed onto her back. He wasn't heavy for her,

but she kept staggering and slipping on the uneven bottom.

The men lined up on the opposite bank, yelling, "Throw him in the water. Throw him in!" But she continued faithfully, her face tight with concentration.

"I'm going to push him over," one of the women decided, and she headed out toward them, but they reached the bank before she could do it.

Their morning by the river was over. On the way back they saw a coyote in the distance. It was a small animal, and it ran out of sight when it saw them, but it was wild and unfamiliar and they found it frightening.

"They won't attack when they're alone," someone guessed. "There have to be a lot of them before they attack."

The walk back to the restaurant made them hot and tired. They had some lunch, and cold beers to quench their thirst, and then they lay under the trees to nap through the heat of the day.

When it got cooler, they got up and started to drink. They all drank beer now that Jorge had finished his brandy.

Ileana didn't like it, not with serious business ahead. "When are we leaving?" she asked Jorge. "I don't want to have to sit around and watch you get drunk."

"Then don't look," he replied. "I won't miss you. We have to wait here until the guides come. So it's a fine time to drink. You ought to try it. It would do you some good."

At dinnertime the women ate. Most of the men continued to drink, and they got louder. Flora came to tell Robles that their Ricardo was getting drunk and she couldn't stop him. Robles went over to tell the boy that that was enough, but since Robles had been drinking himself, it wasn't very convincing.

"Leave me alone," Ricardo answered angrily. "I'm spending my own money."

"Let him do what he wants," Robles told Flora. "He'll make himself sick, and it will teach him a lesson."

Groups of strange Mexican men had come in the restaurant and sat around drinking beer. More Dolls. They were a large gang and ran the border for hundreds of miles in each direction. Some of them were waiting for another group due later that night. The Salvadorans had to stay until the bosses came and Jorge closed the deal.

An hour later one of the drivers came looking for Robles. "Is that little one related to you?" he asked.

"He's my nephew."

"Well, I don't know if he's going to make it. He's pretty drunk, and you people are going to have to walk a bit." Jorge and a few others were also getting sloppy.

Finally the men in charge came. They sat with Jorge and bought him another beer. They made the Salvadorans nervous. They looked at each of the travelers individually, assessing them. There was too much interest in their eyes. When Luisa walked by their table, one of them reached out and grabbed her wrist. "Is she traveling with you?" he asked, pointing at Ileana. "Ask her if she wants to cross with me, in my car. It will be real easy, and she won't have to walk like the others. I have a green card for her. She can cross as my wife." His meaning was clear.

"She can't cross with you because she's coming with me," Luisa said curtly.

That made him furious. "You just tell her what I said. I didn't ask for your answer." A number of people turned to watch. But when Luisa relayed his message, Ileana turned away with a look of disgust that left no room for discussion.

Emilio leaned in through the front door. "We're having prayers outside," he announced quietly, "for a safe journey."

Only a few came and joined the small ring of travelers kneeling on the sand in the dusk. They bowed their heads and Don Cruz led them, *"Padre nuestro . . .* Our Father, who art in heaven, Hallowed be Thy name . . ." When they finished, he prayed, "God, we need your help and guidance on this trip, and we ask . . ." Then he started crying. No one knew what to do. "We left everyone," the old man sniffled. "Our families, everyone . . ." He wiped his nose on his handkerchief. "We're so far from everything and we don't have any idea what will happen to us. How could you all be so happy and wild?" He started crying again. Then he got up and walked away. The others looked unsettled as they went back into the restaurant.

Inside, Josefa and Ana were also approached by the coyotes. The two women wanted to go with them. They liked the idea of not having to walk and the men didn't seem that bad to them. But the Lugo sisters were appalled. They hovered around the women and whispered urgently to them, "Don't do it, it's too dangerous. These men will lie to you. Something terrible could happen." The women had practically agreed to go, but now they became cautious and then changed their minds completely, leaving the men alone again.

"You stupid bitches!" one of them raged. "If you had any sense, you'd come with us. But by the time you see what kind of a mistake you made, it will be too late, because I won't be there with my nice new car to give you a ride." And he stalked off.

Those who were not drinking were busy packing. Rollers put her hair up for the last time, with a feeling of ceremony. With any luck, by tomorrow night she would be in bed with her husband. She crossed her fingers that he had no unpleasant surprises he had been saving to tell her. Sometimes people put off saying difficult things over the phone.

One of the drivers told them that they would probably have to walk for a few hours through the desert, and he didn't think everyone was ready for that. Many of the women had on high heels. The group was dressed for the airport, which was what they had originally expected.

"Everyone who doesn't have walking shoes had better come with me," he said. It was only a few miles to Sonoita. In minutes they could be at a shop that sold tennis shoes, buy something cheap, and get back. He left with a small group of women and was back, as he said, in little more than half an hour.

That afternoon, during the naptime, Francisco had taken Felícita for a short walk to find a shady tree of their own. They sat quietly, close together, talking little. He knew they would probably part the next day and never see each other again, but that moment felt good just the same. After a while he told her he thought he loved her. She took the news without any particular sign of interest. But that evening, while Guadalupe was nervously absorbed with final packing, Felícita came over, put her hand in Francisco's, and drew him into a corner. "I bought you something," she said, and she gave him a black leather wallet from town, where she had gone to get tennis shoes.

Antonio went outside to get away from the noise. He was looking at the stars when Pagán came out, and they stood there together, both contemplating the sky. "You've already been to the U.S.?" Pagán asked quietly. It was the first time they had ever talked.

"Yes, I was in San Francisco."

"Do you know this way across?"

"No, I only know Tijuana."

"What do you think, are we going to walk much?"

"In Tijuana we walked only two hours. But I don't know this part of the line."

"I'm afraid," Pagán confessed. "The desert, the Migra, the coyotes . . . none of us knows anything about these things."

"We'll be all right. It always works out somehow."

"I don't want to be sent back," Pagán said. There was no answer to that.

Just then a group of people, mostly women, came out and started rummaging through a garbage heap alongside the restaurant. Antonio asked what they were doing. "The driver said we had better hurry and get our water," Ana told him with annoyance. "No one ever told us we would have to get our own water."

They collected some of the discarded gallon-size plastic milk containers, which they washed and filled at a faucet on the building. There were thirty-three of them making the crossing, but only eighteen gathered the plastic jugs they called *pichingas*. Most of the men were drunk and paid no attention to the announcement. The jugs were heavy to carry, and even those who took them wondered if it was worth the trouble. And those drinkers who did think about it, decided that for a short walk through the desert at night, it wasn't. Someone had said it would be about ten miles across. But Jorge told them it was only a half-hour walk, a bit more if there was trouble. The "trouble" was never specified, and no one expected any. They were all combing their hair to look nice when they arrived.

Luisa was putting on makeup when she saw Ileana lugging in a full *pichinga*. "Why are you bothering with that?" she asked.

"You don't know the problems we had last time. I'm not taking any chances."

"I think you're being silly."

"Luisa, leave me alone." Ileana set her jug carefully with her things.

Finally Jorge ushered them out of the restaurant to the two pickups with Arizona license plates waiting in front. Jorge was loud and overbearing, and when some people climbed into the trucks, he grabbed them and pulled them roughly about. "Wait a minute," he yelled, "I'll tell you when to get in. First we have to separate you into two groups. All the women will be going in this truck, and the men in this one." It appeared that he was in the mood to make Pagán's humiliation complete. Jorge pushed in between the couple, waving the wife to one side where the women's truck was parked. When Pagán tried to follow her, Jorge blocked his path. Pagán was angry, but Jorge was quite drunk, and with the strange coyotes standing behind him in the dark, he looked menacing. Everyone turned to watch the two men silhouetted in the dusty aura of the trucks' headlights.

"Why is this necessary?" Pagán asked.

"The women are going an easier way than the men," Jorge snapped.

"That doesn't make any sense. We should all go the easier way. And I want to be with my wife."

"You'll be where I tell you to be," Jorge said, enjoying the moment. But to his surprise, Pagán suddenly started marching straight toward his wife.

The coyotes shouted at him, "Get back! Get back!" and stepped forward out of the darkness to block him. They raised their fists, shouting at once, furious at the challenge to their authority. They didn't want to start the trip with a successful mutiny.

But Pagán bent down, picked up a large bottle by the neck, and held it like a club as he marched forward. He was clearly ready to use it on anyone who came within reach. They had not expected this, and in their confusion they let him pass. Pagán turned and looked back defiantly at them, one hand around his wife's waist, the other still holding the bottle. And then the rest of the men surged along after him. Now that they thought about it, they, too, were skeptical about the need to separate the men from the women as they went into the desert at night with a bunch of strangers. The coyotes shrugged and gave up their plan, whatever it had been, and the two groups were one again. The travelers climbed into the trucks according to their preference, and Jorge had nothing more to say.

4
BORDERLAND

They rode for fifteen minutes through the warm night. Then the trucks bounced off the paved highway and wandered in the desert without their headlights. The moon was a little more than quarter full and the pale surface of the ground reflected its light. They drove among the dark shapes of great plants and stopped near a tree.

The mood was one of intense anticipation. With an intuitive feeling for ceremony, Pablo went up and thanked the driver for the ride. They shook hands, and then waved as the truck pulled away. But suddenly Pablo realized that his guitar was still in the back, wrapped in an old shirt to protect it from scratches. "Wait!" he called. The driver stopped while Pablo ran puffing to the cab. "Just a minute, please. I left my guitar in your truck," he said. The man turned and looked. Sure enough, the guitar was lying safely in the corner. He pressed his foot on the accelerator and sped away. The group watched as Pablo stood dejectedly in the dust. Then he turned and trudged back to join them, ignoring their sympathetic looks. These weren't good signs: the attempt to humiliate Pagán and then the stealing of the guitar. It was no way to start the crossing to their new lives.

Jorge cut the mood short. "Never mind that," he told them. "Come over here. While we're waiting for the guides we have some business to take care of. I want an address for each of you in the United States." Most of them owed Jorge more money. He wanted to know where to find them, or at least their families. They squatted in the smooth, sandy soil under the big tree and gave him in turn what he wanted.

Antonio had been preparing for this moment. "I'll tell you my address once we're safely there," he said dryly. "Besides," he reminded Jorge, "I live all the way up in San Francisco. It's too far for you to come for a visit."

Antonio had already decided that when they got to Los Angeles he would walk away from the group, and keep going. Jorge had never returned the hundred dollars he had promised to exchange for Antonio in Guatemala, as well as failing in many other promises. And Jorge realized that Antonio was not going to pay him another cent, but Antonio was not someone he wanted to argue with in front of everyone. He was too self-possessed, too clever, and too popular. Others might decide to follow him. The trip was too close to success to risk a mass rebellion. It was safer to let Antonio do whatever he wanted, as long as he did it quietly.

Finally, even though there had been no sound of a car, a whistle sounded from the dark. Jorge whistled back and two men came out of the desert. One was in his mid-twenties, tall and thin, with straight black hair and a cold, unfriendly appearance. The other was an old man with a worn face and a much kinder look. They didn't introduce themselves, but stood looking over the group. They didn't seem pleased with what they saw.

"You have a hard walk ahead," the young one warned. It was the first time anyone had told them that. Still, a new life was worth more than a hard walk. "We won't get there before dawn."

Antonio calculated quickly. He had been told it was ten miles. If they walked at three miles an hour, they would have been there before midnight.

"Let me see your water," the young one demanded. He addressed them directly, rather than through Jorge. He didn't seem particularly impressed with Jorge. His manner said that *he* was now in charge and he expected to be obeyed by everyone. He counted their jugs. There were only eighteen gallons for thirty-three people. He didn't like that. For a walk like he anticipated, a gallon per person should have been the absolute minimum. He and the old man moved a few steps away to discuss their options. There weren't any.

The trucks had left. To send for more water would mean a long delay. This area was well-patrolled and they wanted to complete the crossing before daylight. If they were seen, they would be arrested. Or perhaps mistaken for drug runners, who also used these routes, and be shot at. They decided it was more important to go at once, to travel rapidly, and to be done with a bad business as soon as possible. Neither of them carried any water. They were experienced and felt the trip posed no problem for them.

"Come with us," the young one commanded. "And keep quiet. As soon as we get to the line there could be Migra anywhere. If they hear you, we'll all be arrested."

They had an easy walk of only a few minutes to reach it. When she saw it, Flora felt a surge of panic mixed with exhilaration. Here was the line. On one side was fear and poverty. On the other was opportunity. But to get there she had to walk into wilderness with two complete strangers, men whose faces she couldn't even see clearly in the darkness. Even for so much, was it worth risking such helplessness? she wondered.

The border was only a barbed-wire fence about six feet high, and no obstacle for them. Two of the men pulled the strands apart and held them while everyone stepped through. They went slowly and carefully, helping each other. On the other side the young guide counted them, unaware that he was frowning.

No one said it aloud, but this was the climactic moment, what they had struggled and suffered to achieve. Antonio turned and gave Francisco his hand, helping him ceremoniously onto American soil. Then he rested his palm on the boy's shoulder and looked at him. They all felt it, and everyone waited for Antonio to speak the first words in their new land. "You're in the United States now," Antonio said solemnly, "do you know what to do?" Francisco shook his head. "Well, you'd better run like hell, you little bastard."

It broke the tension, and Francisco loved him for saying it. A few minutes later he turned and said, "You know, Antonio"—Francisco was the only one who didn't call him Squirrel—"wherever we go, I hope I'm near you."

"Yes," Antonio answered, touched by the compliment, "I'd like that too. We understand each other pretty well."

Since they didn't know the names of the guides, they called them the young one and the old one, although they learned that the old one was Felipe Vidal. He lived in Sonoita, and the young one was his oldest son. He was a mild man, with a straw hat to protect his deeply weathered face.

The young one was in charge. "Papa, you have to stay at the back," he said. Felipe was to make sure they didn't lose any stragglers in the night, and to listen for the sound of anyone coming after them. He carried a branch and stopped from time to time to sweep out their tracks, especially when they crossed one of the dirt roads used to patrol the area.

Francisco walked with Felícita, reaching out to take her hand from time to time. They talked about their plans. Felícita said she was looking forward to getting married and settling down, and Francisco automatically wished her much happiness. Then he said more earnestly, "*I* want to be your boyfriend."

"That's impossible," she answered in her soft, precise way. "You know someone is waiting for me."

"But . . ."

She put her hand to his mouth to stop him from arguing. Feeling her fingers against his lips, he thought, This is almost a kiss. He stood without moving until she took her hand down and started walking again. Their conversation shifted instinctively to the past, to life in El Salvador and away from the troublesome future that was so strongly implied by the border. Felícita described her mother and her home, and Francisco told her about his. She tired quickly, so he helped her carry her suitcase for a while.

Guadalupe was not with them. She was having trouble walking. Her usual routine of housework had not in any way prepared her for this. She was wearing a pair of dress sandals with thin soles, and the ground was hard and rocky. The bottoms of her feet had already become bruised. Now she was sorry she hadn't bought tennis shoes too, but these had been comfortable enough back at the restaurant. And besides, she had wanted to look her best for her arrival in the

United States. So while younger and more vigorous people moved confidently to the front, Guadalupe sagged to the rear with the woman called La Gorda, the Fat One, and old Don Cruz. They gave each other encouragement and sympathy and kept alive the desire to struggle on.

Jorge Dávila also had trouble walking, and he leaned heavily on the obliging Espinoza. Jorge was drunk, and liquor and exertion made him sweat. But the arid atmosphere somehow snatched the moisture away before it could cool him. "It's too hot," he complained, "but you know, that may be good. The border patrol won't be expecting us this time of year." The alcohol was dehydrating him, he could feel it. And when he stopped, he pissed a huge puddle that quickly disappeared into the earth.

The water jugs had grown too heavy. Because Luisa hadn't seen the need to take water, they had only Ileana's to drink, and they decided to save most of that for when they were really thirsty. But Luisa still didn't feel that the extra weight was worth the trouble. "Will you take this back, please?" she asked Ileana. "My hand is tired and I can't carry it anymore."

"Give it to me," Ileana said crossly.

But Jorge, who was right behind, surprised them by offering to help. "Don't worry, I'll bring it for you," he promised. Luisa gave it to him gladly.

The hiking became even harder for the bulky Luisa when they left the flatness of the desert and climbed into the Puerto Blanco Mountains. No one was prepared for this. Even young athletes like Francisco, Emilio, and Raúl had grown soft after sitting motionless for days in the bus. None of them had the sturdy hiking shoes they needed, a legacy of Jorge's fantasies of private airplanes. Not one of them had a map of the area. Among them all, only Pagán and old Felipe, the guide, even had pocketknives. They were totally dependent on the two Mexicans to take care of them.

The guides wanted no loud talking or calling out in the desert. Felipe and his son communicated with sharp little whistles that passed like darts through the darkness. They used them to judge the distance from front to back, to keep the group from getting too spread out. The travelers followed the sounds. If someone wandered off the path, they whistled for help, and the others whistled back until they were together again. The night hid everything. There was no way to tell who or what was waiting out there, so they tried to stay close.

Their cautious silence was soon badly disrupted, however, because in the darkness they couldn't always see the cactus. That was their first inkling that this was going to be more than a simple walk to freedom.

They had crossed the border undetected because they were in the desolate territory of a nature preserve. They had entered a park, but nothing any of them would have recognized as such. To them a park was an area of flowers and grass around the bandstand in a town's central square. But they had entered the Organ Pipe Cactus National Monument, which protected a prime section of the Sonoran desert in its natural state. It is the only area in the United States where the organ-pipe cactus grows. This is a cousin to the giant saguaro, that huge humanoid plant that lives for hundreds of years and is also abundant there. The organ pipe differs from the saguaro by branching into many thin arms near the base, instead of a few thick ones higher up.

But it was the cholla that was the worst by far. Scattered everywhere and growing up to human height, their branches were chains of loosely attached segments, each the size of a fist and densely covered with particularly vicious spines. The spines grew so thick and pale that they deceived the eye, appearing like a fluffy cloud which enveloped the plant. Merely brushing against one would sink numerous needles into one's flesh. Then as one pulled away in pain, the segment, or *bola*, would detach from the plant and ride along on one's body. The plant was so dangerous that Mexicans taught their children that if they even came close to one, it would jump out and attack them. They called it the "leaping cholla."

Berta was the first. Everyone heard her scream. Marching confidently near the front, determined that her short legs and heavy body would not handicap her, she was unprepared for this assault. The spines went immediately through her clothing and anchored deep in her upper arm. Pablo was close behind and he ran to help her. She was groaning and he wanted to do something quickly. So he grabbed the pincushion and yanked it out.

The spines are constructed so that they grip. When he pulled at the cactus ball, her skin lifted and small shreds of flesh were torn away by each spine. A lot of blood seeped through her sleeve, and now Pablo had his hand pierced with thorns, and no way to get rid of them. He tried to pull them out with his mouth, and discovered that they went into his lips as easily as they had entered his palm. Carefully and with considerable pain, he removed them one at a time with his teeth. He tried to keep his tongue far back in his mouth while he worked, but it was stuck a number of times. Before he was done, his face and hands were smeared with his own and Berta's blood. But he kept working stubbornly because there was nothing else to do. He was learning the first lesson of the desert: they were on their own.

Raúl also suffered the torments of Saint Sebastian as he walked. If the spines hurt as they went in, they were even more painful as he pulled them out. But he thought the worst pain came when he had one halfway out and lost his grip. As soon as it was released, it seemed to be sucked back in, reentering the same wounded flesh. His shoes had been old when they started, and now he realized they were rapidly wearing thinner on the rough ground. The thinner the soles, the more easily the spines entered his feet when he missed his step in the dark. I wish it wasn't my feet, he thought. There was nothing like this in El Salvador, no cactus, and no desert, and neither he nor Emilio was prepared to deal with them.

Fortunately Felipe came by and helped free him. He showed Raúl the technique of pinching the thorns between two rocks and tugging them out without touching them. When a whole ball of cholla was attached to one's body, the best method was to slide the teeth of a pocket comb between the skin and the cactus, and flip it away with a sharp jerk.

Other dangers crawled through the area as well. That desert is the only place in the United States where both the black widow and the brown recluse live, the two most deadly spiders in the country. And only in the Sonora can one find the Gila monster, one of two venomous lizards in the entire world. There are many rattlesnakes. They inject their toxin through fangs like hypodermic syringes, but the Gila monsters have a more difficult time poisoning their victims. Because they have short teeth, they hold on like bulldogs and grind into the flesh until their saliva mixes with the venom and seeps into the wound. The area also shelters tarantulas and scorpions, but they are scattered so thinly and live so cautiously that few people ever see them.

Emilio and Raúl had been more careful than most, and they had each brought a jug of water. After climbing for several hours, Emilio said, "We'd better drink only from one, and save the other for later. When they start fainting, we'll need it."

"Why should they be fainting?" Raúl asked him.

"I think there's going to be a lot of trouble," Emilio said. "It's already hot and very hard. We didn't start out with enough water in the first place, and these people are wasting it terribly." It was true. The men who had been drinking beer earlier now guzzled from the *pichingas* constantly. The alcohol had made them thirsty. And because they were still drunk and thoughtless, they poured water liberally over themselves to cool off.

Ileana called to Luisa for the *pichinga*. "Jorge has it," Luisa replied.

"Jorge, give me the water. I'm getting thirsty."

"What water?" he asked.

"What do you mean?" Ileana was excited. "You said you would carry it for us. Now I need it. Give it back to me."

"Look, I'm sorry, Ileana, I drank your water. I didn't mean to finish it, but I was very thirsty, and before I knew it . . ."

"That's not funny, Jorge. It was a stupid thing to do. That was all we had . . ."

Ileana and Luisa stopped in anger, letting Jorge go ahead so they wouldn't have to walk near him. And while they stood there, they realized it would be good to sit for a few minutes. As the tail of the line caught up with them, others joined them on the ground for a rest.

The Lugo sisters had tired quickly and were near the back now. Don Cruz, in addition to being old and weak, was starting to suffer from his asthma and found the walk a great struggle. Guadalupe and La Gorda were limping and tired. And last of all, shepherding them patiently through the night, came the steady old Felipe.

"How much farther?" asked Ileana.

Felipe squatted next to her. "To tell the truth, I'm not sure," he said. "I don't know this way. My son does, so we'd better ask him." But when they got to their feet and looked for the trail again, they didn't know which way to go.

They panicked. Being lost in the desert was worse than being discovered by Immigration, and they began to scream as well as whistle. "Help!" they yelled. "Where are you? Come back and get us!"

They kept it up for several minutes, but finally the young guide stepped out of the darkness. "Be quiet!" he commanded. "You can be heard for miles. What's the matter?"

"We couldn't find our way," Felipe told him.

"Then don't stay so far behind. Keep up with the others if you don't want to be lost." And he marched off in irritation.

It got even steeper and Luisa had trouble climbing. Ileana carried her things when she could, and took her hand to pull her up. Much of the time they were scrambling on their hands and knees now, sliding back on the loose volcanic stone that covered the hills. "How much longer do we have to do this?" Ileana asked. No one near her knew. "Ask the Mexican coyote," she insisted. "Pass it up the line."

The question moved from person to person, and Ileana could hear that the others were out of breath too.

Then the answer came back. "The next mountain is the last. The boss will be waiting there with the trucks." After that there was only the long ride to Los Angeles.

But when they finally struggled to the top of the next one, what they saw in the moonlight was another, higher mountain. The trails grew narrower, and in places the drop-offs were quite steep. "I can't cross that ledge," Luisa said. "There's no way I can walk across a little thing like that."

"Of course you can."

"No. I'm too frightened. It goes down forever."

"You have to," Ileana told her. "You can't go back, and we can't leave you here. You have no choice." She went ahead and turned, offering her hand to her sister-in-law. Luisa inched her way across, trying not to look down so she wouldn't get dizzy. But the loose rock crumbled under her foot. "I'm falling!" Luisa screamed. Ileana leaped forward and grabbed her by the wrist, but Luisa was too heavy and she slid farther over the edge. Past her body the mountain disappeared into the blackness below. The rocks they kicked loose as they struggled clattered and smashed themselves to bits far out of sight. Robles, who was the next one to cross, jumped onto the narrow strip. Together he and Ileana slowly hauled the frightened Luisa back onto the path and slid her across to firmer footing. Luisa gasped and wheezed as the three of them stood aside, the rest of the group filing tiredly past them.

The next mountain wasn't the last either. "When are we going to get some water?" someone asked the guide. "I'm thirsty."

"Right after this hill is a big lake. If we keep going we'll be there in a little while," he said. So they stopped asking. The idea of a lake out there was preposterous, and it was clear he would say anything to keep them moving.

At midnight, Emilio's nose began to bleed. "It's nothing, it happens all the time," he said. It was true. Raúl had seen him bleed from heat, from fatigue, and from extreme nervousness. At first they wet a handkerchief to wash off the blood and to help stop the flow. But as the bleeding continued, they felt they were wasting too much water. "Maybe if we wet a rock," Emilio suggested, and that worked just as well. The wet rock held the cold and used only a fraction of the water necessary to soak a handkerchief. As he walked along, Emilio held the damp stone under his nose to help clotting.

There was a lot of complaining now. It seemed as if some-one was always saying, "I can't walk anymore," but they kept walking because they were afraid to be left in the dark. The Lugo sisters were having a hard time. They had only one suitcase between them, and they were supposed to take turns carrying it, but Juanita, the youngest, had a tantrum. "I can't do it," she said. "I'm too tired. You take it. Or just leave it here." But Inés, who had just carried it, didn't think that was fair and insisted that Juanita take her turn. "No, you're bigger than me. I shouldn't have to carry it as much as you," Juanita objected, and she put the bag on the ground and refused to pick it up. Alicia, the oldest, had to come back and settle it by taking it herself. Even then Juanita had not vented all her misery. She continued to whine as they walked. "Why did they lie? Everyone lies to us," she said mournfully. "They said it would only be a few hours, but it's a long, long time." And it *was* beginning to seem very long.

Finally the guide signaled them by banging two rocks together. When they had assembled he announced that they would take a good rest before they went on. "It's only a little farther," he assured them. "We're almost there. Keep going a little longer and we'll be all right."

Luisa slumped next to Ileana. "I don't want to walk any-more," she said. "I'm staying here. When it gets light, maybe I'll go back to Mexico, but I can't keep going."

"You have to," Ileana said. Felipe was sitting near them. "Do you know anything about this?" Ileana asked tiredly.

"I don't want to lie to you," he said. "I don't know this way. I don't even know where I am. I told the boss, 'I don't know that route. I don't want any problems. I don't want to get everyone lost.' But he said, 'Don't worry about it. Just do what I tell you. Go ahead.' He sent us this way because he was angry that the women wouldn't go with him. I think he wanted to teach you a lesson."

"How stupid!" Ileana exclaimed. "Doesn't he have any idea what kind of problems he has caused? How could he do that?"

"I told him I wanted to go by another route. I know one that is much easier. I told him, but the boss said, 'No, I don't care what you want. Go this way.' So I don't know how much farther it is."

The young one, who had been listening, said, "It's true. This is a terrible way. But it's not too much longer. We have to keep going. We can't be caught here in the daytime."

Francisco and Felícita sat together, leaning against the same rock, their shoulders touching. They had stopped talking. In fact, at times they were hardly even aware of each other. As the struggle against pain and fatigue demanded more concentration, they withdrew more deeply into themselves to find strength. Her headaches had returned. When the guide stood up and signaled by clapping his hands, she said to Francisco, "I'm holding you back. Go ahead for a while. It will be easier if you can walk faster and don't have to worry about me."

"No, I want to stay with you and help you."

"I'm all right. Sometimes it's better for me to be alone. Go ahead, please. I'll catch up with you later."

Luisa also wanted the others to go ahead, but she didn't speak as softly and several people heard her. "Please, Luisa," Flora said, "you can't stay here. Something terrible might happen to you. You have to come with us, for your own sake."

"But I can't. I can't go another step. And I don't care. I'd rather take what happens than keep going like this."

"Flora is right," Ileana said. "You *have* to walk. You can go slower, but you have to keep going."

"No. Get out of here and leave me alone. Maybe you can walk, but I can't."

"Give me your hand," Ileana ordered. "I'll help you up." But Luisa refused, crossing her arms and burying her hands in her armpits. "Then I'll have to make you get up," Ileana said. She grabbed Luisa's belt and hauled her to her feet. Luisa protested, but she didn't even have the strength to put up a fight. When they were both standing, panting from the struggle, Ileana gasped to Felipe, "You'll have to wait for her. She can't walk this fast, but she'll do the best she can."

Now Ileana regretted the long rest they had taken. She felt more tired and stiff than she had before. But they were in the United States now, and the worst of it was already over. She was not going to stop until she was with her husband again. She changed her grip on Luisa's belt so she could pull her along and up the path.

As Guadalupe struggled by on sore feet a few minutes later, Felícita stepped back onto the trail to join her. "Where's Francisco?" Guadalupe asked in surprise.

"He had to go ahead," Felícita said. She didn't look good. The smell of stomach acid on her breath made it clear she had been vomiting again, and Guadalupe wondered if that had anything to do with the separation. As they walked quietly near the end of the group, Felícita began to cry in barely audible little gasps.

"Why did I come here?" she asked Guadalupe. "Why didn't I stay in my own country? I wish I was back with my mother." She was wearing her pink dress and new white tennis shoes, a tall, pale girl who suddenly looked much too fragile to pretend she was an adult in the face of so much trouble. Guadalupe hugged her protectively, and even though she had to reach up to stroke her head, she felt the girl collapse gratefully against her.

Emilio and Raúl, who had stopped to work on Emilio's nose, now came upon Felícita in Guadalupe's arms. The young girl looked unsteady to them. "Have you anything to drink?" they asked her.

"Our water has been gone for more than an hour," Guadalupe told them.

"Here, we've been saving this," said Emilio. Felícita was embarrassed, but the young men insisted and passed them their last *pichinga* for a long grateful drink.

Francisco had moved to the front of the group. Felícita had been right, it did feel better to go faster and it was easier to walk without her holding him back. Francisco's way of dealing with unpleasant situations was to face them and try to end them as soon as possible. His efforts brought him up with the young guide, and they strode along together. "Are we all right?" Francisco asked. "Everyone is complaining that this is worse than we were told. Has anything gone wrong?"

"They're just not used to walking," the young guide replied sourly. But the longer they struggled, the more nervous he looked. He refused any more talk with Francisco, and then he speeded up, so Francisco had to follow.

The dark had been bad, but dawn was also discouraging. Now they began to see each other. The vague forms that had been stumbling along, bumping into cactus and each other all night, now became people they knew. They were each a graphic record of what had happened to them.

Then the sun came up, looking huge. They felt the heat immediately. The night had been in the high eighties but under the July sunshine the temperature would soon rise to between 110 and 120 degrees. And the ground would be twenty to thirty degrees hotter, especially where the earth was dark.

But at least they were leaving the mountains. They stood on a slope that reached down to the Valley of the Ajo. Below them the desert unrolled into the distance until it was blocked by another range of dark mountains. Now that they could see the ground, it was much easier to walk and the downward slant carried them forward. This was their way out. Somewhere ahead lay Route 85, which ran north to Gila Bend, where it crossed Highway 8, to San Diego. But there was no sign of it in the distance. On the way down, La Gorda, her legs weary, slipped and fell badly on the loose rock.

It wasn't really better in the desert. Whatever they gained by leaving the mountains they gave up to the sun. Felícita vomited again, losing fluid at a much faster rate than the others. And then Inés Lugo, the middle sister, vomited too. The young coyote, trying to pull them along by his example, was already far ahead, only a dark mark beginning to waver in the heat.

"I have to stop," Luisa said.

Ileana looked at her and agreed. "Tell the guide to come back," she called. "We have to rest."

Luisa sat heavily on the ground. "I don't want to rest," she said, "I want to die."

Jorge and Espinoza were walking by and heard them.

Espinoza sat down, and Jorge, of all people, ran partway up yelling, "Come back. There are problems here." The young guide finally turned around. It was a long way back, and even in the distance they could see he was impatient.

Felícita sat down with Luisa. "I want to die too," she said with tears in her eyes. "I don't have the strength for any more."

"What a stupid place to stop," the young coyote stormed as he walked up.

"They couldn't walk, so they had to stop here," Ileana replied crossly.

"But there's not even shade. A little farther on there's shade. And I think there's water. Besides, Immigration patrols out here and they could see us."

"If it's only a little farther, maybe we should keep going," puffed Pablo, who had just staggered up.

"Yes, we should," the young coyote said. But just then Don Cruz walked by, rolled his eyes up, and passed out next to them.

Pablo opened Cruz' shirt, and Espinoza fanned him with his hand. When his eyes opened, they pulled him up to a sitting position and talked soothingly to him. But suddenly everyone scattered wildly when Jorge yelled, "Migra!" And sure enough, they could hear the beat of a patrol helicopter heading their way.

"Hide!" yelled the young coyote. "Everybody get behind something, quick!"

They ran to take the nearest hiding place, only to discover that there was none. The ground was fairly even, and the plants and rocks were too small to conceal them. So they took what they could find, any slight depression, the flimsiest bush. Some scooped dirt quickly over themselves to dull the colors of their clothing and help them blend into the ground. Even Don Cruz, too weak to crawl away, cringed back and covered his head with his arms. Only the two women, Luisa and Felícita, sat in the open and watched the approaching aircraft without expression.

It came along a slight ridge, several hundred yards away,

the throbbing getting heavier until they could feel it against their skin. "Guadalupe, they can see you!" Jorge screamed.

Guadalupe had been crouching like a rabbit behind a mere twig of a bush. But when she heard Jorge, she panicked. She jumped up and ran swiftly along the trail. They watched her in amazement. A minute before she had been exhausted, barely able to walk, and now she was sprinting by them in a blur. But even stranger, she had walked right through the bottoms of her sandles, and now she was essentially barefoot, the tops still fastened to her ankles by the straps and flapping wildly as she streaked by. But despite all this, the helicopter continued right past them and flew rapidly into the distance.

Jorge laughed first. And then they all started, even Guadalupe, who didn't know why. It was a miserable joke, but it was all they had, and it was such a relief to let out some of the tension.

"Well, I guess we might as well rest here," the young coyote decided. "It's not much of a place, but we can take half an hour."

He looked at his father and raised his eyebrows. What do you think? his expression asked.

Felipe pulled off his wide-brimmed hat and ran his fingers fretfully through his gray hair. It's not good, the gesture replied. They were in agreement.

"They're stupid," the young one muttered under his breath. "We'll miss the rides for sure. That means another whole day out here. They have no idea . . ." The old man looked at him sadly and shrugged. There was nothing they could do.

It was almost eight in the morning and they had been walking since nine the night before, eleven straight hours. Robles laid his head on a rock, because it was still slightly cool, and stretched out. He sighed several times with fatigue, but he couldn't relax. He couldn't forget the dusty feeling in his throat. All around him people were trying to nap, groaning softly as they felt the wounds and bruises they had accumulated.

A few feet away Antonio put his head on his arms, shut his eyes, and began snoring. Just before curling up, he had placed his *pichinga* on the ground close by his head. He had been rationing his water. Now the sunlight struck it and Robles could see more than three inches gleaming in the bottom.

He raised his head and looked around. No one was watching. Antonio was fast asleep. Slowly Robles crawled over, cursing silently as the pebbles bit into his knees and palms. He picked the jug up carefully, pleased by the weight of it. He uncorked the top, watching Antonio, calculating an escape route in case of emergency, and took a long drink. It was wonderful. He had planned to take only a sip, but now he sat there with the jug in his hands and nothing to stop him from having more. He decided that nothing Antonio could do would be so bad that it wouldn't be worth another swallow of water. He tipped his head back and let it gurgle between his crusted lips. Then he carefully returned the jug.

But as soon as he put it back, another hand was ready. A woman who had been lying on the other side of Robles had crawled over for her turn. She too took two long swallows. Originally, Robles had decided that he owed it to Antonio to save him some, but if this woman was going to drink it all anyway, then there was no virtue in leaving it to her. So he took another drink.

"You bastard! You're stealing my water," Antonio suddenly shouted.

"No," Robles insisted, "I didn't take any." But Antonio snatched the *pichinga* and tilted it into his own mouth. Only a trickle came out.

"Damn!" he yelled, throwing the container on the ground. "You can't trust anyone." He slapped the jug as hard as he could.

That wasn't the only conflict about water at that time. Luisa was having trouble breathing and Ileana lay next to her, listening to her wheeze. She knew Pagán had some water left and she didn't look forward to asking him for it. But Luisa was getting worse. Ileana crawled to Pagán and knelt beside him.

"Please give me some water for my sister-in-law," she asked.

He pulled the gallon in protectively and placed it between

himself and his wife. "I don't have any more," he said. Ileana looked directly at the jug. "I only have a little bit, and I have to save it for my wife," he amended.

"But Luisa is sick," she explained. "Please, just a little water for her."

To her surprise he said, "Yes, give the poor thing some water," and he picked up the jug. "But just a little. Only enough to wet her lips." He poured a capful for Ileana to take to her. Then he saw several other thirsty eyes watching him hopefully, and he gave each of them a tiny sip as well.

They were supposed to stay only half an hour, but they rested double that. Then the young guide called, "Wake up, it's time to go. It's not unbearably hot yet and we can still walk. Later we won't be able to move. Let's finish this, and then you can sleep all you want."

They followed him, but they were seriously tired now. Flora needed help. Robles loosened his belt so she could grab it from behind and be towed along. And when he saw Ileana look at Flora enviously, he let her hold him by the shoulder and he pulled them both for a while. Robles was refreshed by the long drink of Antonio's water, and he also felt a little guilty about it. He thought he should pay back the group through good deeds.

At one point Felipe caught up with them and walked along. "You know, there's a plant here that will help you," he said in his offhand way.

"What is it?" Robles wanted to know.

The Mexican pointed out a tree that was "good." It didn't *look* good. The branches were brown and dry. "If you break off a twig and chew it, it helps you. It makes saliva."

Felipe was convincing because he never pressed his views. So Robles took a piece of the wood and chewed on it. It had no taste, but in a moment his mouth was comfortably moist again as the saliva started to flow.

Robles went back to the tree and broke off some branches. Then he walked around, giving pieces to everyone. He even went up to Pagán and said, "Here, don't throw this away. Chew it and it'll make saliva." This was the first time they had talked since the Big Fight on the bus. Pagán was polite.

He thanked him and put the stick immediately into his mouth and chewed it vigorously to show that the gift was not scorned. Soon everyone chewed on one of the sticks as they walked along.

By midmorning the water was gone. Only Don Cruz still had an inch in the bottom of his jug. He allowed himself a tiny capful every so often, just to wet his mouth. Survival experts consider that an inefficient use of water. They feel it is better to drink as much as you need, as you become thirsty. But this way Don Cruz extended the psychological comfort of knowing it was there. And no one insisted that he share his last drops; he was so old, and it was too little water to make any difference.

The next time they stopped, something different happened. Robles picked up a stick and attacked a giant saguaro with it. It was the first time any of them had taken independent action to help themselves. Until then everyone followed the coyotes more or less passively, trusting that they would be cared for.

It was difficult work. The skin of the saguaro is like the hide of a rhinoceros, and just beneath it runs a layer of sturdy supporting ribs. It was one of those ribs, from another cactus that had fallen and rotted away, that Robles used as a club. All that armor was designed to protect a pool of moisture that would have attracted almost every living thing for miles around if they could have gotten to it. The capacity of a saguaro to store water is incredible. Several tons may be gathered by the wide, shallow net of roots after a single rainfall. But this hoard must be guarded for months, even years. The plant was obviously effective because the larger ones around them were over two hundred years old, as old as the nation that now protected them.

Everyone sat on the ground watching Robles exhaust himself in the sun. He finally knocked off an arm. When they saw that, they joined him, swarming over it with sticks and rocks like a Stone Age tribe hacking their prey to pieces. They expected the sweet moisture of the tropical fruit back home. The cactus flesh was wet but bitter, with a heavy aftertaste of minerals, like chewing aspirin. Even to them it was an unpleasant way to moisten their lips and they spit it out.

The group, which had stayed close, marching single-file during the night, now stretched out like taffy in the heat. Because it was no longer dark, Felipe moved up from the rear. And the mood had changed. Stragglers would have to look out for themselves from now on. The old guide looked tired but his sinewy legs still jerked him forward.

He was walking with Emilio and Raúl when they sat down for a moment on a cluster of rocks to gather their strength. He was surprised to see that there was still an inch of water left in Emilio's *pichinga*. The two friends each took a carefully measured sip and then passed it to the old man. Felipe swallowed quickly and then took several deep breaths. "Ah, that's good," he said. "Do you think I could have one more?" They all took another sip and it was finished. "Oh, hell," Felipe said. "I feel sick and tired. This is too much. That's the first drink I've had since we started." He and his son hadn't taken water with them because they thought the hike would be easier and quicker than this.

Everyone was noticeably weaker now. They felt it in themselves and they saw it in the others around them with a growing, unspoken sense of doom. It was early afternoon and the sun was extremely strong. They could feel it searing them right through their clothing. The guide saw it too, and where earlier he had urged them along by saying, "You're not walking as fast as you were. Hurry up, we have to get out of here," now he said, "Don't panic. It's no use to panic. Let's go a little farther and we'll rest again."

There was a continuing argument as they walked along, an argument that was disjointed and protracted because they were never together in a large-enough group to resolve it. Some wanted to stop, to relieve the pain they felt from walking in that heat without water. And some wanted to continue at any price, to end the accumulating horror and pain of wandering in the desert. The young guide was one who wanted to stop at the first available shelter.

"What about our rides?" Pagán's wife asked. "Won't we miss our rides?"

"You've already missed the rides," he answered impatiently. He had answered that question several times, but every half hour there was some new voice, plaintive and complaining, to ask it again. "When we don't show up, they'll realize something happened, and probably come back again tomorrow."

"We're not going to make it until tomorrow," she cried out. She was usually quiet, but she was frantic now. "Look at us. We can barely walk."

"That's why I want to stop," the coyote explained wearily. "I want to save whatever energy you still have. You'll be able to walk a lot farther when it's cool again. Tonight we can go to the road and hide and wait for them."

"Tonight we'll be dead!" Pagán tried to soothe her, but she wouldn't stop crying. The hopeless sound frightened them all.

"Maybe we should keep moving while we can," someone suggested tentatively. They had noticed the guide's uncertainty, and their confidence in him had dropped as their troubles increased.

"There's no shade here anyway," someone else said.

The guide was angry that they had refused his advice, and he felt the implied criticism. It was all the more painful because he had presented himself from the start as totally in charge.

They're stupid, he thought, not for the first time. They have absolutely no idea. But he stalked off, accepting their decision, and they stumbled after him. Farther back he could hear someone calling him, the exhausted voice of some woman who wanted to stop. Everyone belonged to either the "stop" or the "go" faction by now. At the back, Felícita, Luisa, and La Gorda kept going only because of Ileana's determination. While up front Francisco, Raúl, and Emilio were just as desperate to continue. They were young and suffered less, and they still feared being returned to El Salvador more than what might await them in the desert.

Actually the young guide was no longer as confused as he had been earlier. The route he had been forced to take through the mountains was unfamiliar to him. It was only by using stars and a good sense of direction that he had kept them on the right way. But now in the desert again, he had his bearings. He could see Montezuma's Head, a prominent, sharply pointed peak in the Ajo Mountains, which bounded the northeast edge of the desert. A direct line to it would take them across the Valley of the Ajo to Highway 85, somewhere near Alamo Wash Bridge, where they were supposed to meet the men with the trucks. It was only a matter of getting there, of enduring. He moved with more confidence now, and it was ironic that he had just lost their trust when he had finally found his way.

They had been on the trail for more than fifteen hours. "We're walking too much," Pagán complained to Jorge in another version of the stop-and-go argument. "We should have been there a long time ago."

"Shut up," Jorge answered. "Be quiet and walk."

But Pagán still had his capacity for outrage and wouldn't be silenced. He had paid good money and he knew he was entitled to better treatment. Jorge plodded on with his head down and ignored him. In fairness to Jorge, he was now in as much pain as the worst of them. Because of his drinking the night before, he still had a double thirst and a vicious hangover to deal with, in addition to everything else. And, of course, he was deprived of the satisfaction of having anyone else to blame.

In one little group that stopped, Guadalupe suddenly remembered she had put some fruit from the restaurant into her bag for later. There was a small bunch of grapes and an apple. Everything was smashed and rotten from the heat, brown and soft. But they each ate their share. It was wet. The sweetness made their salivary glands ache. It soothed their mouths, but when it was gone, they felt worse, a sense of loss. It made them remember water with painful clarity.

While most were moving automatically, trying not to feel, Robles was suddenly touched by the suffering around him. Emilio walked by, bleeding from the nose again. Flora, who had been helping others all along, was wearing down and having trouble helping herself. Suddenly they seemed precious and fragile to him. Behind him Ileana was staggering, and he decided to go back to get her. He carried her bag and let her lean on him until he could put her under a little bush with some shade. Then he went back to get Flora.

They have the faces of dead people, he thought as he looked around him. Flora wasn't even strong enough to hold on to him. He put one of her arms over his neck and half-carried her. Now he began to give out too. "Give me courage," he prayed.

When they reached the bush, Flora said, "Put me down. I can walk." She took a few steps and fell forward, unconscious, into the shrub. Robles' first fear was that she had blinded herself on the short, sharp branches. He pulled her out and laid her flat on the ground, shading her with his body. There were gashes in her cheeks but nothing near her eyes, he saw with relief. She was very pale, limp, and heavy. He lifted her up to a sitting position, hoping that might revive her, but his arms were so weak that he dropped her. He didn't know what to do. He slapped her face and got no reaction. He pulled off her blouse, hoping to cool her.

"Hey, what happened to Flora?" asked Paleface. His fine skin was now bright pink with sunburn.

"She fainted," said Robles anxiously. He leaned over and tried to blow into her mouth, remembering something vague about CPR.

Paleface opened his suitcase. He had a bottle of Coca-Cola. "Give her some of this," he said.

None of them had a bottle opener. They hadn't even brought keys with them. All their locks were in El Salvador. Robles pried at the cap with his teeth at the risk of breaking them off. But after a minute he had the cap in his hand. There were some tiny, clear drops of moisture clinging to the inside lining of the cap. He pointed his tongue and licked them. When he picked up Flora's head, she still seemed unconscious. "Put some on her face," Paleface told him. Robles patted Coca-Cola on her cheeks until she opened her eyes. Then she took a few sips. When she had had enough, Robles gave the rest scrupulously back to Paleface, but Paleface offered him a drink. Then Ileana fainted and they repeated the entire treatment with her. They had sunk to an entirely new level, he realized: they felt truly horrible.

As the last people in the line limped by and saw Flora and Ileana on the ground, they sat down to help and give comfort. Don Cruz came, his Bible and jug under one arm, his small valise under the other. When he saw Flora crying in Robles' arms, he stepped over and said kindly, "Here, drink this. It's concentrated water," and gave her his jug. She took a long swallow, but when she realized it was urine, it backed up on her and she vomited.

"No, no, no," Cruz pleaded. "You should drink it. It's good for you." That was the first they saw of bottles of urine, but as they thought it over, they realized it would be urine, or nothing. Some of them had kept their empty *pichingas* in case they found water. Now they started to use them. It marked another step in their acceptance of the desert, and of their status in it.

Someone brought out a tube of toothpaste and they passed it around to freshen their mouths. Meanwhile, Pablo was still struggling to come in last. They saw him fall in the distance. He was not able to get up again. Every time he put weight on his legs, his knees buckled. Espinoza and Robles went back again to aid him. It was a long, slow trudge, and all the while Pablo lay there as helpless as an overturned turtle in the sun. "Can't you walk anymore?" Espinoza asked.

"No, I can't. I'm going to die here," Pablo said with a break in his voice.

"We won't leave you," Espinoza assured him. "Try to get up. There's a bunch of us just ahead. Let's go stay with them." They could see the others, all facing back toward them, sitting almost a quarter of a mile away.

Together they pulled him to his feet and braced his arms over their shoulders. Because his legs still wouldn't hold him, they half-dragged him for the first few hundred yards. Then Robles' legs buckled too. He staggered out from under Pablo's weight, leaving it all to Espinoza. "I can't," he gasped. "I just can't," and he looked at them in apology.

Pablo slumped against Espinoza. His breath was shallow

and rapid with fear. "I can't leave you here," Espinoza said. "You'd be dead in two hours." He shifted Pablo's weight entirely onto his back by pulling both arms over his shoulders, and then he staggered off. They stopped often to rest, but he never dared to put him down, and finally he hauled him the entire way.

When they reached the others, Espinoza lowered Pablo to the ground and fell beside him. As soon as he caught his breath, he eased off his cowboy boots. They were not made for hiking and his socks were wet with blood. Carrying double weight had scraped the skin off the bottoms of his feet. I owe him my life, Pablo thought, and he tried not to imagine how it would have been if he were still lying back there alone while everyone moved on without him.

Flora, the first to pass out, was also the first to recover and insist on continuing. This curious leapfrogging of energy was to continue. People who had been unconscious or totally exhausted would recover for a time, lead the others on some ambitious attempt, and then collapse again. Flora thought it was important to rejoin the main group, which seemed to have settled about a quarter of a mile ahead in a low area that hid them. But she insisted they could not leave without her cousin, Ricardo, who was now unconscious. Occasionally he came to, complained of a terrible headache, and then passed out again.

Finally they agreed with her. They would walk to the other group as soon as Ricardo could go. But when he finally came to, he found he couldn't stand. And then they realized that neither could the rest of them. The strongest could half-rise, knees bent and feet spread, struggling for balance until they dropped forward to their hands to avoid a fall. In the end everyone crawled the entire distance on their hands and knees.

Up ahead things hadn't been going much better. Francisco, one of the youngest and strongest, had been walking near the front, peering around for some sign of hope. Around noon the strain had begun to affect him and he started seeing things. They were only little things, far away, but they sent thrills of relief through him. The struggle was over. They had made it. They would all laugh about this soon. It had seemed so terrible, but now it was all right because . . . there was a house . . . or was it a farm? Several times there were roads, real roads that cut through the middle of this wilderness. And people, people who would help them. He was sure. Each time he was sure. And each time the road was a strip of different-colored sand. And the houses and people in the distance became bushes as they approached. And each time the realization of nothingness was so disappointing that he swore he would never make the same mistake again. But he was desperate, and his imagination was beyond his control.

By one o'clock he stumbled into another dry riverbed. He fell and lay panting. The earth fried him, but he didn't have the strength to stand and there was nothing to sit upon. He hadn't had saliva in his mouth for hours. One by one, as they followed him into the wash, bodies dropped around him. They all had the same silent thought and one woman was unable to suppress it any longer. "I'm dying . . . I'm dying," she moaned. On his other side someone sounded like he was having trouble breathing. Francisco tried to stop his own panic.

When the young guide appeared, he also looked quite worried. "Have you seen my father?" he asked. "I saw him only an hour ago, but then he disappeared." No one knew where he was.

"We can't go any farther," the woman next to Francisco said.

"We'll stay here," the guide agreed. "There are people way out ahead. Someone has to go and tell them."

That job fell to Roberto, who was still strong despite his heavy drinking the night before. It was a long walk. On the way he passed Paleface, who turned back when he heard the message.

Later the others saw Roberto coming and sat down to wait for him. They were now out of sight of the main group. "Everyone's going to wait back there," he told them when he finally caught up.

"We think we're lost," was Antonio's reply. "It shouldn't be taking so long."

Roberto looked around in panic. There was nothing to see but desert. Desperation gave them a surge of energy, but they had no way to use it.

"We'd better do something," Felipe said, "before it's too late."

"Do you have any idea where to go?" Roberto asked him.

Felipe put out his hand, palm down, and rocked it back and forth in equivocation. "More or less," he said.

"Why don't we go?"

Emilio and Raúl were too tired. They decided to stay and rest, and then go back to the others. Felipe was tired too, Antonio and Roberto less so, but they were all frightened, and they got up and moved slowly off. They headed more directly east now. Felipe remembered that was the direction of the highway, and anywhere they could cross it would be fine with them. The two young Bible scholars watched them grow small in the distance. Then they turned and looked back. It was impossible to see the others.

Back in the wash people moaned and twisted on the ground in pain. The young guide looked increasingly nervous, walking up and down, climbing out of the gully to look around, and then coming back again. "I told you we shouldn't walk in this heat," he scolded them. "Now you're in trouble. I don't think you're all going to make it unless I can get some water." That got their attention. "I know where I can get some. It will take about two hours to get there and back."

"I want to go with you," said Berta quickly. She was not going to lie there in the desert and let him walk away, even though she was afraid to go off with him.

The guide didn't answer her, but she got up anyway. "Don't stay here too long," he told the others. "Try to keep going. I'll find you on the way back. But the farther you go now the easier it will be for you later."

The group watched silently as the two climbed the bank and disappeared over the rim. Not one of them had the strength to follow. Now they remembered what they had heard about people abandoned by their guides. They knew the disaster stories even though they usually tried to ignore them. Such things did happen.

Suddenly Francisco saw the impossible. Pagán sat next to him, mouth open and eyes dazed,   his side a jug with an inch of real water in it. "Pagán, please let me have a sip of your water," Francisco pleaded. Pagán shook his head. "What do you want for it? I'll give you all my money."

"This water is for my sons."

Josefa, sprawled on the other side, had been listening. "But your sons are not here," she said, pointing out the obvious.

"No," he flatly refused.

"Then let me do it," she persisted. "If you don't want to give it to him, give it to me and I'll give it to him." But Pagán became angry that she was pressing him. He moved his *pichinga* between his legs where he could protect it.

Josefa was shocked. This was the first time she had seen anyone refuse to share water and it suddenly gave her a different understanding of their situation. The worst of it was that it was so pointless; the man wouldn't even drink it himself. She reached into her valise and took out her Bible for comfort, but as she opened it, she burst into tears. "What's the matter with you?" she cried out. "Can't you see he's dying?" But Pagán shook his head stubbornly and crawled away, dragging his jug with him. Josefa went back to her suitcase for a tidbit she had been saving. She brought out two battered, lint-covered figs. She crawled to Francisco, brushed them off as well as she could, and put them both in his mouth. She patted him on the cheek and watched sadly while he ate.

It was hard for Francisco to chew and swallow. The food made knots in his stomach as his body struggled to dissolve it, but he was determined to show Josefa that he appreciated her gift. He had no idea how harmful it was to eat when his body was so deprived of water.

Late that afternoon Flora's group began one at a time to slide down the bank and join the others in the wash. That was when they learned that the young coyote had gone off to look for water and old Felipe hadn't been seen for hours. So it had finally happened: they were lost and alone in the desert. That awarness now became the emotional background for everything they did.

Jorge lay back against the bank, bloated and surly. When

he saw his old friend, Pablo, he called out, "Come here and take off my boots."

"I don't have the strength," Pablo answered.

Espinoza ignored Jorge's unpleasant tone and took pity on him because he was so helpless. "Does that feel better?" he asked.

"Yes, some," Jorge told him, "but I think I'm dying. I tell you one thing, if I ever get out of this alive, I swear I'll change. I'll become a revolutionary." It sounded like a late and pitiful attempt to bargain with fate, and no one made any comment.

It was there that Pablo first drank urine. Unlike Flora, he thought it was a blessing. The ground was searing hot and they were spread about, barely able to stand the sight of each other. Everyone's lips were burned, swollen, and split open If they touched them, it only made them bleed. All around Pablo people cried out to heaven, just to release their hopelessness.

It was in that mood that they started drinking urine. When the jug came to him, Pablo was amazed that it felt so good. He wanted desperately to stay alive, and the urine was a fantastic relief. It gave him hope. He wasn't troubled in the slightest by the taste or the thought. He could feel immediately that it was helping him. He kept an empty bottle, and when he had to urinate, he saved it and swallowed it later.

Anyone who asked for water was now given urine without comment. With the recognition that this was their most important resource, the values of the group shifted accordingly. Everyone sacrificed their fastidiousness and urinated in front of the others, collecting every drop in a *pichinga*. The group suspected that anyone who went off alone was hoping to hoard his or her urine, and the pressure to remain all together was quite effective.

Putting aside social reactions of disgust, there are significant differences regarding the two major human wastes. It is quite dangerous to consume human feces, or even to fertilize crops with them unless they have been treated so the disease-bearing organisms have been killed. That is not the case with urine. Only two common diseases are transmitted through urine. If it is known that the donor is free of hepatitis and typhoid, then the urine is generally safe to drink, since in other regards it is likely to be aseptic and a good source of salts lost through sweating. In some ways the replacement of those salts is as vital as the need for fluids, since the loss of the salts upsets the body's electrolytic balance and affects the functioning of all organ systems. Pablo's instincts were quite life-preserving.

But Felícita couldn't drink it even though she felt quite sick. She had already vomited several times in the wash and her headaches had worsened. Flora came over twice to wipe her face and neck with skin lotion to cool her. About five o'clock she came back with an Alka-Seltzer she had found. She broke it into little pieces and passed them out, saving the largest for Felícita, because of her headaches. But their mouths were too dry to swallow and there was no urine left to take them with. Robles and Jorge Dávila peed into a plastic cup and they passed that around. Only Felícita wasn't able to swallow the Alka-Seltzer and urine. She forced it down, gagged, and coughed it up again. "It's no use," she said, and after that, she didn't even try it again.

The sight of the women drinking gave Pablo an inspiration. He searched his suitcase until he found his bottle of Old Spice after-shave lotion. He tipped it back and swallowed half the bottle. It was a terrible mistake. His cracked throat absorbed the alcohol as if it had been poured into an open wound. He fell to the ground screaming. Flora yelled in fright, "Help! Come help, Pablo is dying!" But her efforts exhausted her and she fell beside him. No one else came, and he arched in pain until he too became unconscious.

Ileana couldn't tell if she were awake or not. She felt feverish and rolled restlessly on the ground. Her body was numb, but she could still feel the cactus spines as they accumulated. They pressed deeper every time she rolled on them. She cried for her husband and heard Flora in the background, crying for her mother. Espinoza crawled over, put his arm around her, and pulled her into the shade of the bank. He unbuttoned her blouse and took it off. "You'll feel better this way," he said. "Calm yourself, please calm your-self, Ileana."

La Gorda had been lying silently on the ground, her bulky body swollen and red in the heat. Suddenly she rolled onto her back. Her eyes stayed closed but she called for water, strange little cries, like the barking of a small dog: "Water! Water! Water!" The effort was pointless and there was clearly something wrong with her, but the group was too confused to realize it. When she yelled, "Water!" instead of coming to help her, someone would say, "Water? Do you see water? Did the guide come back with our water?" And that would start someone else crying out. No one could sit up now, and those who were conscious were not rational. La Gorda began to sputter and make sounds that were not words. Then she went into a seizure.

Espinoza had evidently heard her, even though he hadn't been able to respond. But later he crawled over. She had pinned up her dark hair to keep her neck cooler, but it had become undone and was twisted across her face. He wiped it carefully away, brushing off the dirt that also stuck to her, and the muddy patches where she had drooled on herself. Then he massaged her shoulders and neck. She seemed more relaxed after that and her breathing returned to normal.

Espinoza crawled back to his place and put his head on his arm in fatigue. A gray weakness shrouded the group and they lay inert and silent, as if they had finally become a part of the desert. When La Gorda began a second seizure, there was no one to help or notice. She flopped on the ground, her muscles so tight they vibrated. And when the tension finally released, her collapse was complete. Before she died, she kicked her leg over Ileana's chest.

As Ileana woke, she had trouble breathing. It took her several minutes to realize that it wasn't her body that was at fault, but the weight on her ribs. When she saw it was La Gorda's leg, she screamed. She woke the others. They had rested while unconscious and now poured their new strength into their terror. They yelled for the Migra to come and take them. Through all the pain and fear they had endured they had not believed that anyone would really die. Not one of themselves, such sensible, ordinary people, and not on such a routine crossing. But in that instant their expectations changed. Now they felt it would be remarkable if any of them survived.

When they had exhausted themselves and grew quiet, Espinoza told them it was foolish to scream. No one would hear them. The Migra probably weren't even working that day. It was some big American holiday, he said, Fourth of July, Independence Day.

Felipe had only "more or less" known the direction of the road, so Antonio picked a mark to keep them traveling in a straight line. He chose a prominent peak ahead of them, and whether it was coincidence or he intuitively realized the young coyote had also used it, he chose Montezuma's Head.

"I have some relatives in Ajo," Felipe said. "If we can get there, they'll help us."

"What will happen if the Migra catches us?" Roberto asked.

"Forget about the Migra," the old man answered. "Just walk."

They walked. The plan was simple, to head for the tall mountain until they crossed the highway. But the sun made it impossible. Time after time they forgot to look up, and when they did, the mountain was no longer in front of them. They became lost in daydreams, in wishes and regrets, and they wandered. They stumbled into cactus they didn't see and collected more spines. Repeatedly their concentration failed them.

By four they found a dry little tree and huddled under it for the illusion of shade. The heat was fierce. Roberto took off his shoes because his feet were burning. When it was time to go, his feet had swelled and he was too weak to pull his shoes back on. He had to take out the laces. When he got up, he fell down. There were always cactus underfoot, but he almost didn't care now and was content to lie on them while he caught his breath. The others changed their minds about moving on and sat down. Then they lay down, and all went to sleep. They slept about an hour.

When they woke up, Antonio found a single Chiclet in his pocket. He bit it in half and shared it with Roberto. "This will help you," he said, but it gave them cramps under their tongues as it forced out saliva.

"Let's go," said Felipe, and they walked on. They were rested, but still they staggered. And Felipe became confused. He couldn't even remember the direction. That's when Antonio told them to stand still and be quiet.

"I think I can hear a car," he said. Through the quiet of the desert at dusk came the distant sound of a motor. Antonio chose the direction carefully, and they set off again with new strength. Every few minutes they would fall or sit, and they would have to rest. But they heard cars pass several more times, each time a bit closer. Finally, falling over each other with fatigue, they came to the road, a simple double lane of black tar lying empty in the moonlight.

"A car will come by and we'll get water," Antonio said hopefully. The old man had finally lost the strength that had carried him so far. He lay where they placed him, on the ground just off the road, unable to move. But they saw headlights in the distance, and then they heard the motor.

Roberto was ecstatic. It seemed like years since he had seen an automobile. He ran into the road and yelled, "Water! Water!" over and over. He waved his arms and jumped up and down.

The car swerved around him and kept right on going. But several hundred yards down the road it slammed on the brakes and stopped. The driver's door opened, an arm reached out, and set a *pichinga* of water right in the middle of the road. Then the car drove quickly away again.

Roberto laughed hysterically. "They left us some water!" he yelled, and limped rapidly toward it along the highway. He kept repeating "water" to himself. Antonio followed more slowly, dragging Felipe with him.

When Roberto came to the jug, he was amazed to see that it had a film of moisture on the outside. He put his hands on it. Not only water, it was *ice* water. "Water, Antonio," he yelled down the road. He thanked God for giving them water and crossed himself. Then he took up the jug and hurried back to the others with it in his arms.

But Antonio gasped, "Water," in a different tone when he got there. He grabbed the *pichinga* and started to guzzle it.

"Wait," Roberto panicked, "save some for me!" And he managed to pull it back. When they had both drunk, they went to Felipe. They found him unconscious. They poured water on his face until he came to. He mumbled, "More, more . . ." every time they tried to take it away. The level went down quickly and they wanted another drink. Again they struggled over it, balanced in a tug-of-war, until one of them said, "Careful, we'll drop it," and they decided to share it.

Another car came. Again they yelled, and this time the driver pulled off the road near them. "Where're you from?" he asked in Spanish.

"From the south. Have you got any water?" He had a cooler jug in the car and gave each of them a glassful. Again it was amazingly cold.

"Why do you look such a mess?"

"We've been walking in the desert," they explained. They each had another glass of water. "Could you give us a ride to Ajo? We think we could get some help there."

"No way," he told them. "It would be too dangerous for me. You people are illegal, and if I get caught with you, I'll be in bad trouble."

"You can't just leave us here," Roberto said. "We barely made it this far."

"I'll get someone to help you. Sorry, but that's the best I can do." He had a CB radio in the car. He called the border patrol and told them there were three men on the highway by milepost 65. He wished them good luck and drove off.

Half an hour later a car came for them. They were searched for weapons and none was found. Then they were handcuffed and driven to the hospital in Ajo. They were treated well by a friendly staff that spoke Spanish. Antonio was put in jail, because he was now in the best condition. Roberto was put in a private room, watched carefully, and given juice, milk, and hot water. The doctor told him, "If you had drunk any more ice water, you might have died." The following day he was put in jail with Antonio. Felipe stayed in the hospital, in serious condition. Although the hospital workers went over them carefully, the men continued to pull cactus spines from their bodies for many days.

When they were questioned, they told the truth about everything except that there were others. They said they had come alone and they had come by bus. They knew how badly the others wanted to avoid being sent back, and they thought everyone had a chance to walk out. When they had left, no one had yet died.

Back at the main group the endless day somehow turned into evening. Flora felt strong again and kept busy helping those who called out. She brought them urine, and after they drank, moistened a rag with it and laid it on their foreheads. There were no more suggestions that they move on. Everyone rose and fell on mysterious cycles of energy: up into consciousness and pain, down into delirium, and back to oblivion.

Robles woke up. His face was pressed into the dirt and small pebbles had embedded themselves in his skin. He got up and looked around. Salvadorans were quite conservative about nakedness, but he was surrounded by partly dressed women. Pagán's wife had taken off her bra. Flora was in her panties. Even the young sisters had stripped to their underwear, and only Felícita still wore her pink dress. But it was meaningless. Robles had finally gone beyond interest in women.

All he wanted was a drink. As he crawled to the jug he saw that Ileana's pants were bloody. "Are you all right?" he asked. She told him she had her period, on top of everything else. The urine was a different color than the last time he had seen it, a dark, oily brown, and he wondered if someone could be bleeding internally. It smelled more rancid too. This was at least the third time they were drinking it, he realized, and it was hot from the sun. He rinsed his mouth and swallowed a bit experimentally. The look of the stuff made him cautious, but it still felt good. When he was done, he passed the jug to Flora.

Flora had helped Francisco a number of times that afternoon. He was feeling stronger now, and when he saw her make a disgusted face as she forced herself to swallow some urine, he decided to do something to help her.

"Maybe we can fix that so it's better to drink," he offered. "Maybe we can purify it with a filter."

Flora was relieved at the thought. She needed to drink something, but she could barely bring herself to swallow the dark, foul-smelling liquid in the jug. They took Francisco's shirt, placed several handfuls of sand and rock in it, and poured the urine through. They caught the drippings in a cup. Instead of coming out clear and tasteless, the urine dissolved minerals and dust in the dirt and dripped through darker, cloudier, and even worse-tasting than before. The experiment was a failure and there was no way to replace the liquid they had lost.

Julio Espinoza, who had passed out while La Gorda was dying, now opened his eyes. "Make a fire," he croaked to Flora. "Someone might see it. It's our only chance now." She moved around unsteadily, gathering fuel and placing it in a pile. Espinoza stood up to help her, but fell over. He crawled around on his hands and knees searching for scraps that might burn. He did not have the strength to go far. Then he turned to Pagán. "Give me your lighter," he said.

"No," Pagán replied. "It's too soon for that. Maybe we can still get through."

"What's the matter with you?" asked Espinoza, dumbfounded. "Don't you realize what's happening?"

"I understand as well as you! And do you know what can happen if we get sent back?" Recently there had been rumors that two planeloads of returning refugees had been unloaded in a remote area of the airport, lined up, and shot by government troops. The bodies were dumped in ditches along the same airport highway where the corpses of the Maryknoll nuns were found. "The guide could still come back with water. I don't want to bring the Migra down on our necks if we don't have to."

"You're living in a dreamworld," Espinoza accused. "No one is coming to help us. We'll be lucky to survive the night. Give me that lighter!"

Pagán wouldn't, and Espinoza tried to take it by force. The two men rolled on the ground, grunting in a feeble, slow-motion fight. Finally Espinoza pushed the exhausted Pagán onto his back and crawled away with the lighter. He made sure the fire was well started, all the time cursing Pagán for using up all his energy. Then he slumped to the ground and left the fire for Flora to feed.

At first no one helped her. Then, as it grew larger and brighter, Robles, Josefa, and Ana all started to throw on branches and dried plants to make a huge bonfire. It felt crazy to be making a fire in the midst of all the heat, which matched the look of the naked, disfigured travelers lying in the shadows. "Come and help us," Josefa called, but no one else could move.

Lying there semiconscious, Pablo thought about the futility of it. Why did they bother? he wondered. It was over already. All this is just a part of death, he thought. Everyone is waiting to die.

But not everyone was. Success with the fire gave Josefa courage. "I can't stay here," she said. "I have to go. Who wants to go with me?"

"Don't make things worse," said Espinoza. "This desert is dangerous at night. There are snakes and animals. Stay with the group."

"Oh, no, the fire will bring the Migra, and they will send us back. I already went back once and I don't want to do it again. It's cooler now, and I'm going to try to get out."

"I want to go too," said Ileana, who did not want to stay with the dead woman.

"I don't want to die here either," said Luisa. But when they tried to get up, neither of them could. Several others also tried without success. But Ana stood up.

"I'll go with you," she said.

"Please don't. You'll only get lost. We have a better chance if we stay together," said Espinoza.

"Why not give me your address book?" asked Josefa. "When I get to Los Angeles I'll call the families." He gave it to her and warned her once again. "I don't care," Josefa responded. "I feel I can walk, and I want to do it. I don't want to end up like her." She pointed at La Gorda.

"Do what you want to do," he told them.

They picked up La Gorda's blue overnight bag, waved once, and walked off into the darkness to the east.

They talked about La Gorda because they were constantly more aware of her. A sweet and nauseating odor had been growing stronger until it could no longer be ignored. She had been lying there in only bra and slip since afternoon. She had been exposed to the full sun for several hours and it had been enough to greatly speed up putrefaction.

"We have to get away from her," said Ileana, "or we'll get sick." Everyone agreed.

Flora and Francisco gathered clothing from the ground and carefully covered her body. There was no possibility they could bury her, but neither could they abandon her completely without protection. Already she was darker, rounder, and smoother as bacteria and fungi did their work and the gases of decomposition began to inflate her.

Then they moved their camp. Those who couldn't walk leaned on those who could. Whenever possible, they dragged their baggage with them. Last of all they took burning sticks from their fire and held them over their heads so they could see the way. In a limping, torchlight procession they slowly moved several hundred yards up the wash. Then they put the burning sticks back together again in a pile and lay down, exhausted by their effort.

Raúl and Emilio had watched with mixed feelings while Felipe, Antonio, and Roberto went off to look for the highway. The young men rested for the walk back to the main group, but sitting on the open ground in the sunlight, they only grew weaker. And when they looked for the way back, they found they had left no trail on the hard earth. They began to search in a direction they assumed was generally correct, but since the group was down in a wash, they realized they could pass quite close to them and not see them. "If we have to put out all this effort anyway, why not try to find the road?" asked Emilio. So they turned in the opposite direction.

Raúl was failing, but Emilio was still strong. At least they had had the sense to stay dressed, even keeping their long sleeves rolled down. Raúl fell regularly, and his hands became sore from the impact. His friend always stopped to help him and gave him a shoulder to lean on as they walked. Several times they thought they might have changed direction without realizing it, for places they passed seemed familiar. And Raúl's vision began to blur. That was when they saw Berta and the coyote in the distance.

They were outlined against the sky, walking along a ridge to the southeast of them. They were headed in the same general direction, the tall, thin young man and the short, stocky woman determinedly at his heels. They moved at a good pace. "We have to hurry," Emilio told Raúl, and he led his friend off at an angle to intersect the other two, as fast as he could.

It was a long, stumbling footrace. Emilio pulled and supported his friend. Finally the others saw them. They waved, but did not stop or change direction. "Wait for us," called Emilio, but the guide only made a sweeping gesture with his arm, telling them to come along. He kept going, but now that they were on the same track, they could at least stay within sight of each other. And after Raúl got a second wind, they began to close the gap.

The two young men had not been talking, concentrating instead on the struggle to avoid being left behind. When they finally joined Berta and the guide, Emilio asked, "Where are you going?"

"To get water," they told him.

"Is the road this way?" They said it was. "Good. Then you can look after my friend for me. I want to go ahead but I don't want him to be left alone." And leaving an astonished Raúl, Emilio walked on in front of them. Raúl saw him striding sturdily into the desert, determined and marvelously vigorous, until he disappeared. Raúl plodded along, stupefied. It wasn't until his friend had gone from sight that it occurred to him he could have simply said, "Wait, please wait for me. I want to go with you." They were never to see each other again.

Berta was having trouble walking too, and the guide had an arm around her waist to help support her. That was what had finally enabled Raúl and Emilio to catch up with them. But Raúl didn't trust the guide. He wondered what might have happened to Berta if he and Emilio had not come along. It would certainly have been easier to leave Berta than to carry her.

"We're all right now," the guide told them. "If we head for that mountain, we'll come to the road."

They covered about two miles in the next hour, and then they took a rest. Sitting in the quiet desert with the two men made Berta uneasy. There was no one anywhere in sight but these strangers. When Raúl moved, she flinched. "You'd better not do anything to me!" she exclaimed. Raúl was surprised. He took her hand and held it.

"While you're with me, you'll be all right," he promised her. "Have patience. We'll make it." They didn't say any more, but when they left, Raúl asked her if she needed any help, and she put her arm around him and leaned on him as they walked. The guide seemed happy to be freed of that burden. Unable to control his impatience, he walked far ahead of them.

Before he left, he had seemed upset. He was frightened for the people still in the desert and he didn't want the blame for what he knew was coming. He talked to himself, and from time to time he cursed out loud. "You guys really screwed up this whole thing," he said. But later he admitted, "We got lost. That was *our* fault. That, and the water. We screwed up because of the water."

At times Raúl and Berta changed roles. When he became tired, she put his arm over her shoulder and supported him for a while. She was a strong woman, but her strength came and went. As they continued into the heat of the afternoon, Berta began to see visions. "There are cows over there," she would say eagerly. Or "I can hear the sound of cars. Listen! You see? There are men's voices too."

Raúl felt a struggle inside himself when she said these things. Part of him wanted to give in and believe, and the other part refused, warning him that it was the way to madness.

But they did finally get to the road. And they probably passed close to Felipe, Antonio, and Roberto somewhere along the way, perhaps while they were sleeping. They all came out near the same point, but Berta's group came out hours earlier. Then they sat by the side of the road, shrunken with dehydration, and waited to see whether the next person to pass would be a friend or a jailer.

The first thing they saw was a large American automobile. The guide ran light-headed onto the pavement, falling over himself like a drunk, but the man stopped. "Listen," the young coyote said, "we need a ride to town right away. It's a matter of life and death."

"Are you kidding?" the driver replied. "You folks are wets. I could get in a lot of trouble for taking you anywhere." He was a middle-aged Chicano and he spoke to them in Spanish.

"Please, please," they begged him. The guide got on his knees. The man refused, but since he didn't walk away, they kept on trying.

"Oh, get in the car," he finally said. "But keep down, for God's sake. I don't want you to be seen."

The first thing they noticed in the car was a six-pack of Coca-Cola on the seat next to the driver. They grabbed the bottles without asking and twisted the tops off. The sodas were hot from sitting in the sun, but they didn't care. They drank them all without a word while the man looked nervously at them and wondered if he had taken on more than he could handle.

When they got to the edge of Why, he pulled off the road and said, "You've got to get out here. There's a border-patrol station in this town and I'm not driving through here with you in the car." Several hundred yards ahead of them was a three-way intersection with a gas station. Directly off the road about fifty yards away was an abandoned shack.

"Let's go to that house," the guide told them. "When you get out, just walk naturally and don't look around." They thanked the nervous man, but all he wanted was for them to get out quickly. The house had no door or windows. They ran inside.

Raúl thanked God that they had made it safely. Then he thanked God again when he saw a row of ten *pichingas* full of water lined up along a wall. Apparently someone was expecting another group to be stopping there. They each took one and guzzled with relief. When they were done drinking, they splashed water over themselves and even did a little washing. It made them feel new again, and it pushed back the ache of death, which had seemed so close for so long.

The shack was covered with black tar paper and it was quite hot in the sun. But the little front porch was shielded by a waist-high wall. They crawled out there and lay in the shade where they could feel the occasional bits of breeze. Compared to what they were used to, it was quite comfortable. As soon as they relaxed, they fell asleep. Without anyone keeping guard, they slept for several hours. When Berta woke up, she was very hungry. "There's a store near here," the young coyote said, but when they checked their pockets, they realized that none of them had American money.

"Have you anything valuable?" the guide asked. Berta hesitated and then gave him her favorite gold bracelet.

"Here, get some food for this," she said.

He appraised it and put it in his pocket. "I can't take this to the store," he said. "Tomorrow, I think I know a place I can use it." Until then they would just have to live with the grumbling of their stomachs.

While there was still light to see, they went back into the house. It was filthy. The place was open to any kind of casual visit and the litter ranged from empty cans and liquor bottles to condom wrappers. There was a collection of broken furniture: two torn sofas, a padded rocker with exposed springs, some long planks of wood from an abandoned construction project, and a dirty box spring. Raúl had a clean sheet in his bag. He spread it over the box spring and all three of them lay down on it.

Berta and the coyote went right to sleep again. Raúl did not. It would be safer to have someone awake, just in case anyone came by, he decided. But also, he didn't trust the guide. When he imagined all the terrible things the guide could do to them in the night, it kept him awake.

In the morning the guide said he was going to look for his friends. They watched him walk out to the highway, trying to look casual. Then he turned toward town and they lost sight of him. It was nine o'clock. They sat and wondered for three hours. At noon a truck drove up and he got out in front of the house. The bosses, who looked like Mexicans in traditional Western clothing, stayed in the truck while the guide talked to them.

"Those are my friends," he explained, "and everything is all right. But we can't take you out of here yet. There are too many Migra around, it's too dangerous."

"We can lie down in the back. You could put a blanket over us," Berta pleaded. "We can do it," she assured him.

That was not what he wanted to hear and it made him uncomfortable. "No, not now. Later. We'll be back." He edged out the door and hurried into the truck. The bosses drove off without saying a word to them. They hadn't brought any food or returned her bracelet.

"We have to get something to eat," Berta decided. Raúl still had some Mexican currency. Maybe someone would take it. They couldn't think of anything else. He walked to the gas station. Raúl spoke almost no English and he felt quite nervous. While he looked over the selection of snack foods, the attendant went to the back and made a call. Raúl put down his handful of bills and looked questioningly at the man. He nodded, accepting it, and Raúl left with sodas and cake.

As he stepped outside, a man drove up in a plain American car and got out, looking suspiciously at him. Raúl walked away, trying to be calm, and the man followed him. Raúl walked faster. "Hey, you, wait!" the man commanded. He walked up. "What's your name?" he asked in Spanish. He was a tall, muscular gringo and his clothes didn't tell Raúl anything. "Where do you live, where are you from, who are you?" the man asked rapidly.

"I'm from right here, I live nearby," Raúl answered nervously.

"Where?"

Raúl pointed quickly in the first direction that came to him. There weren't any houses in that direction. There were hardly any houses in any direction and there was little chance of bluffing, but he had nothing else to try.

"Tell me, what's the name of this place?"

"Well, I haven't lived here very long. As a matter of fact, I just moved here, so I don't know the name yet."

The man took out his wallet and showed him identification. He had a metal badge and a card from the border patrol. Raúl had to lean spread-eagled against the car while the man searched him. Then he turned him around and handcuffed him.

"I don't feel good," Raúl told him. "Can I sit down?" He slid to the ground, suddenly weak. All they had gone through, everything had been for nothing. And he couldn't even think about going back to El Salvador yet. The man watched him carefully to see if he was all right.

"May I drink one of the sodas?" Raúl asked him. The man opened one and handed it to him, and Raúl drank it with both hands manacled together.

The man got in the car and radioed back to headquarters. Then he came and squatted in front of Raúl. "Look, we know there's a group coming through," he said, "and there are probably more people out there, but we don't know where. Are you with a group?"

Raúl shook his head.

"We already got three of them," the man went on patiently.

"Last night they were sitting by the road, too weak to move. In terrible shape. They couldn't talk much and we took them to the hospital. But you can talk, so I want you to tell me about the others."

"Yes," admitted Raúl, "I was with them."

"Did they come out with you?"

"No, I'm here by myself."

"How did you get out?"

"I just kept walking. They were too tired and they stayed to rest. I walked until I got to the highway."

Two other agents, these in uniform, drove up and got out quickly. "Where were you going just now when I caught you?" the man asked.

"Over there." Raúl pointed nearby. "I wanted to find a place to sit and drink the sodas."

"Better hold him here," the officer told one of the new men. He took the other and cautiously began to backtrack Raúl, heading in the direction he had been walking when intercepted. They were pointed directly at the small shack. They went in, and a minute later came out with a tearful Berta.

"Is that your husband?" they asked her. She was handcuffed too and they took her to the car. By the time she got in, she was crying too much to be questioned. She couldn't bear the thought of all she had endured for nothing. If only the coyotes had taken her in the truck when she begged them, she would have been all right. She had never seen American Immigration officials before and she was frightened.

They took them both to the trailer office. From the time they found Berta, they ignored Raúl. Perhaps it was because he had told such obvious lies at first. Or because they thought Berta, a woman, would be so much more accessible as an informant. In any event, Raúl's confession about the people in the desert was ignored, and they were wrong about Berta. She had no idea that anyone had died, and in her exhausted and confused state she became tenaciously secretive. It seemed the loyal thing to do. And Raúl now followed Berta's lead and offered nothing.

It took Hector Ochoa several hours of exhausting effort before Berta yielded. Then he left with her immediately. Raúl was put in jail.

Back at the main group the night had stayed hot. Some of them were unconscious and the others lay on the ground in pain, wondering what would become of them. At one point, old Don Cruz thought he could hear an animal in the distance, sniffing and grunting around the corpse of La Gorda. He offered up a prayer for her soul.

The sky turned from black to deepest blue. Espinoza, who had been thinking for some time, sat up. "We can't just give away our lives. We have to try something," he said.

"What?"

"Walk a little more. That's all I can think of. Maybe we can find help. Or at least a little water, so we can survive." Espinoza pushed himself to his feet. He meant to go now, while he could. One by one, other men joined him. Pablo rolled onto his stomach and began to struggle to stand. Then Pagán surprised them by hugging his wife and getting up too. That left eleven women with Don Cruz and Jorge Dávila, lying on the ground, watching eight men prepare to go off.

"You can't walk," Espinoza said as he came over to Pablo. Pablo had one arm extended, as if he were balancing on a ledge rather than standing on solid ground. "You should stay here with the women."

"No," Pablo said stubbornly. "I can walk." There was no point in arguing. They would find out soon enough.

"Why should we stay? We can walk too," said Ileana. Flora agreed with her.

"No," Robles objected. "We'll be moving too fast. This way we'll have a better chance of finding water and getting back quickly."

The women didn't like that. But Luisa didn't intend to walk another step, and Ileana didn't want to go without her. Flora didn't want to leave anyone behind either, so the question settled itself, after a fashion.

"If you're leaving us here, then you should pee in our cup

before you go," Ileana told them. "You may find water up ahead but we won't have anything else."

"I don't have to pee," Robles objected.

"Force yourself," she insisted. "It's important." And they agreed. One by one the men took the cup they were using and spent a minute concentrating, coaxing their kidneys to let down a few drops of fluid. As Robles waited his turn, Alicia Lugo reached up and pulled at his shirt.

"Give me some," she said with difficulty.

Robles urinated a tiny bit into her hand. There was a single drop left hanging from his penis and he touched it with his finger and transferred it to his tongue.

"Hey, what about you, Jorge?" the men asked. "Come with us."

"No way," Jorge scoffed. "You'll only get lost out there. I'm going to rest here. And then I'm going back to Mexico. I've had enough of this shit." They thought he said that because he didn't want to admit he couldn't walk, so they left him alone.

"How will we ever get back here after we find the water?" Paleface asked nervously. "We may never find this place again." It was true. The endless repetition of similar plants and rocks made the desert confusing.

"Toilet paper," decided Espinoza. "We'll carry several rolls and drop sheets along the way."

"And if the women feel stronger later they can follow our trail," Paleface said hopefully.

Pagán's wife was standing now, holding her husband. "You don't have to go," she grumbled. "Everything is bad enough without you leaving me in this godforsaken place."

"Nothing is godforsaken," Pablo rebuked her piously. "He always knows."

They were the only couple. It made the rest of them aware that the people they loved were far away, without the slightest hint of what was happening. There was only one way to get back to them. They turned and scrambled up the wall of the wash.

Felícita lay very still, her arm over her eyes. She didn't

look up as Francisco left. She was haggard now, and she had been sick repeatedly. Although she couldn't bear for anyone to see her that way, there was nothing she could do to control it. Her only privacy came from covering her face.

"I want to come too," the voice of Don Cruz called after them. They didn't want him. He was obviously too old and feeble to go far. They were afraid he would slow them down, but no one wanted to shame him by saying so. It took him forever to get on his feet.

"Don Cruz, why don't you stay with us? We need some men here too," Flora urged.

But Don Cruz replied politely, "It is my duty to go for help if I can." What he said was also a rebuke to Jorge Dávila. But in spite of his determination, the old man was not able to climb the embankment. And even when Espinoza reached down and gave him his hand, he grunted with exertion as he was hauled up. The women watched him anxiously, but the men turned away. He made their vulnerability all too obvious. Flora gave them a sad wave. Robles looked down at her and shrugged unhappily. Then the men turned and walked off toward the east, just like all the others that had gone before them. In front of them the sky was glowing.

They focused far ahead as they walked, trying to stretch their determination toward the horizon. So they were surprised by the sounds that came from behind. They had forgotten Cruz. He was trailing the group and had already stumbled. They waited while he got up. Then he fell again.

This was what they had hoped to avoid. Now even he saw that despite his courage, he was too old and weak. The men who stood watching were in torment. They all knew this was their last chance, for everyone. They no longer had the energy to go back and help. Every movement had to be forward now.

Don Cruz understood. "I can't walk anymore," he called out. "So pray for me. I'm going to stay here."

"God bless you!" someone called emotionally.

"Don Cruz, go back to the women," Francisco urged. They could not see or hear the women now that the embankment was between them. "They don't know you're here. Go back to them." There was nothing else they could do, except to extend their pity across the gap that widened as they walked away and left him.

Francisco was afraid that the old man would die alone in that vastness if he didn't return to the others. He kept looking back. But each time he saw Don Cruz struggling onward. He would crawl a few yards after them, dragging his Bible and urine bottle along the ground, and then drop and rest again. Each time he had the energy, he used it to pull himself farther out into the desert, away from the comfort of the women. He continued to crawl and drop until he couldn't rise to his hands and knees anymore. But he still twitched forward on his belly with little movements of his arms and legs, a swimmer slowly drowning in the sand. Until finally Francisco looked back and he had sunk out of sight.

No one had truly felt hopeful when they started out, but after this they were even more discouraged. They walked, strung out in a long ragged line, their heads down. Francisco kept thinking about Cruz and he moved back to talk with the failing Pablo. "What makes you so sure that God knows all this?" he asked.

"We see proof all the time," the little man replied. "Like that poor woman who gave us her last water when we first got to the desert. That's God's goodness." It didn't satisfy Francisco.

"I've seen it personally," said Pablo. He decided to tell Francisco his favorite story. "When I was only fifteen I worked as a mason on top of a three-story building. One day I slipped off the scaffold. I fell straight down on a pile of bricks. And the foreman came over and said, 'Oh, no, we have another one dead. Call the ambulance and let's get him out of here.' But I was alive and conscious. Just confused from falling. They took me to a doctor and there was not a bone broken. Only some bruises on my hands and knees . . . So I know He won't abandon us."

They stumbled on and on. The heat grew rapidly once the sun rose. Robles came up and took Pablo's urine jug. The other jug held urine the color of maple syrup, but Pablo's was deep green. The night before, Espinoza had found an old pill in his pocket. It was for treating a kidney disorder, he said. Pablo asked him for it. He reasoned that kidney medicine might strengthen his kidneys, and any strength he could give his body might help him survive. But the medication dyed his urine deep green. Robles was not impressed by the pill story. "We'd better not drink out of Pablo's jug anymore," he told them. "He's falling apart on the inside. It will make us sick." That thought made them uncomfortable, so they stopped drinking from Pablo's jug.

"The truth is," Robles admitted a little later, "I'm sick and tired of urine . . . I don't want any more urine. . . . Let's make an agreement. Whoever dies first, even me, we'll cut him open and drink his blood."

That was too much for Miguel. He was only seventeen and the things he had seen already made him feel weak and vulnerable. So it really panicked him to imagine that he might lie down to rest, or even pass out, and wake up with his veins cut open and someone sucking out his blood. They walked steadily and the heat stole their strength. But each time they flopped on the ground, Miguel, no matter how tired he was, managed to stagger a few extra steps so he would not fall within reach of Robles.

But other prey came into Robles' clutches. Once he saw a snake and chased it wildly through the sand. He wanted to eat it, but the snake easily outdistanced him. Francisco, of all people, was the one to find the drab nest hidden in a bush. Inside were two terrified birds, still too young to fly. He took them. They will help us, he thought. We can eat them. He handed one to Robles, automatically sharing what he had found. But Francisco, feeling the trembling body in his hands and looking into the bright little eyes, couldn't go any further. Robles decided to tear his apart and eat it immediately. He twisted the wing, breaking it, but he was unable to pull it from the body. Francisco couldn't bear the sight. If *we* can't pity the helpless, he wondered, then who can? He placed his bird back in the nest.

Robles, too, hungry and desperate as he was, found himself unable to tear apart the tiny being. He set the nestling on the ground and walked rapidly away so he wouldn't see it squirming in the sun.

By midmorning Espinoza spotted something in the far distance, the first thing they had seen that was not part of the desert. It was a row of wooden poles connected by electric wires. They could hardly believe it. The struggle had paid off. Power lines ran along roads, and roads were filled with traffic. Or if not exactly filled, at least someone came along every so often, and that was so much better than where they had been. They would find some way to endure and they would be saved.

Pagán was especially relieved. Now he was the weakest. At times he looked dazed and not totally there. But he took strength from hope and pushed on as fast as he could. They were all relieved that they had been spared a slow, painful decline like Don Cruz.

But as they came closer, a different truth was revealed. There was no highway but only a little-used dirt road for an occasional service vehicle. It might be weeks before one came by again. There were just the barren poles marching through the desert, and the smooth geometric arcs of wire between them, a garland of technology to show that people had once been there.

But Pagán couldn't face that. "It's a railway line," he insisted childishly. "We have to wait here for the train." It made Francisco's skin crawl to hear it, but no one contradicted him. If Pagán could see the tracks, then what could anyone say that would be half as convincing?

They continued to the nearest pole because that way they had at least reached something. It rose out of a shallow depression and they crumpled into it. No one could move. Now that hope was gone, their walk was over. None of them suspected that the real road, which had regular traffic, was only a mile farther in the same direction.

Espinoza sighed, "Well, this is it. We can't walk anymore . . . God has forgotten us." This time Pablo didn't contradict him. "Might as well face it. Find your own little place, because that's where you'll stay."

They looked for a good place to die. A bit of shade was all they wanted. Pagán took off his shirt, hoping he would be cooler. And then the rest of them followed his example, stripping down to their underpants. The sand was hot on top but cooler underneath. They scooped out shallow trenches to lie in and then heaped sand on themselves.

Robles found an animal burrow and decided to use it. He pushed his head inside, leaving his almost-naked body out to roast in the sun. The air was cooler in the hole, it was easier to breathe, and he was a little more comfortable. No one lay near him because of what he had said earlier about drinking blood, but he didn't care. For once he felt like being alone and he was glad his head was in the dark where he couldn't see any more of their suffering.

Francisco saw what Robles had done and thought it was a good idea. He searched until he found another hole, under a small tree. It was too narrow for his head but by scraping the dirt away with his fingernails he was able to widen it enough to protect his face. He felt better with his face shaded, but his thirst was still painful, so he stuffed rocks into his mouth, trying to force a little saliva to flow.

Pablo was still determined to live if he could. He sorted through the few belongings he had dragged with him, hoping he had forgotten some bit of salvation. There was only some clothing, a towel, and a can of spray deodorant. One by one he took them out and threw them at the pole in disgust. And the deodorant he threw the farthest and angriest, remembering his ghastly experience of drinking the after-shave lotion. But Espinoza, despite his morbid speech, still found himself unable to give up hope entirely. He was watching Pablo, and the sight of the spray can flying through the air gave him an idea.

"Come help me," he called, but only the tall Paleface paid any attention. "Spray deodorant burns," Espinoza reasoned. "We can use it to set fire to the power pole. The wires must carry electricity to someone. If the power goes off, they'll notice immediately and look for the problem. If they come soon enough, we can still be saved."

They were enthusiastic about their plan and staggered off to put it to work. They sprayed the pole and held Pagán's lighter to it. The flames flared, clear and almost invisible in the bright sun, and then died. The pole was lightly charred but the wood had not caught. They tried again, using the rest of the deodorant, and the same thing happened. Their efforts gained them only a patch of blackened wood. The wires, high overhead, were untouched and unreachable. "Those people will never know we tried to send them a message," Espinoza said. He remained their leader to the end, and when he saw that his final plan had failed, he called, "If we have to die, let's at least die together." And those that could, crawled toward him to gather for the last time, preferring not to face death alone.

There were eight in all: Pablo, Robles, Paleface, Pagán, Miguel, Ricardo, Espinoza, and Francisco. As Pablo crawled back to the group, he passed Pagán moaning on the sand. He looked half-dead. His skin was filthy and peeling off in places. One ear was full of blood and more was dry under his nose. "Would you like a little toothpaste to freshen your mouth?" Pablo asked sympathetically. Pagán couldn't answer, and Pablo, having nothing else to offer, took the tube and opened Pagán's mouth to squeeze a little inside. He was shocked to find it full of dirt. Pagán's tongue lay in the dry dust like some fat lizard. Pablo's stomach turned. Forgetting the toothpaste, he decided he had better bring Pagán back to the others with him. He wanted to help him to his feet, but Pagán was much taller and heavier than he was and it was impossible to lift him. Then he tried to drag him along the ground, but Pagán was too limp and heavy, and no longer cared.

Finally Pablo said good-bye and staggered on. When he passed the towel he had flung away, he picked it up and brought it with him. He draped it over a bush near the group, making the only little patch of shade they had, and everyone who could, crowded in with him there. Ricardo came, and Francisco, and Miguel and Espinoza. Robles lay silent and unmoving, his head still buried, and Miguel was greatly relieved that he stayed there. The kindly Paleface, usually one of those with the most energy, had not been seen since the attempt on the pole. The assumed he had collapsed somewhere. There was no one who could go after him.

Miguel, weak as he was, tried to shove Pablo out of the shade. Pablo kicked him back. "What's the matter?" Miguel whined. "Do you want to suck my blood too? Leave me alone. Let me lie here." They continued arguing over the merest shadow until Miguel, growing wild, suddenly threw himself on Pablo and bit him fiercely in the upper arm. He took Pablo by surprise and succeeded in biting a chunk right out. Pablo bellowed in pain and threw him off. Miguel sat back, chewed the piece of flesh thoughtfully, and swallowed it. That seemed to settle down the seventeen-year-old. He curled up on the ground and went peacefully to sleep in the sun.

Pablo stared at the ragged wound and the blood unbelievingly. Then he took out the all-purpose toothpaste and smeared a large gob on the spot to soothe it. He was now so dehydrated that he couldn't really bleed. That gave him another idea, and next he carefully covered his face and neck with a protective coating of the white paste.

In his dark separateness, Robles drifted in an intense world of images. It was a little past noon and outside the burrow his body felt like it was cremating slowly. But the earth shut out the groaning and sobbing of the others and left him with his memories. He remembered walking through the shadowy rooms of his home in El Salvador. He pictured a bottle of ice water, just as it came from the refrigerator, and then a few minutes later, after it gathered a film of droplets around itself. He saw a spring that had been nearby, and heard the marvelous, gentle sound as it flowed from the ground. He remembered when he took a bath, how much water he used. And when it rained, how the puddles stayed in the streets. But when he imagined his daughter playing in the water, he remembered where he was and what was happening. And he prayed she would not find out how he died.

Finally, perhaps because their minds could no longer find any excuse not to, they started dying. Between periods of unconsciousness they babbled incoherently. Pablo and

Espinoza called out to their wives and children with sudden, loud, disconnected cries. Nearby someone was praying, but not Pablo.

"Why do You abandon us now?" Pablo complained. "You're so great. Why don't You do something?" He rolled from side to side in misery. Then he saw Francisco next to him, watching with concern. "Will you kill me?" he pleaded. "Right now! I don't want to go on like this anymore." Francisco reached out to reassure him, but Pablo started sobbing. "I can't suffocate myself. I don't want to die that way. *You* should kill me. Use a rock or something. Please . . . please . . ." He felt humiliated, begging for such a thing, but he could no longer control himself.

Pablo had always been so full of life. Francisco was shocked. "You're the one that talks so much about God! You should know you can't ask me to do that." He put his arm around the plump little man. "I know we're going to get out of this. We'll find some way. When it gets dark, we'll walk some more. We're near a little house, I know it. When we get there they'll give us water and they'll help us. We'll be all right, I promise you. I'm not going to die without seeing my mother again."

Pablo stopped crying and became very quiet. Francisco lay there listening to the weakening groans of his companions. It was becoming like a dream. Death is not so bad, he thought with relief. After all, soon they would get into a little car. They would drive to the house. They would stay in the house with the two children and play with them, because they didn't have anyone to play with. The images were soft and comforting.

To his surprise he heard Pagán again. "Give me water. Please, give me water," he said, but he was talking to no one.

Then Francisco first realized that it was July 5. It was his birthday. Without anyone knowing, he had become twenty years old. To celebrate he slid into unconsciousness with the rest of them.

They were awakened late in the afternoon by the tremendous sound of a jet airplane flying close overhead. The roar brought even Robles out of his burrow. "A plane! A plane!" Espinoza croaked. "Help me signal it." He had a shirt in his hand and was trying unsuccessfully to get to his feet.

Robles felt drunk. He couldn't coordinate his movements, but he was desperate to do something. He too picked up a shirt and a stick from the ground, and he put the shirt at the end of the stick. He waved it twice in a circle and then dropped everything. He couldn't pick it up again and he lurched around, stumbling over the bodies of the others, fighting to stay on his feet. The plane was already gone, but he waited and hoped. A minute later they heard it again. "God, let them see us!" he called. The sound grew overwhelming as the plane flew by. "They see us! They see us!" Robles screamed. He was crying with happiness. He sat down to wait. After a while he became too tired and hot. He crawled back to his hole and put his head into the ground again.

They didn't realize that the park was used as a practice range for the air force. People who crossed that way often mistook the planes for border-patrol searches, but these pilots looked at the ground only to skim it as low and quickly as possible. They never saw the people below.

But the Salvadorans didn't know that. They waited patiently and their faith was rewarded. In the early dusk someone called excitedly, "Immigration is here!" Pablo actually saw them first. He was looking out toward the road when he spotted Berta and the uniformed agents getting out of the jeep. But he was so overwhelmed he could only stand there and cry, his round face sad and pale like the moon.

"Don't worry, we're here to help you," a tall man in a green uniform told them. "Don't move, just stay where you are and don't exert yourself."

The air became thick with voices. "Give me water!" people were crying. "Please give me water."

"There must be others around here," one agent said. He sounded very concerned and began circling the group anxiously.

When they pulled Robles from his little cave, the first thing he did was to tell them about the women. They questioned the other men immediately. "How far away are the others?" they asked. "And in what direction?" The men were eager to help, but they were hopelessly confused. Someone got on the radio and called for more help.

The agent who was holding Robles poured some water onto his hand and cleaned out Robles' mouth. Then he took his handkerchief and wiped it out again. Finally he tilted up his head and put the canteen to his lips. "Don't drink too much," he cautioned, but Robles grabbed his shirt to keep him from getting away. The man had to warn him again, "I don't want you to kill yourself. Take a little at a time, slowly. There's plenty here." After a minute he put him down and went to another man. It was confusing. Robles sensed many people, horses and vehicles, and ambulances with nurses and hospital equipment.

When they picked him up and he felt their clean, freshly pressed uniforms against him, Robles became aware for the first time how totally foul he smelled. It was not only the dirt and the urine, but the smell of the dead also clung to him. The determined Pagán and the kindly Paleface had not survived.

In the ambulance they took his body temperature, his blood pressure, and started an IV. They gave him his first soda, an ice-cold 7-Up. "Drink slowly," the nurse warned him. It was one of the most beautiful sensations imaginable, the cold bottle in his hands, the cold glass rim against his lips, the cool flow that went right into him. They put Berta in the ambulance with him and drove to the hospital. Robles was too exhausted to talk, but he lifted his breath in long sighs.

Berta was also feeling weak again. They gave her water, soda, soup, and juices, along with the rest of them. When they examined her, they decided her condition was serious and put her in bed. Most of the men were transferred to the jail, but Berta stayed in the hospital for eleven days.

Espinoza let them put an intravenous in his arm, but when they wanted to undress him, he insisted they cut off his pants because he didn't want to take his boots off. He struggled and they had to call two orderlies for help. In his right boot they found a wad of bills that counted out to over $4,000. The hospital director put it in his safe.

The nurses undressed Robles completely and put another intravenous into his arm. Then they put him in a special bed with ice in it and covered him with more ice, even his eyes. "Do you feel anything?" someone asked him.

"No, I don't feel a thing," he said contentedly. "But I'm still thirsty." They brought a glass of orange juice and put the straw into his mouth. They did everything for him, and all he had to do was stay alive. He remembered that someone regularly monitored his temperature and that doctors came and again cleaned out his mouth, this time with swabs and instruments, working very carefully. And cleaned out his eyes. And then he didn't remember any more.

Early that morning, after the men had gone, the women were quiet. If they had been by themselves they might have talked, but the sight of Jorge, lying there with his belly up, made them self-conscious. So they waited in silence for the sun to rise. And the sight of it, looking like it could roll across the desert and crush them, made Ileana say, "We'd better pray to God."

There were eleven women with Carlos: the three Lugo sisters; Felícita and her aunt Guadalupe; Flora, Ileana, and her sister-in-law, Luisa; Pagán's wife; the pleasant woman they called Chalatenango (after the province she came from); and Rollers, who still had her hair up for her reunion with her husband. They knelt in a ring. They were mostly naked, except for their panties, because Espinoza, whom they trusted, had told them it would be better. Their bodies were marked with sunburn, scratches, bruises, and cactus thorns. Only Jorge lay where he was. He felt prayer was women's work and he didn't care to join them.

"We are all very bad. But please, God, forgive us, because we don't want to die," Ileana led them off. It was a group confession and they were frightened. They sifted through the past, searching for the causes of their punishment. For twenty minutes they took turns admitting whatever meanness or falseness in their behavior most shamed them. But the heat was already up by the time they finished repenting and they didn't feel any better.

In the silence that followed, Guadalupe surprised them with an announcement. "If we're ever going to look for water, we'd better do it now, before it gets any hotter," she said. It was true. Everyone was already weak and later it might be impossible to do anything to help themselves.

"I'll go with you," Rollers offered. The two women had been companions in their little group during the whole trip.

"Jorge, you come too. You're a man and you should help us," Guadalupe said sternly. That made it difficult for him to refuse. He got up begrudgingly and followed them. But they were back in only ten minutes. They were empty-handed and they looked annoyed.

"What happened?" Flora asked.

"After two minutes he said he couldn't walk anymore," Guadalupe said sniffing. "He couldn't wait to get back. He's no help at all."

In the rising heat they sipped steadily at their small supply of urine. They no longer had a *pichinga* to collect it in. Perhaps the men had taken them all, or they had lost them in the last move, but they were gone. Instead, they squatted over a plastic cup and then shared it around with a small stainless-steel spoon, a sip for each. When the cup was full, they would urinate onto rags held between their legs and then wipe their faces to refresh themselves.

Pagán's wife brought out a sack of sugar cubes. They ate them, but that only made them more thirsty. So Chalatenango donated her tube of Colgate, and they ate that. Nothing stopped their thirst.

Chalatenango was a tall, attractive woman. She was about thirty-five, educated, and reserved. Several of the men had flirted with her, but she had not responded. She was not looking for romance. And while she had her light-brown hair pinned up to stop it from blowing, she did it also to keep herself from looking too soft and accessible. She was a friend of the Lugo sisters, and a member of the clan. Lately her pale skin had become flushed and she was quite tired.

Felícita was worse off than the others because she could not bring herself to drink the urine. Guadalupe pleaded with her, but Felícita refused to try it again, even after she started passing out. Every few minutes now her eyes would close and she would lie there unresponsive when they called her and shook her. Finally Guadalupe couldn't stand it. She begged Luisa and Rollers to help. They held Felícita's hands while Guadalupe forced the girl's head back and her mouth open. She worked quickly and firmly, as if she were only dealing with a stubborn child. She placed the cup against the girl's lips and poured some urine in, but the girl spit it back immediately. "I don't want that," she gasped. "I just want to die now." The women let her go. Guadalupe held her niece's head and wiped her face gently with the rag. She pulled the long chestnut hair away from her neck to make her more comfortable. And then she just sat there with her arms around the girl, both of them quiet and resigned.

From that moment *everything* became confused. Waves of unconsciousness continually swept over the group. *Nothing* was certain in the nightmare that followed.

In the accelerating pain that came with their thirst they put smooth stones into their mouths to force saliva. It was a trick that had always been used by desert people, but now even the simplest things went wrong. They heard gagging and looked up to see Chalatenango turning a ghastly dark color and trying to force her hand into her mouth. She had swallowed her stone and she was choking. Flora rushed over and tried to get it out with her finger, but it was too far down for her to reach.

Jorge came, pushed the woman forward, and pounded furiously on her back. They had never heard of the Heimlich maneuver and didn't realize they were knocking the obstruction more deeply into the passage. Chalatenango started to spasm.

"The spoon!" Jorge shouted. "Give it to me!" Everyone was relieved that he knew what to do. Juanita ran for it and gave it to him with trembling hands. The woman had gone rigid. Jorge used all his strength to force her jaw open. Then he dug in, trying to jam the spoon behind the rock. Blood spurted out of her mouth as he perforated the wall of her esophagus. He couldn't see a thing. He worked feverishly, guided only by the scraping of the spoon against the stone. He felt the flesh tear but reasoned that any damage was justified by the emergency. The minutes passed. When he finally noticed she was limp and still, he gave up. He withdrew the spoon from the ravaged opening and wiped it on a rag.

Juanita was crying and Alicia comforted her. The others had their heads down, not wanting to see. Flora noticed a Bible lying on the ground. It was stained with blood, like an omen, and when she opened it, the first thing she saw was Psalm 91. Her mother had spoken to her of that psalm just a week before. It was a prayer for travelers, she said, and Flora read it aloud in an uncertain voice. "A thousand shall fall at thy side, and ten thousand at thy right hand; but it shall not come nigh to thee. . . . No evil shall befall thee. . . . For He shall give His angels charge over thee, to keep thee . . . they shall bear thee up with their hands. Because He has set His love upon me . . ." She started crying and sat down, burying her face in the book.

Jorge rolled over next to her and tapped her on the thigh. "I won't do anything to you," he assured her confidentially. He seemed quite matter-of-fact, untouched by what had just happened.

"What do you mean?"

"You know. We made the last trip together." He kept squeezing her thigh unconsciously. Flora was wearing only her underpants and she felt very vulnerable with him feeling her. "You're almost like my sister now. I promise, I won't touch you." But his whispered reassurances did anything but comfort her.

At first they were paralyzed by the second woman's death. Then there was a burst of panicky activity. Guadalupe climbed out of the wash to see if anyone was coming back for them yet. The Valley of the Ajo shimmered in the heat, barren and pale all the way to the distant mountains.

Rollers said they needed a sign of some kind, but she couldn't think of one they could use, and who, after all, would see it?

Because she also needed to do something and had no outlet for her impulse, Luisa started sorting through her suitcase. She took everything out and piled it on one side, and then put it all back, a piece at a time.

Inés Lugo, who was watching her, spotted her makeup kit just before it disappeared back into the bag. "We should use that," she said. "It could help protect us from the sun." No one had any better ideas. Because it was their only plan, they all wanted some, even Jorge. They clustered around Luisa and helped one another plaster their faces with makeup base. It was ironic that the hair clan, which had met so often, so peacefully and companionably, should have another frantic gathering in the desert on the edge of total disaster. Last of all they painted each other's puffed and broken lips with Estée Lauder Riviera Red lipstick. It was a bizarre touch, as if they were preparing themselves for some final rite.

Jorge fidgeted with the need to do something else. "Rollers is right," he announced, "we need a sign. I'm going to set fire to those bushes." With the dead woman lying among them as a constant reminder, it felt better to keep busy. Ileana, Guadalupe, and Rollers went with Jorge to help him. The others felt too dizzy to get up. Everyone was relieved that Jorge was showing some leadership. Because he was supposed to be in charge, everything felt more normal and orderly when he acted his part.

"We need a big fire and lots of smoke," Rollers said. Their suitcases seemed like the best fuel. The women searched the area. They emptied every traveling bag, dumping the contents onto the ground, and stacked the suitcases against a dry bush. Jorge put his lighter under the branches. He tried several times, but it did not catch so he gave up. He didn't seem especially concerned that his project had failed. When he returned, he lay in a new place, on the other side of Flora, squeezed in between her and the three naked sisters.

He didn't really want to make a fire! Flora thought angrily. It was just an excuse to get next to the girls. She squirmed away so his hairy body wouldn't be pressing against her. She lay there tensely, wondering what he planned to do.

Most of the women were huddled under a paloverde, a tall bush of bare green sticks. In the desert plants lose their leaves in the summer, because it is from the sun that they most need to protect themselves. Guadalupe expanded their shade by throwing clothing over the branches. She found a bright-red blouse and placed that as high as she could, in the hope that it might be seen from the air. That single gesture was their only attempt to rescue themselves.

Where the sun touched their skin, it felt like fire. Luisa started making rasping noises while breathing. "Ileana, I think I'm dying," she gasped. Ileana crawled to her immediately. "I'd like to die," Luisa moaned. "If only I can do it soon."

"No, you can't. You have a child to think of," Ileana protested.

"I don't care," Luisa said. "I feel too hot. I'm too thirsty. I miss my mother and my father." She talked about the father of her unborn child, who was still in El Salvador, and her fiancé, who waited in Los Angeles. "Please tell him I love him," she asked. "If you see him again, tell him I died trying to come to him."

"Don't say such stupid things. You have to live. You have to come with me and tell him yourself."

"I can't, Ileana. I really feel like I'm dying. I think I'm going to go very soon."

"No," insisted Ileana. They were both crying. "You'll be all right."

"I hope you'll forgive me. I acted very badly to you. I told my mother and father all kinds of nasty stories."

"That's all in the past. It's not important anymore," Ileana told her tearfully.

"I need your pardon before I die."

"I've been bad too," Ileana assured her, "but I don't think *I'm* going to die, so why should you?"

"You're a good mother. I know you love my brother, and you have to live for your children."

"You too, you'll be a mother soon," Ileana said. "A *good* mother. Please don't talk anymore. When you talk, you just get thirstier." And it was also depressing to hear her. She turned to Jorge. "Jorge, please give me some peepee for Luisa," she asked. Jorge had taken personal charge of the urine cup, dispensing the sips with the same spoon he had used on Chalatenango.

"Tell her to come and get it herself," Jorge answered.

"She can't. She's too weak. Please let me get it for her."

"No, I know you. You want it for yourself."

"It's for her," Ileana protested. "I promise you!"

"This woman is bad," Jorge told the others. "We'll have to kill her."

That sent a shock wave through the group. They were all afraid to speak. Ileana thought Jorge was losing his mind. She waited a few minutes and then asked, "Jorge, can I have a little peepee to drink?"

"O.K., come and get it," he offered. When Ileana crawled over, Jorge looked at her angrily before he put a spoonful into her mouth. "But the next time you pee, I want to catch it in a rag and give it to me," he commanded. "That's the only reason I'm letting you have this." Ileana nodded placatingly. The women watched her protectively the whole time she was within his reach in case he tried to do something to her.

Ileana crawled back, and when she thought he wasn't watching, she passed the urine from her mouth to Luisa's. Jorge didn't notice. A little later, when she felt she could urinate, she did it into a blouse. When it was saturated, she swabbed Luisa's face with it. But Jorge saw her that time. "I told you to give that to me!" he screamed in a rage. "You'd better start doing what I tell you, and not what you want, or I'll beat the hell out of you." He sounded fierce, but he lay where he was and the threat passed.

Luisa had plans of her own. When she searched through her suitcase earlier, she had found something no one else had noticed. Flora suddenly screamed, "Ileana, stop her, she has pills!" Luisa had hidden a bottle of Tylenol. Now she was trying to cram a handful of the tablets into her mouth. But she was very feeble and it was difficult to swallow with a dry throat, so she was slow and clumsy. Ileana jumped on her and pulled most of them away. She grabbed the bottle and threw it as far as she could. Then she picked up the pills that had fallen to the ground and scattered them out of reach.

"You can't do that!" Ileana told her. "I won't let you! I'm taking you to Los Angeles with me," she said desperately.

"No, let me!" Luisa sobbed. "Then, *you* kill me. Please. I don't want to suffer anymore. I can't stand it."

"You want to die?" Jorge asked Luisa. She nodded, still sniffling.

"Jorge, don't say that," Ileana demanded, but that only made him more defiant. He had hated Ileana for months, and the last minutes had only made his anger more intense.

"Can I kill you?" he asked, creeping closer. Luisa nodded again, watching him with frightened, fascinated eyes.

"Jorge, don't try anything," Ileana warned.

Jorge crawled deliberately toward Luisa, and Ileana moved frantically to intercept him. Instead of grabbing Luisa, Jorge lay down next to her. He suddenly threw his leg over her, locking his broad thigh over her face to smother her. Ileana shrieked. The other women were too frightened or too weak to help her. She jumped on Jorge and began hitting him. Then she pulled his leg until she had moved it off Luisa. That enraged him. Ileana had interfered with him all through the trip and he was not used to defiance from a woman. He kicked her furiously, stomping her repeatedly in the face and chest with his shoe. When she turned away to protect herself, he continued kicking her in the back. Then, with his enemy silenced, he picked up a fat stick and hit Luisa several times in the face and neck. "All right, die!" he yelled at her. "You want to die, so die." And he jammed the stick against her throat and leaned down on it. Ileana tried once to get up, but the pain overwhelmed her and she passed out.

The women who were still conscious watched in horror. When Jorge finally got up from Luisa's body, she lay without moving, without breathing. Jorge didn't seem particularly affected. He dropped his stick and turned toward the women. When he came toward her, Flora slid frantically backward to escape him. But he wasn't interested in her. He had his eyes on the three sisters. They were huddled together, too weak to get away. He stumbled slowly across the space and stood over them.

"You shouldn't feel bad about her." He pointed back toward Luisa's body. "She's the lucky one. She doesn't have any more troubles." He got down on his knees to be closer to them. His movements were slow and stiff. "You know we're all going to die," he confided as if it were an intimate secret. His voice got low and hoarse and his eyes moved from one young face to another, looking for acceptance. "If you want, you can kill me first," he told them. "Or I can kill you, one by one, and then I can kill myself. It's better to die now. The ones who live the longest will only suffer the most." Still his eyes moved restlessly among the three of them, trying to decide which one he wanted.

"No, Jorge," Alicia pleaded desperately. "Help us, please . . . you promised you would help us see our mother."

"Hold her," Jorge ordered Pagán's wife. He had made his choice.

Pagán's wife had become as crazy as Jorge. Earlier she had emulated Flora, helping the others when she could, dragging herself around with the cup and spoon and putting sips of the dark liquid between the lips of those who were too weak to reach for it. But after a while Jorge told her to stop. "Don't give it to everyone," he commanded. "Just the ones I say. Don't give it to anyone. We're going to die anyway."

That had been enough to unbalance her and she turned from helper to tormentor. Not only wouldn't she pass the cup anymore, but if she saw anyone trying to drink their own urine, or to wipe themselves with it, she crawled to them feverishly, her large ungainly body naked except for her red-and-white-striped panties, and tried to knock the rag out of their hands. She frightened everyone.

"Hold her down," Jorge repeated. "After they're all dead we'll share the urine, half and half, just you and me, and we'll survive. Trust me. Do what I say."

Perhaps she had been trained to obey the commands of men without thinking (she was used to going everywhere with her husband and doing whatever he said), or perhaps she believed the offer Jorge made her, but she came immediately, scurrying across the hot earth on her hands and knees. She grabbed Alicia's wrists and held them tightly together above the girl's head. Alicia, who had been Berta's good friend on the trip, was the oldest and the liveliest of the sisters. But she was weak now and unable to free herself from the crazy woman's grip.

Juanita, the youngest, screamed, "Flora, help me, he's killing my sister." Flora was feeling sick. She had used up the last of her energy in running away from Jorge, but now she balanced unsteadily on all fours and crawled slowly back. Guadalupe and Rollers also got up and headed that way. But it was little Juanita who was the most effective. She got to her feet and picked up the stick Jorge had used on Luisa and then thrown away. The two older women were struggling with Jorge, trying to pull him off Alicia, and he was shoving them away with bearlike sweeps of his large hands.

Pagán's wife looked devilish. She was enjoying Alicia's terror, her eyes shining and her mouth twisted in a cruel smile. Juanita attacked her furiously, swinging the stick with all her might and cursing constantly. "You stupid, wicked bitch," she screamed again and again as she hit her. Pagán's wife tried to duck the blows, but she couldn't get out of the way because she refused to let go of Alicia's wrists. Juanita struck her over and over, in the face, on the shoulders, on the chest. Everyone was screaming at once now and nothing was distinguishable.

"Leave her alone, you dumb shit," Jorge yelled. "Stop that."

Flora reached Jorge, but he swatted her away. A heavy blow from the back of his hand landed directly on her face. It went numb and she wondered if he had broken something.

Jorge tried to be reasonable. "Don't be so stupid," he told them. "It's no big thing. Everybody is going to die anyway. I just want to have sex with you all before we die. I want to do everything before it's too late." Before she passed out, Flora saw Pagán's wife collapse, covered with blood, almost unrecognizable from the beating she had received. And Juanita fell beside her in exhaustion.

Guadalupe pulled back out of Jorge's reach. "We have to

get out of here," she yelled to the other women. "We have to find the men. These girls are dying and he still wants to have sex with them." In her horror she grabbed her niece by the arm and started to drag her along the ground. "Felícita, get up. Please, come with me or you'll be next," she said. Felícita was only semiconscious, but Guadalupe finally managed to get her on her feet. By supporting her weight across her shoulders she was able to stumble off with the girl. Rollers tottered along, the only other woman who could manage to escape.

"Guadalupe, don't go," Jorge called after her. "I want you too." He watched them hobble up the wash together, not strong enough to climb out over the side. "You'll be back," Jorge called after them confidently. "They'll be back," he repeated to the others. "They have no place to go.

"All right, who wants to have sex?" Jorge asked the group. There was only a cringing silence in reply. It was mid-morning. The heat was building toward a crescendo and they were probably the only living beings for miles around who were exposed to the maddening pressure of the full sun. "Ileana . . . Inés . . . Juanita . . . ? Think of it, it may be your very last chance. And it could be wonderful. We may be transported to other galaxies before we die."

He's gone completely crazy, Ileana thought. He was always sick, looking for women every minute, but now he's lost all his sense. He'll do anything, he doesn't care.

"It's *good* to have sex," Jorge coaxed them. "It makes sweat, and sweat cools the skin. When I have sex with you, you can lick the wet off my body. It will be good . . ." No one responded to his offer.

"Well, does anyone want some urine to drink?" he asked pleasantly, holding up the cup for them to see. He was determined to get a positive response and that was the only thing he had that they wanted. There was no answer. "Well, if you don't want to drink something, then let's make love." He moved toward the youngest.

"No, don't do that to my sister," pleaded Inés. "Juanita, come here!" But Juanita couldn't get up. And neither could Inés.

Ileana was fighting to become fully conscious, trying to lift her head so she could keep an eye on Jorge, but her vision was dark. About fifteen feet away Juanita screamed as Jorge came toward her. "You have to do it," he told her unemotionally. "It's good for you, and it's good for me. I'm dying too, and I want to do this. I want to do everything before I go."

Juanita was still screaming but Jorge silenced her by putting his hands around her throat. "I'm going to make love to you. And then I'm going to kill you," he told her. "But before I kill you, please help me. Help me like I'm helping you." And then Ileana passed out and didn't see any more.

Flora partially woke up a little later. Her body felt strange, as if ants were walking all over her, but when she looked she couldn't see any. Perhaps it was the cactus she was feeling, she thought, or perhaps her circulation was getting bad. She heard some grunting and looked across the wash. Jorge was lying on top of Juanita, moving his hips and making the noise. He was holding the spoon in both hands, his thumbs in the bowl, and he was pressing it into her neck, into the small smooth hollow in the center of her collarbone. This can't be happening, she thought as she passed out again. It just couldn't be.

When Ileana woke, there was only the sound of Jorge muttering an endless, rambling prayer. She struggled up to one elbow to look over the group of her fellow travelers. They had all started out so confidently from El Salvador only a week before. Now not one of them was moving. Closest to her, Juanita was lying with her tongue out, her eyes open and bulging. A little farther on, the other two sisters were sprawled awkwardly on the ground. There was no sign that anyone was alive but Jorge and herself, and he still sounded restless with energy. Oh, my God, Ileana thought in horror, they're all dead. I'm alone with him. What will I do? The thought of it was so nightmarishly intense that she felt as if her heart could stop.

Jorge was praying to his wife. "I was bad, my dear Teresa," he moaned monotonously. "And now I'm dying. I don't want to die, but I have to. Please bring my children.

I want to see them one more time. You can do it, you're a saint, the mother of God, so good, so holy, you can help me . . . you can forgive me . . ."

His pious tone, coming after all he had done, was too much for Ileana. She couldn't control herself and she began to shriek. And once she started there was no way to stop it. She wanted to scream until every drop of anguish was emptied out of her.

Jorge turned toward her immediately. "Have you had enough, Ileana?" he asked with satisfaction. "Do you want to die?"

"Yes, Jorge!" she screamed back to him. "Yes, I want to die!"

"No, Ileana!" Flora yelled. She was across the wash, where she had dragged herself to escape. "Get out of there. He's coming for you."

"I can't," Ileana said sobbing helplessly. "I can't do anything anymore."

"Yes, you can. Run away. He's coming. Please. Come away from there. We're the only ones left."

"I can't do it!"

"Yes you can! Come over to me."

Ileana couldn't get up.

"You have to move," Flora insisted. "Roll over."

She still couldn't move, but he could. Ileana was amazed that he had any strength left after all he had done. Jorge crawled steadily toward her. When she was within reach, he grabbed her hair and pulled her head to him. "But first I have to have sex with you," he told her triumphantly. As far as he was concerned, they still had a score to settle.

Ileana rolled toward him, close to the hand that held her hair, and bit him fiercely on the wrist.

"Aieee! You stupid bitch!" Jorge cursed in pain. But he let go. Ileana immediately rolled away. He went right after her.

"Watch out, there's a snake!" she yelled. "A snake! A snake!"

"Where?" asked Jorge.

"By your feet. Watch out, it's coming!" When Jorge shuffled clumsily about, Ileana rolled away again.

"It's a lie." Jorge was angry about that.

"More, Ileana, more," Flora urged.

Ileana rolled over and over on the ground, ignoring the rocks and sharp sticks that bruised her. She had a good start on Jorge, and he wasn't very fast. She didn't think he would chase her all the way over to Flora. She rolled with desperate strength and she was keeping ahead of him until she felt a sudden band of pain completely across her back. She had rolled against a cactus and couldn't go any farther. Her back felt on fire. Jorge kept coming. Ileana twisted around and grabbed hold of the cactus with her bare hands. Blood trickled between her fingers as she pulled herself slowly to her feet.

But Jorge got to his feet too. He had a stick. He hit her with it and she fell backward. Jorge dropped onto her, straddling her body, holding her down while he continued to hit her, with the stick, with his fists, in the face, in the breasts, in the stomach, with all his might.

I'm dying, she thought with some relief. It's finally over.

Long after she stopped screaming and squirming, Jorge continued to sit on Ileana. He wanted to enjoy this triumph. But he was distracted by his pains, and his mind wandered. It was their fault, he decided. These people, with their nagging and complaining, had used up his energy and dragged him down. Everything would have been all right if they had followed orders and kept their big mouths shut. And this one had been the worst. He looked down at the body he used as a cushion. Even now, beaten into an unrecognizable mess, she still bothered him. She made him sick. He threw down his club in disgust, but that didn't help. His stomach heaved. He bent over Ileana, determined to vomit on her, but nothing came up. He was empty, but every time he looked at her he retched painfully, so finally he had to climb off. He swayed on his hands and knees, trying to decide what to do next.

Someone lay directly ahead. She was sprawled on her face, but Jorge recognized the striped panties of Pagán's wife. He could make her do anything he wanted, so he crawled in her direction. She was only a few feet away, but the tuft of a small bush lay between them, and as he maneuvered around it, he fell onto his stomach.

Jorge realized he couldn't get up. He panicked immediately. Gravity felt smothering. "Mother of God!" he called out, begging, but his tongue was swelling and the words were thick. His breath began choking off, and the more frightened he became, the worse it was. I don't want this, he thought, becoming angry to protect himself from fear. "You bitch!" he gasped, but he was not menacing. His body had begun to shake.

He swirled at the center of a great agony. He tried to crawl away, but the earth pulled him down, grinding him closer, belly to belly. The pressure of the warm soil disgusted him. And he was furious at being taken against his will. He tried to pull back. He slapped the ground. He kicked and clawed wildly. Nothing helped him. Straining purple, he couldn't even breathe. A final convulsion struck as every nerve let go. When his body relaxed, it was too late for relief.

Flora woke several times in the next few hours. But it was a minimal, thoughtless wakening. She didn't even disturb the small animals who had slipped from their burrows to nibble cautiously at them. She didn't realize that evening had come, and then night, and then another day.

A few hundred yards up the wash Felícita, Guadalupe, and Rollers lay where they had fallen. A plane passed over, slowly and quite low. The noise woke Guadalupe. Felícita and Rollers lay with their heads resting on their arms. Guadalupe wanted to tell them about the airplane, but when she touched them, they were past caring, both stiff. Rollers still had her hair up . . . hoping.

Farther on, Flora, too, was conscious. A man in a uniform carefully lifted her head and wiped her face with a handkerchief wet with real water. Around her there were people rushing everywhere, and others charging in on horses, jeeps, and motorbikes. Helicopters landed, dust swirled in the sunlight, and the noise was incredible. The man who held her seemed unbelievably tall and handsome. Deep inside her something bubbled up out of control. She started crying with happiness at being alive. I may be dying, she thought, but I'm still looking at him.

But joy was too exhausting and Flora started to sink into unconsciousness again. The man holding her became alarmed. "Oh, no, come back!" he shouted over the noise. "You've got to live!" And he gave her a shake. Supporting her with one arm, he took his canteen and began splashing water on her. Flora smiled. As she felt the water sliding over her body, she began washing herself. She spread the precious liquid over her neck, her breasts, and her stomach, her eyes closed, delighted with the feel of her wet skin, until a nurse came and took her arm so they could give her fluid intravenously. When the press helicopter landed, the border-patrol agent wrapped his jacket around her before they started taking pictures. Everyone was so very kind. She relaxed, completely in their care.

As she passed out, she could hear Ileana screaming somewhere behind her, delirious but still full of fight. "Those rotten coyotes," Ileana cursed furiously. "They ran off and left us. They just left us out here!" But then the anger was eclipsed by a sorrow that chilled the men working around her. "My babies!" she wailed. "Where are my babies? Oh, please, I want my babies!" A number of them converged on her, working desperately to lower her temperature, to raise her fluid level, and to interrupt her delirium. They tried to restrain her, hoping, for their own sakes as well as hers, to stop her screaming. They couldn't bear her agony. But she continued keening pitifully as they waited with her for the evacuation helicopter, the IV already in place.

"Oh, my babies. Please . . ."

5
THE AFTERMATH

The press helicopter arrived only minutes after the women were discovered. Randy Collier, a reporter for the *Arizona Republic*, and Mike Ging, photographer, were the first to climb out into the murderous heat, just ahead of the TV cameras. They looked around and tried to understand what they saw.

Bodies were everywhere.

Only three women were left alive from the entire group.

The youngest girl had died clasping the hand of an older woman. They were lying on their backs, looking up. Their eyes had shriveled from the sun.

Someone pried open the fist of a dead middle-aged woman with her hair full of rollers. She was clutching an empty perfume atomizer.

Mike Ging worked rapidly, trying to capture the feelings at the scene. He took a photograph that showed Ileana and Hector Ochoa in an intensely emotional moment. Ileana, her eyes still full of pain and death, was cradled tenderly in Ochoa's arms. The picture subsequently appeared on the front pages of newspapers all over the world. Its power came from a clarity of instant recognition: the eternal theme of suffering and comfort was retold in a modern Pietà. The photograph was nominated for a Pulitzer Prize. It multiplied the impact of the Salvadorans, moving all sorts of people to action.

Ileana was still raving when they put her in the evacuation helicopter to fly her to Ajo. She told a reporter that some of the women had threatened to kill her if she didn't share her urine with them. She said they had decided they should all urinate in one spot and would kill anyone who didn't. Ileana thought she had survived because she had secretly taken a sock, stuck it in her crotch, and urinated on that. She had sucked out the moisture when they weren't looking.

Since Ileana had been screaming for her babies, once emergency care was under control, the officials launched a frantic search for them. Agents probed every possible hiding place in the vicinity. Ochoa backtracked the group on foot for three miles, following the trail of abandoned belongings, and the marks where they had fallen and dragged themselves. It was only several days later—when Ileana recovered enough to talk coherently—that they learned her children were still in El Salvador. And it took several more days before they discovered the connection with the group of women and children who had crossed near Yuma with Esteban Alvarado. As usual, the children had been dosed with sleeping pills to keep them quiet. According to one account, they had been sprayed with insecticide by a crop-dusting airplane as they slipped through some fields at dawn, and everyone became sick.

After the survivors were evacuated, work at the desert site became grim and methodical. The scene was carefully mapped and catalogued. The position of each body was described and photographed from several angles. Distances between bodies were paced off. All personal articles and their locations were listed, and then the items were collected for possible use as evidence. No one was sure yet what had happened there, but a criminal investigation was obviously needed.

The notes concerning the body that was later identified as Jorge Dávila's read, "Adult male was lying facedown, his arms pulled up under his upper torso. This deceased was lying under a paloverde tree with 5 other deceased. The deceased was clad in dark pants, no shirt, no shoes or socks. Post-mortem lividity and rigor mortis were present. . . ." A later note mentions that his fly was unzipped.

The women had been found about ten in the morning,

which is late on a summer day in terms of heat. Decomposition had accelerated at an explosive pace. The stench became steadily worse. The evacuation team had large body-bags made of heavy-gauge plastic with full-length zippers. The bodies were already stiff, and they loaded them into the bags with difficulty. Everyone was careful not to get the body fluids on themselves. They warned each other that decomposing bodies were very unhealthy. They had rubber gloves, but there weren't enough to go around, and those they had were used up quickly. Their hands sweated badly in the heat, and the gloves trapped the moisture and made them feel clammy. When they removed the gloves to dry off, they became fouled and were not reusable. So they carried the bodies using clothing. As they worked for the next few hours, they saw the corpses change dramatically. Faces swelled and dissolved and the tongues puffed out. The full body-bags were stacked in pickup trucks.

Eventually the media left, the agents with motorbikes drove off, and so did the trucks with the bodies. Most of the belongings had been collected and the area was almost back to normal. The last two at the site were Hector Ochoa and Jerry Scott. They felt physically and emotionally exhausted. It had been frustrating to work so hard and long to save those people, and then to have only three survivors, and so many dead. Perhaps the two agents had intentionally remained behind when the others left, for the cleansing solitude of the desert. The sun sank behind them and the sunset was florid. It became too dark to ride the horses out safely, because of the cactus, so they led them slowly back to the highway. There was nothing more to say. They had a long, quiet walk through the southern Arizona evening. One chapter had closed. A whole new and complex phase was beginning.

At the time the Salvadorans were discovered, the town of Ajo was already involved in a crisis of its own. Situated deep in the desert, the only reason for its six thousand inhabitants was the Phelps-Dodge copper mine, one of the largest open pits in the country. And only a few days earlier the workers had declared a general strike. A long, hard time lay ahead, and no one would have been surprised if the people of Ajo had been quite uninterested in a group of illegal immigrants suddenly thrust into their midst. But their troubles had only made them more sensitive, and they reacted with great concern.

An ad hoc committee for the Salvadorans' relief immediately formed. Offers of food, money, and jobs poured in, and the committee became a clearinghouse. Another group started organizing legal-aid assistance for the survivors. Petitions circulated asking that they be granted political asylum. Ajo had adopted them. "We all care," said a sergeant in the sheriff's department.

A Salvadoran exchange student had attended their high school the year before. While he was in Ajo, he learned that three of his friends at home had been killed. Because the town went through the experience with him, they thought that perhaps they understood more than most Americans did. (The only exception to this spirit of understanding was the company hospital, which sent the indigent survivors a bill of six thousand dollars for emergency-room treatment.)

People also responded in many other places. When she heard that the Salvadorans would later be brought to Tucson, Lupe Klein, a sheriff's deputy there, offered to take in all the women. She was officially overruled because it would be a conflict of interest with her work, so she turned to another need. Most of the group had only the clothes they had on. In her official capacity as president of the Tucson Lioness Club she called the local radio stations and asked them to announce that she was collecting for the survivors. Her phone rang constantly and huge quantities of clothing arrived at her home. The tiny town of Elfrida sent an entire pickup full.

Phone calls and reporters came from all over the world. Sweden, Italy, Australia, South Africa, England, Germany, and most of Latin America were represented, as well as all the wire services and many of the major newspapers of the United States. A long poem written in their honor was published in *El Diario de Hoy* of San Salvador. These lines are extracted from a much longer work:

Their bodies covered with thorns,
Their hearts occupied by flags
Because someone told them that the world was their
   country . . .
They can be found drinking in the morgue . . .
Drinking eternity with their bright eyes . . .
Those who move away like shadows
Over the burning dream of Arizona.

Ironically *El Diario de Hoy* (The Newspaper of Today) had carried Jorge Dávila's original advertisement, which had led them into the desert.

When they were taken to the hospital, Miguel was close to coma and Espinoza was delirious. He thought the devil had come to attack him, and he fought back desperately. Francisco felt anxious because he couldn't communicate with his family. He knew they were suffering, wondering if he was alive. The men were given food, but they couldn't eat. Their bodies resisted. And although they were able to drink so much that the anxiety of not getting enough fluid finally left them, they found they were unable to urinate.

Flora and Ileana were flown to Ajo in the same helicopter. Ileana went back into shock. As they passed over the desert, she screamed, "I'm going to die! I can't take any more!" They were treated together in the emergency room, but after it became clear that they would live, they were separated and put into private rooms. Nurses went over them with pincers and pliers, pulling cactus spines from every part of their bodies. Even so, it would be weeks before they were free of the last of them.

The first night in the hospital Flora hardly slept. Too many people wanted to talk to her, and every few minutes a doctor or nurse would come in for treatment. The women were attached to EKGs, which bleeped electronic heartbeats in the background. Someone came by frequently for blood samples. I'm dying and they're still taking out my blood, Flora thought. The nurses told them they had been only minutes from death.

The first visitor was Father Maurice Roy, a Canadian priest serving in Ajo. He wore ordinary shirt and pants and carried a Bible. He brought each of them a rosary. "Can you recite the Lord's Prayer with me?" he asked. Flora shook her head. She was too weak to speak and her throat pained her. "Don't worry, they won't deport you," he assured her. "Everyone will help you. You must be a fine person. They say you saved many lives through your kindness."

Flora whispered, "What happened to my uncle and my cousin?"

"I'm not sure," Father Maurice told her. "I think they're in jail. I'll go and tell them you will be all right. Would you like me to send some message to your mother?"

Flora promised to write a note for him as soon as she could, but it was two days before she felt strong enough. When she did write, Father Maurice sent it to her priest in El Salvador, who brought it personally to her home. It was the safest way to communicate. Because of the publicity, their exodus had become a national embarrassment to their government, even though most of the refugees were not politically active.

"Do you really love the poor?" one of the Salvadorans asked Father Maurice.

"Of course, that's why I come here," he replied.

"Then for sure, they would kill you in our country," he was told.

The priest made many patient rounds, giving comfort and solving whatever problems he could. Much later Ileana would write to him, "The help you gave me in my necessity was more soothing than water . . ."

The next visit that night was Hugo Orantes, the Salvadoran consul general. "Nobody wanted to talk to him," Flora remembered, "but he came anyway." She didn't give a very flattering description of either his appearance or his manner. Several complained that he acted like they were enemies of their government. He asked them what had happened, but significantly, he never asked why they came. So they were surprised to hear him announce on the late news that they were not political refugees at all, but had only come to make a lot of money. They wanted to return to El Salvador, he said, and his government would help them.

The last visitors were two homicide detectives who were investigating the case. The doctors explained that the women were too weak to talk, so the detectives returned several days later.

On the second day, when Flora could speak a little, a nurse told her she had a long-distance phone call. The nurse helped her into a wheelchair and pushed her to the telephone. It was an aunt in Los Angeles. When Flora heard the familiar voice, she began to cry. The two women cried together, long distance, for a number of minutes. "Everyone thought you had died," her aunt said. The first thing she wanted to know was whether Flora had been raped. "Imagine, that was the first thing she wanted to know!" Flora later exclaimed. But Ileana was also preoccupied with that question. The reassurance she received from the doctor was very important to her.

At one point, Pablo came to visit. He gave Flora a big hug. "I'm alive because of you," he told her. "You were one of the people who saved me." After four days of bed rest Flora and Guadalupe were transferred to the jail. Ileana stayed in the hospital for several weeks, recovering from her beating.

The Salvadorans' deaths were caused by heat and dehydration. Humans are much more sensitive to a rise in body heat than to a drop. Surgery patients have been medically cooled to 40 degrees Farenheit, but with a rise to only 102, people commonly become nervous and irritable, and 103 brings confusion. And with only a degree or two more there can be delirium. (The same 1980 heat wave that engulfed the Salvadorans eventually caused 1,265 deaths in the United States.)

Sweating effectively lowers body temperature in the desert. The lack of humidity makes evaporation rapid, and that provides maximal cooling for the blood passing under the skin. (This blood then circulates into the interior, lowering the temperature of vital organs.) But water lost in this process has to be replaced, and so must the minerals that go with it. One way to adapt is to try to slow the rate of sweating.

Instead of undressing, the Salvadorans should have covered as much of their bodies as possible, like the desert-dwelling Bedouins, whose loose robes are thought to create a separate miniclimate between the cloth and the skin. This would have also helped to prevent sunburn, which is dangerous because it can injure the sweat glands and interfere with their vital function. It is especially important to shade the head and the neck with a bandanna or wide-brimmed hat. Major blood vessels pass through there and quickly absorb extra heat on their way to the brain. The lightest-colored clothing available should be used. Black can be 30 to 40 degrees hotter than white at midday in the desert.

Once the Salvadorans had entered the desert without adequate water, proper equipment, and local knowledge, they had already accepted a grave risk. The odds are always against being able to rely on the desert for subsistence, and many of the clever survival techniques that are common knowledge do not work. The widespread belief that all one has to do is to find a barrel cactus and cut its top off to have an abundant supply of water, is not true. The amount of fluid the cactus yields is fairly small. The sap is milky and extremely bitter, and it congeals quickly. Many of those who have tried it say it is not drinkable, and some experts claim it is not healthy. The cactus skin is extremely tough, and unless one is carrying a machete, one may use up more body water in opening the cactus than one gets back from it. In one experiment it took forty minutes of hard work to cut the top open with a pocketknife, and those who drank the cactus fluid threw up afterward.

The Salvadorans could have traveled twice as far on the water they had if they had rested in the shade during the day and walked at night. The young guide had suggested this to them, but they overruled him out of impatience and panic. However, if night walking is to be attempted, it is important to protect the eyes from sun blindness during the day. Prolonged exposure to ultraviolet radiation significantly reduces night vision. This may be why they stumbled into so many cactus in the dark.

Sometimes desert people seem to adjust to conditions that

are fatal for others. Felipe and his son trusted their ability to travel without water (although they misjudged the distance, and Felipe ended up in serious trouble). During World War II, when much of the fighting took place in deserts, the army questioned whether it was possible to learn to function with less water. Men practiced going without water for various lengths of time. They never managed any improvement. Each time they dehydrated they showed the same symptoms. Water is necessary for life.

However, acclimatization can be a help to survival. People who live in hot areas like Arizona generally have body temperatures a degree or two higher than normal. The British army prepares troops for transfer to hot climates by keeping them in overheated barracks. It helps them adjust to sweating more rapidly, to producing greater quantities of sweat, and sweat that is less salty. In a study of long-distance runners on a hot July day, it was found that the winners had begun sweating first and had produced the most sweat.

Women generally start sweating more slowly than men and have higher heart rates to begin with. These are important handicaps and may have contributed to the fact that many more women than men died in this crossing. In addition, middle-class women from El Salvador are not prepared for prolonged exertion, while the men routinely take part in strenuous sports and physical activities. If the women who crossed had been peasant women, used to long hours of hard work in the hot fields, or American women, with their enthusiasm for fitness and activity, the outcome might have been different. But the Salvadoran women's traditional roles, and perhaps their expectations of themselves, did nothing to help them survive when the situation became difficult.

In a sense Mary Lou Harris was involved with the Salvadorans from the minute she saw them on television at her vacation cabin. But when she returned to her office on Monday she began in earnest a project that was destined to last years. There is an ethical ban on attorneys' soliciting clients, but Legal Aid workers are excused from it. That's because they're not seeking fees and because the people they serve often don't realize what their legal needs are. The first thing that Mary Lou and her co-worker, Nancy Tyson, did was to draft an identical letter in Spanish for each of the Salvadorans and send them to the jailed and hospitalized survivors. They were told that if they were poor, they could have lawyers without a fee, and if they had money, they could get the names of private counsel they could contact.

The letters were sent special delivery to Ajo, in care of Lieutenant Garchow, the officer in charge. They arrived just after the Salvadorans were transferred to the Pima County jail in Tucson. Even so, Lieutenant Garchow took the letters to Tucson and delivered them. That quality of meticulous care continued throughout the case. Representatives of the border patrol and the sheriff's department, who were supposedly in an adversary position, acted as though they had a special trust to fulfill in the protection of these people.

The lawyers were told to report to the Pima County jail on Wednesday morning for their first meeting with the Salvadorans. Mary Lou, who had once sung in supper clubs in San Francisco and was now known as the Silver Tongue, did the talking. They met in the visitors' room, a grim and noisy location that smelled of urine. The eight men, shrunken from their ordeal, stood at the far end, clutching their letters in their hands and watching the lawyers anxiously. They had chosen Robles, now as cautious and wide-eyed as a deer, as their spokesperson.

"Our legal system is different from yours," Mary Lou assured him. "If you choose us as your legal representatives, we promise to do everything we can to help you. We won't represent your country, and we don't represent our country. We'll only represent you."

The men huddled out of hearing and talked. From time to time they would all stop, look up, study the two women, and then talk some more. Finally Robles came forward. "Yes," he said, "we do want to talk to you. And we want you to represent us." The defense had begun.

From eight in the morning until late in the afternoon they talked nonstop, interviewing them one at a time. From the background came the constant clamor of steel doors and the yelling of prisoners and guards. They had to raise their voices to talk and there wasn't much privacy. When the sheriff had a pitcher of ice water and some cups brought for them, Mary Lou sent back a request for a quieter location. It was granted and they were quickly moved to a nonsecurity area on the visitors' side. But now the situation became surrealistic. The room was quiet, but there was a huge glass window along one wall with noses pressed against it. The world's press was in the waiting room, watching their every move. Each time one of the lawyers went out to make a call, reporters would mob her and press notes into her hand.

"Please give this to the Salvadorans," they would beg. A typical note read, "I am your friend. I speak Spanish. Please talk to me at your earliest convenience." Outside was pandemonium, people screaming over each other and waving their arms to attract attention. Then the door would close and it would be silent again, with only the contorted faces at the window to suggest the frenzy.

Sheriff Clarence Dupnick had jurisdiction over Pima County, where the refugees were found. For the Salvadorans, he became a personal hero. He made critical decisions early in the case and stuck to them. When he learned of the unpleasant effects of the Salvadoran consul general's first visit to the hospital, Dupnick gave orders to the guards he had posted that there was to be no repetition of that incident.

Next Consul Orantes asked for a list of the names of the Salvadorans on the trip and for photographs of the corpses. He said they would be published in Salvadoran newspapers so relatives could come forward to help identify the bodies. An officer in the sheriff's department, apparently thinking this was a routine request, offered to provide the materials. But when Orantes returned to get them, he was informed that the officer who had made the offer was "on vacation." Dupnick had decided to deny the request. "I'm suspicious of them," he remarked. "In the past they've made examples of Salvadorans who've left the country." Consul Orantes said he would complain to his superiors when he returned to his home base in Los Angeles. Dupnick explained that there was no need to publish the photos since he was confident that the medical examiner's team would be able to identify the bodies.

Next, Orantes asked that the corpses be sent back to his country. But a pathologist in the coroner's office said the bodies were in no condition to be moved. He suggested that if the remains were to be returned, they should first be cremated and then sent back. Everyone seemed to be responding to rumors that identification of the bodies in El Salvador could lead to retribution against family members still in the country. "It is becoming increasingly obvious to us that the tragedy unfolding here in the desert is due in part to social and political problems in El Salvador," Dupnick commented.

"I'm puzzled, because in the beginning all the information was offered and now they don't want to say anything," Orantes complained as the blackout became complete. He claimed he was quite concerned about what might happen to Julio Espinoza, one of the Salvadoran coyotes. When a reporter informed him that Espinoza was due in federal court on smuggling charges only half an hour later, Orantes looked amazed. He fumed that ordinary reporters knew more about the situation than he, the consul general, did. Orantes protested vehemently that the Salvadorans who came to the United States illegally were only poor people who wanted to take advantage of America's wealth. "I do not think they are political refugees, because political refugees look for help in embassies," he asserted.

That remark was quickly contradicted by José Maldonado. Señora Lugo was unable to come forward to claim the bodies of her three daughters because she was here illegally, so their uncle, Maldonado, came instead. Maldonado, an engineer who had been in the United States for twenty years, said he had gone back to visit El Salvador that February. He was shocked by the violence. He tried immediately to arrange for the legal entry of Alicia, Inés, and Juanita into the United States, but it was impossible to get into the American embassy. So many Salvadorans wanted appointments that embassy officials had been giving out numbers to those outside. Even the people who dared to sleep all night on the sidewalk (a very dangerous practice, since it both violated curfew and called attention to themselves) were not able to get in. He said that numbers for appointments were routinely sold on the black market. Maldonado asked Sheriff Dupnick not to turn over the girls to the consul general for shipment back to El Salvador. He said the government wanted to display their bodies to intimidate others who wanted to leave. Sheriff Dupnick said he had refused Orantes' requests and would continue to do so.

After the lawyers finished talking to the men at the jail, they waited for Flora and Guadalupe, who were transferred from Ajo that evening. Then the same process of interviewing and case-building began all over again. Dupnick had given his liaisons instructions that the Salvadorans should get any help possible. The women asked if they could have clean underwear and a few basic cosmetics. They looked exhausted and frightened, and they were still covered with the marks of their injuries. They got their requests, and a few minutes later the jailhouse cook sent in a huge platter, three feet long and two feet wide, heaped with sandwiches. They were ham and cheese, salami and cheese, and all the crusts had been cut off. In addition, several Sara Lee pound cakes had been sliced and arranged attractively around the edge. And to top it off there were pitchers of Kool-Aid. They had been given the very best the jail had to offer. The lawyers hadn't eaten anything since breakfast. The four women ate the huge platter clean.

At this point the Salvadorans were being held as material witnesses in the trial of the coyotes. The court automatically appoints an attorney for material witnesses, and they picked Rick Gonzales, a bright, young, bilingual Tucson lawyer. Rick immediately tried to get his clients out of jail. Material witnesses are held until trial, or until they pay a bond that guarantees their appearance. But the Salvadorans had no money for a bond, and even if they did get out, they had no place to stay. Rick went to Magistrate Raymond Terlizzi and tried to work out a compromise that took these realities into account.

Magistrate Terlizzi had the reputation of being tough. He

treated everyone alike, and that meant he didn't make excep-
tions. But Rick convinced him that it would not be humane
to keep the Salvadorans in jail until the trial. The magistrate
agreed to a unique arrangement. He decided that they would
not have to post bond, and they could be released, if the
proper custodial families could be found in the local community. This was a novel and creative approach, because
release to custodial families is usually reserved for small
children. The conditions were strict. The families had to
accept responsibility for the care and feeding of the Salvadorans at their own expense; they had to keep them within a
twenty-mile radius of Tucson; they had to promise to get
them to court and to all appointments with their attorneys;
and they had to report to the court instantly if any of them
left their custody.

Then Rick went to the local Spanish-language station,
KXEW-Radio Fiesta, and they broadcast an appeal. The next
day when the Salvadorans and their lawyers walked into
court, the room was already full of people who had come to
offer their homes to these strangers. Most of them were
working-class Mexican-American families without the luxuries
of extra money and space.

But the Salvadorans' problems were not over. As soon as
they were released as material witnesses, federal immigration
law would come into effect. Then they would immediately
have to pay an immigration bond of $2,500 apiece, or go right
back into custody. And that would make their situation even
worse, since there was no federal prison in Tucson and the
Salvadorans would have to be jailed in Phoenix, or they
might even have to go as far as El Centro.

Now Mary Lou, their immigration lawyer, swung into
action. She called Gus Gustafson, district director of Immigration in Phoenix, and convinced him that it would be
heartbreaking to have these people released from one jail
only to have them immediately sent to another. Especially
since it would take them an impossible distance from their
attorneys.

For a start, Gustafson promised not to seize the Salvadorans as long as they remained in Terlizzi's courtroom. Then they began to negotiate over the bond and the conditions of release. Finally the bond was tentatively reduced from $30,000 for the group, to $500 apiece, if all conditions could be met.

The ten refugees had to remain in the sanctuary of the courtroom until the bond could be raised. (Ileana and Berta, the remaining two, were still in the hospital.) Mary Lou immediately contacted a number of human-rights groups that had promised unlimited aid. None of them was able to deliver on the promises. The search went on, the lawyers calling everyone they could think of. The Salvadorans and their new families waited patiently. At one point someone came in to tell Mary Lou that everything was all right, they had the money. A man in the hallway had promised to pay the entire bond. Mary Lou rushed out to meet him, but it was only the reporter from the German magazine, *Der Stern*, who had been following her everywhere for several days. "Look, I'll give you the five thousand dollars if you'll only give me an exclusive interview with one of the women," he promised.

Mary Lou blew up. "I don't sell my clients!" she told him, and stalked off. The hall was full of reporters looking for a story, and the incident was mentioned in all the evening papers.

By late afternoon another solution had been worked out. A Catholic church in Phoenix and Saint Mark's Presbyterian church in Tucson put up their trust fund to make the bond, and Pima County Supervisor David Yetman contributed five hundred dollars of his own. Reverend Paul Sholin, pastor of Saint Mark's, said his congregation decided to put up the collateral because they felt so sympathetic to the Salvadorans. "We consider the mess in El Salvador to be so dangerous," he said, "that anybody who could get out would want to."

At 5:30 P.M. the Salvadorans finally walked out into the fresh air of Tucson. They stepped into gusty winds and a pelting rain on the way to their new homes in America. The U.S. marshals tried to stop reporters from taking pictures. "You want to get someone killed, don't you?" one of them told the photographers. The families scattered, and some of them eluded the press, but others were followed right to their doorsteps.

For the next few months Mary Lou carefully followed the details of the official investigation, since the outcome would ultimately determine whether criminal charges would be filed against her clients. In the state of Arizona the medical examiner is responsible for the investigation of all deaths that occur under unusual circumstances, or when there is no attending physician. The dead Salvadorans fell into both categories. The sheriff's department, as an agent of the medical examiner's office, sent Detectives Miranda and Dufner to Ajo. As the survivors became well enough to talk, the detectives interviewed each of them to establish a detailed chain of events, and to help with the problem of identifying the corpses. They plotted the sequence of the last days on a large map of Organ Pipe Cactus National Monument and constructed an outline of the entire trip.

Although Julio Espinoza was a partner of Jorge Dávila, investigators didn't think he should be held responsible for acts Jorge had committed. Espinoza, it was decided, had done everything possible to get the Salvadorans out of the desert alive. He had forceably taken the cigarette lighter from Pagán to start a signal fire; he had tried to ignite the power pole to bring help; and at several points he had carried others long distances, probably at considerable risk to himself. The Salvadorans felt quite protective of him, and several apparently later denied evidence they had initially given against him.

The investigation concluded that if crimes had been committed, there was no one left to prosecute, since Jorge Dávila was dead. But that was one of their more predictable conclusions. The complete inquiry was long and complex, and some of their findings were quite surprising.

On July 6, at 5:50 A.M., a Customs patrol helicopter had found Emilio's body while searching the pole line. He was only wearing his underpants and his right sock. The rest of his clothing was bunched up underneath him. There was some indication that he had run south for two miles along the service road, which could easily have exhausted him and caused his death. There was no rational explanation for this behavior since it was not along his line of travel, which would have led straight to the highway at half the distance.

Chief Border Patrol Agent Jerry Scott doesn't believe that this was really Emilio's body. He thinks Emilio benefited from the misidentification because it ended the search for him. "I just know he's in Los Angeles somewhere, but I have no way of proving it," Scott said. He points out that Emilio was described as "*fuerte,*" rugged and strong, and could walk much faster than the rest of them. Given his strength and his direction, he couldn't have missed the road if he had kept going. During the trip he repeatedly said that he couldn't allow himself to be sent back, and he was described as a "revolutionary" by some of the others, although it was not clear what they meant. "So when that body remained unclaimed, there was nothing else for his brother to do but to come forward and say, 'This is my brother.' But I don't believe it to this day," Scott asserts. (The sheriff's department's notes disagree, stating that there was a strong resemblance between the "brother" and the corpse, and that the identification was "positive.")

The questions surrounding Don Cruz are just as problematical. During the last week in July, five detectives from the sheriff's department returned to the desert scene for a quadrant search. They systematically crisscrossed the entire area at arm's length from each other, looking for supportive evidence and for Don Cruz' remains. They worked for most of the day. They were properly prepared, with hats, hiking shoes, and water, and still found the operation quite difficult. Their feet were sore when they finished, and their legs were tired, because the ground was too hot to sit on when they needed to rest. All they found were jackrabbit and coyote bones. There was no sign of Don Cruz anywhere.

I asked Paul Thompson, chief of Visitor Protection at the park, if a body could disappear in the desert, from natural causes, so that the search party would not be able to find a trace of it. "There's a possibility," he said, "but it's very low. After a week in the desert, maybe you couldn't see it, but you certainly could smell it. A rotting human body is much more pungent than a dog or a horse, for some reason. And the area out there isn't mountainous or doesn't have deep canyons or heavy vegetation. When you're flying a search pattern you can clearly see a gallon jug lying on the ground, or a man's shirt. That's from a fixed-wing aircraft. In a helicopter you can go much lower. And they grid-searched that area on foot and on horseback as well." Thompson presumed that if Cruz wasn't found, he wasn't there.

But a survey of the survivors indicated complete agreement that he must be there. In their opinion Don Cruz *definitely* died in the desert, although no one actually saw his final moments. Throughout the hike Cruz was very weak. The others felt that he would be the first to die. They didn't think there was any way he could have escaped in his condition.

And there are other details to consider. On July 5 a man staggered out of the desert at the park headquarters, the only place to get water in that season. He was described as being an older man, in terrible shape. He drank a lot and filled the plastic jug he carried with him. Then he wandered across the road and back into the desert. It was an extremely bad direction to go. He walked out a short distance and then sat down. A ranger who talked with him briefly didn't know if he kept going into the desert or changed course. No one knows who he was or what became of him.

Also on July 5, the border patrol received a radio call that there was a man down at the highway sign eight miles from the Mexican border. He was lying in the road, covered with dust. The caller thought he might be dead. The park rangers, who monitor the same frequency as the border patrol, got there within five minutes. He was already gone. Apparently someone had picked him up. There is no further information about him, and it is not known if he was the same man who was seen earlier at park headquarters, only a few miles away.

According to unofficial information from a government agency, Don Cruz' wife was greatly troubled by the mystery surrounding her husband's death and the disappearance of his body. She decided to hire a private detective to clarify the situation. He searched the Latin neighborhoods of Los

Angeles and found a man he thought was Don Cruz. The man was living with Ana, the woman who left the desert with Josefa in the middle of the night. Ironically, Ana was reported to be a cousin of Jorge Dávila.

Next the private detective took a Los Angeles relative of Cruz with him, who supposedly identified the man. But the man insisted he was not Don Cruz, and walked away. None of this behavior fits with Don Cruz' previous history of religiosity and devotion to his family. Don Cruz' wife couldn't believe that he wouldn't have contacted her if he were all right. She feels he must have developed amnesia from his experience in the desert.

A year later, Flora says a priest called a friend of hers in Tucson to say that Don Cruz was definitely alive. No one knows who the priest was, and it is not possible to verify the story. When the survivors were asked about these reports, they felt it would be miraculous if Don Cruz had escaped the desert.

La Gorda's blue overnight bag, which had been taken by Josefa and Ana when they left the women's group, was found along Highway 85, directly to the east. Apparently they were quite capable of negotiating the desert, despite Espinoza's warning that it was not safe for them to go off alone in the dark. The next sign of the women was to the south, at the Mexican border. The manager of the Gringo Pass Motel in Lukeville later identified Josefa and Ana from photographs as the two women who booked a room for two nights with an unidentified man. The man was described as "older," but it was not known if he was Don Cruz, and may have been another, little-known man who was traveling with them.

On the third day, while an intensive search was being mounted for anyone connected with the group, the three fugitives hired the manager to drive them to Gila Bend, where they caught a bus to Los Angeles. The manager later said that Josefa had asked several times whether there had been calls or visitors for her, so the motel may have been a backup meeting place in case of trouble. Most of the permanent residents of Lukeville are government officials who work in the area. There were border-patrol officers sleeping a few hundred yards from the Salvadorans while the massive search went on. They were later reprimanded for not looking in the motel.

The last, and in some ways the most difficult, phase of the investigation took place under the coroner's direct supervision. That was the attempt to identify all the bodies, so they could be returned to the proper relatives, and to determine the causes of death, to decide what crimes had been committed. All the bodies were fingerprinted in the morgue, a process that had to be repeated as many as five times because of the degree of decomposition. In an attempt to preserve the bodies during their transportation to the morgue, they had been shifted to a refrigerator truck borrowed from the Air National Guard, which was usually used to move their produce. Unfortunately the temperature setting was not reliable and the cooling system went much too low. All the tissues were frozen, which further hampered the medical examiner's investigation.

Dr. Walter Birkby of the University of Arizona, a specialist in human identification, was called in to make dental charts of the victims. This was a safety measure. Everyone knew it would be difficult to get reliable dental histories from El Salvador, but these indicators might have turned out to be critical, and then it would have been too late. This phase of the investigation was quite successful. Twelve of the victims were positively identified. However, the thirteenth, Paleface, is still known only by his nicknames, and by his first name, which was Carlos.

One of the newspapers reported that the bodies were too badly decomposed to determine from autopsy whether the women had been raped or strangled. Dr. Joseph Halka, chief medical examiner, emphatically denied this. The evidence is definite, he said, that no one had been raped or strangled.

His conclusion was based on a number of positive and negative indicators. There was no sign of sperm, or seminal fluid, in any of the women. There was an absence of hemorrhaging and soft-tissue damage. The hyoid bone, a delicate Y-shaped structure at the base of the tongue, which would have been crushed during strangulation, was intact.

Some of those supposedly raped were wearing panties when found. There were at least five separate signs he relied on, and if decomposition sometimes obscured some of them, there were always enough left to provide a clear indicator, he said.

He doesn't rule out that strangulation and rape might have been attempted. The medical examiner explains that as the victims became weaker and less able to defend themselves, Jorge would have also become less able to carry through his attack. Even so, Dr. Halka's conclusions seem to contradict the eyewitness reports of the women who survived Jorge in the desert. To an outside observer, it would seem that with severe stress and dehydration affecting the women's judgment, and decomposition and freezing affecting the coroner's work, it may be impossible to ever feel certain about what happened during those last few hours.

The coyotes' trial was heavily attended. People packed the courthouse to hear dramatic descriptions of what had taken place in the desert. But that did not occur, for no one was prosecuted for the deaths of the thirteen, or charged with negligence or abandonment. What happened in the desert was not at issue. The charges concerned the smuggling of illegal immigrants, and once they had crossed the border into the United States, the crime had been committed.

The Salvadorans hugged and kissed one another when they were reunited in the courtroom. Julio Espinoza and Felipe Vidal were not tried. They pleaded guilty and were both sentenced to five years in federal prison. Esteban Alvarado, the twenty-two-year-old who had escaped capture on the first trip and gone off with the women and children on the second one, claimed to be innocent. He said he had not known Jorge Dávila before April of that year. He insisted he had only done minor errands to help pay for his passage, and because he was afraid of Jorge.

All the refugees were material witnesses and all of them testified. Several said they believed Esteban Alvarado was an agent or helper in the travel agency, but it was probably Ileana's testimony that was the most damaging. At critical points in the prosecution's chain of evidence, Ileana had seen significant events. For instance, it was Ileana who said she had seen Esteban Alvarado take instructions from Dávila in Ejido, then hitchhike away, to return later with the Mexican coyotes.

Alvarado's defense was that Ileana's testimony could not be believed because Ileana was vengeful toward him. She had been in love with him, he claimed, had pursued him sexually and emotionally throughout the trip, and had even kissed him against his will.

The prosecutor said he had difficulty accepting this picture of Ileana as a frustrated sex-bomb, but then he wasn't as handsome, as virile, and as attractive as the defendant. He was actually a very distinguished-looking and well-tailored man, and the courtroom had a laugh at the expense of the tattered Esteban Alvarado. A jury of seven women and nine men deliberated only ninety minutes before finding him guilty. He was sentenced to five years for smuggling aliens, and two more for conspiracy, in federal prison.

Following the massive publicity surrounding the refugees, Mexican and Salvadoran police began a crackdown on the gang known as the Dolls. In San Luis, in the middle of July, the federal judicial police commander announced that authorities had seized Silvano Rodríguez Macias, twenty-three, on charges of illegal transportation. Rodríguez Macias was thought to be the one responsible for planning the Salvadorans' disastrous border crossing from Mexico, although he did not accompany them. Mexican police said they were searching for two co-conspirators in the case, two brothers who were cousins of the man in custody.

But only a month before, three Mexican government officials had been released from Nogales prison, where they had been held for over a year on related charges. The three, Manuel Quiroz, Carlos Ornelos, and Gustavo Arevelo, were returned to the San Luis area. Quiroz was then reinstated to his job as Immigration inspector in San Luis. The Mexican appeals judge had ruled that there was insufficient evidence to hold them. His decision to dismiss the charges was made despite the fact that all three had confessed, and approximately twenty witnesses, including two United States border-patrol agents, had testified against them.

Two former members of the Dolls had testified that they regularly paid off Mexican Immigration officials during their smuggling careers to avoid arrest. Smugglers' bribes sometimes amounted to as much as two thousand dollars per day, they said. One former gang member, who is now living in Redwood City, California, said he paid Quiroz $250 per load for over five years. He said it was common knowledge that if the official was not paid, the smuggler would be taken to San Luis jail. The acting chief of the Yuma border-patrol district said that Quiroz' reinstatement was of great concern to the agency.

The current legal status of the Salvadorans is like limbo. They are permitted to remain in the United States until they either choose to leave or their immigration cases are settled. They can travel anywhere they wish, but the minute they cross the United States border their cases will be terminated. They would be considered to have voluntarily deported themselves and would not be allowed to return. Visits to their families in El Salvador are therefore out of the question. They have all applied for political asylum, but their cases are at different stages. Mary Lou Harris currently represents two of them in immigration matters, including Francisco. The others now have their own attorneys. Francisco is awaiting the reconvening of his hearing by the immigration judge. At that time his application for asylum will be discussed, testified to, challenged by the government, defended by Mary Lou, and the judge will make a decision.

It is apparently for political reasons that the Salvadorans have been stuck in the middle for quite some time. If U.S. officials were to order them sent back to El Salvador, it would risk antagonizing the many people sympathetic to their situation. It would also bring to public debate the question of whether the government of El Salvador was harsh and repressive to a degree that justified the search for asylum. But to grant the request for asylum would be a slap in the face of the Salvadoran government at a time when the United States is supporting their political and military programs. At this point only twenty-six out of 12,000 Salvadoran asylum requests have been granted.

The bodies of the Lugo sisters were not handed over to the Salvadoran government. Eventually, through the persistence of their uncle, a number of bureaucratic problems were resolved and they were shipped back to be buried near Los Angeles, finally in their mother's care once again. Most of the remaining bodies were also sent to relatives. Only three were left. The Salvadoran family of Señor Pagán and his wife could not afford to have their bodies returned. And the young man known as Paleface was never claimed. Reverend Glen Jenks of the Chapel of the Resurrection agreed to perform the funeral. A local funeral home offered free burial for the trio.

About six weeks later Reverend Jenks received a telephone call from an Episcopal priest in El Salvador. He said that one of the bodies shipped home, supposedly the remains of a woman, appeared to be a man, when they opened the casket. They suspected it was Señor Pagán, who should have been buried in Tucson. The family asked for an investigation. Pagán's grave in Tucson was opened and found to contain the body of the woman who should have been sent to El Salvador. As the family representative, Reverend Jenks contacted Sheriff Dupnick and asked for a detailed accounting of how the bodies had been handled from discovery to burial. There was a suspicion that the Salvadoran government might have been involved, but the funeral home subsequently accepted the responsibility for the mix-up. There had been a large number of badly damaged bodies, and apparently there had been a simple switch of tags at some point.

Since Pagán was already in El Salvador, the funeral home accepted the expense of sending his wife back to be buried with him. (It was only after her death that her traveling companions learned her name was María Concepción.) That left Paleface unidentified and buried alone in Tucson.

Luisa's condition was finally resolved by autopsy. She was found to have been approximately three months pregnant at the time she died, and carrying a male fetus. That information was relayed to her fiancé.

A visit to Sonoita, Mexico, to find out what happened to Felipe Vidal's son, the young guide, revealed that he was back in the area. A man in a bar agreed to talk about the family as long as he was not identified. It was always possible that the Dolls might decide to take revenge on him. He said that when the son returned alone, the townspeople thought he was a lazy good-for-nothing who had run off and left his father in the desert. Old Felipe used to run their pool hall. He was thought to be quite honest (definitely not a professional coyote), and local people were surprised when they heard he had committed a crime and was going to jail. He had a large, poor family and that was probably why he took the job, the young man thought. Felipe writes home regularly from prison. He says he is taking part in a work project that will help him win an early release.

The young man said that smuggling has been a business in Sonoita for generations. Years before, large numbers of Chinese settlers passed through on their way to the United States. They landed on the Mexican coast from boats and hired guides to take them north. He said that near Mexicali there is an area called Los Chinos (The Chinese), because a group of people that had tried to cross there in the summer had all died. But it isn't really necessary to have a guide, or to take long trips through the desert, like the Salvadorans did. He said if you went to the border station and then walked to the right or left, you could quickly find holes in the fence that were used by the local people. A quick check showed he was right. At the official crossing point on the highway at Lukeville there is an impressive ten-foot cyclone fence topped with barbed wire. But if you go a quarter of a mile in either direction, it shrinks to a simple three strands, like a pasture fence. Only a cow would be stopped by it.

6
LIFE IN AMERICA

After all that the Salvadorans endured, it is natural to wonder what kind of lives their suffering gained for them in the United States.

Berta has had passing contact with several of the women who disappeared. According to her, Josefa now lives in New York. And she once bumped into Ana, who was cleaning tables in a Chinese restaurant in Los Angeles. Nothing more has been heard of Don Cruz.

After a week and a half of intensive care in Ajo, Ileana and Berta were transferred to Tucson, where they were re-hospitalized at Kino Community Hospital.

Recently Ileana has worked double shifts as a nurses' aide and lives with her family in the Los Angeles area. Her strength has returned and she seems recovered from her ordeal in the desert, but she still cries and trembles when she speaks of it.

Berta is living with her family in the same area. She works as a short-order cook in a mobile lunch wagon and has marks up and down her forearms where she has burned herself on the stove in her cramped space. But she likes her job. She has always had a deep appreciation for snack foods and can now put her talents to use. And she is a warmhearted person who genuinely enjoys feeding others. She is also proud of her skill as a cook and of her mastery of English short-order slang.

Robles has been less fortunate. When he was finally re-united with the woman he had lived with in El Salvador, it didn't work out. At one point he fell off a friend's motorcycle and broke his leg. He had no health insurance. About a year ago Mary Lou received a call from a social worker in Los

Angeles saying that his situation was desperate. He couldn't find work, and because he had no status in this country beyond that of awaiting trial, he fell through every bureaucratic crack and couldn't qualify for any kind of aid. He was literally living on the street and close to starving. The court-appointed family he had originally lived with would have taken him back, but he was too proud to ask for help. He finally found work washing cars for $130 a week. Then he got a job parking cars, which paid a little more. His standard of living is considerably lower than it was in El Salvador, but he still likes it better here. He follows the news and knows how dangerous life there is. He hopes that someday he will be able to buy a house and open a business. He says he doesn't care what kind; he just wants to make a living. He's quieter than he was, but he certainly hasn't lost his old sense of excitement. He still likes to tease, and has a look of lurking mischief.

Ricardo, his nephew, lives with family in Los Angeles also. He works as an auto mechanic at a low wage, but seems content.

Guadalupe is a live-in housekeeper, with a family she likes, in northern California. For a long time she had nightmares of watching her niece, Felícita, die in the desert, but lately she sleeps better. She still cries when she talks about it.

Roberto is living with family in Los Angeles, working as a dishwasher, and looks well.

Francisco found life quite difficult for many months because he couldn't get a job. Eventually he was hired for factory work at minimum wage. He is forming sheet metal, manufacturing the casings for computers. Recently his pay was increased to four dollars an hour. He has a good boss. He bought a car and started going to night school to learn English. But the automobile, which much of the world considers the sign of being a real American, has been a treacherous ally. His first car, a Falcon he bought for two hundred dollars, never ran right and drained him financially. The second, a '76 Datsun, was stolen right out of his front yard. The insurance company has refused to settle for the value of the car, so Francisco is still making monthly payments on the stolen vehicle. He is also paying off a '71 AMC Hornet station wagon, which he now drives. Exhausted by debts and maintenance needs, he dropped out of school. Now he putters around the house on the weekend, resting up so he can return to work on Monday.

He misses his mother and thinks of her often. He wishes she could join him, but she won't leave El Salvador. An elderly couple, a great-aunt and -uncle, are in her care. She refuses to go and leave them helpless.

Francisco seems lonely and disappointed. He had come here with a vivid picture in his imagination of the United States as "a beautiful place with many lights and much happiness." But at close range it looks sad to him. He's used to the life in El Salvador, where most people don't have cars. Back there the nights are warm and balmy, and in the evenings the streets are full of friendly people. Or at least they were before the fighting began. Everyone used to stroll through their neighborhoods, visiting their friends. Vendors with lanterns would sell fruit and snacks along the curb, and it was the time neighbors took to invite one another for a soda or a beer. It was his vision of paradise, and naturally he expected to find it reborn in the United States even bigger and better. But here he sees his neighbors are all in their cars. They enjoy themselves alone, or in couples. He is shy and talks with few people. He has lost the sense of belonging that he needs.

Raúl has also had trouble, but he is beginning to find his way. He moved to New York City first, but New York had a record cold spell. He had never experienced anything like it and found it unbearable. He returned to Tucson. For his entire time in this country he has not been able to find regular work. The government has not ruled on his case in over two years, but Immigration has refused to give him a work permit. He cannot get a social-security number and many employers feel, mistakenly, that they would be taking a legal risk if they hired him. So he has subsisted on help from friends and occasionally cleaning out yards. Recently he found temporary work loading a truck.

He misses his family and has had terrible news from home. Two of his cousins have been killed, and when his only

brother answered a knock at his door in the middle of the
night, someone blew his face off. But so far his parents and
his sisters are at least surviving. Raúl would not dream of
going back there voluntarily.

Aside from politics, however, he feels that life here for
ordinary people is harder than in El Salvador. At home at
least there is always some food in the fields. If one had no
work, one would not starve; one could always survive by
eating off the land. One is more likely to go without food in
America, he has found.

But there are wonderful things in his life as well. He still
has his feeling for God. He enjoys the freedom from fear.
And he has met a woman. He says he never believed he would
find someone in America he could love so much. They live
together and hope to get married, but she feels hesitant,
because of his situation and her past experience. She was
married before and found the divorce terribly painful. She
doesn't want to make another mistake. Just the same, they
seem committed to each other, and if he could only find
regular work, it would probably be enough to make them
feel they could go ahead. His parents have written that they
accept his choice, that they know he is mature enough to find
the right woman for him. He is close to his parents and was
relieved to hear that they feel open to his new family. Raúl
also sketches and paints beautifully. If he has the chance, he
will go to the University of Arizona to study art. He says he
has a lot of ambition, and if he is only allowed to, he will
make something of himself.

Miguel, as the only juvenile, was split off from the group
early in the legal proceedings. He has been politically active
in Salvadoran causes.

Antonio still puts his family ahead of everything else and
lives happily with them in San Francisco. He now has three
beautiful dark-eyed children: Enrique Juan, nine; Rafael,
three; and Luz María, named after his wife, three months. He
still works as an auto mechanic.

For many months Pablo was a night janitor at a McDonald's
in Tucson. Now he is the maintenance man for a chain of
exclusive beauty salons. He feels it is a good job for the

present, but he hopes for more from life. Still, he looks good. When he sits in his favorite chair at home you notice his bright, gold-rimmed teeth, his curly black hair and thick dark mustache, his round but muscular body, and he seems solid and relaxed. His one-room cottage is tiny. Every few minutes the jets taking off from the adjacent military airport obliterate all conversation. But the place is clearly home. A photo of his four children hangs on the wall, draped with a rosary. He has an old guitar, which he complains about, but when he sings, his voice is still clear and full of emotion. And there is a fish tank in the corner near the TV. The gentle bubbling of the aerator is a constant reassurance that water is nearby.

He lives with a young woman, a daughter of one of the families that took in the Salvadorans. "The way I see it, I'm here because God put me in his path, to help him," she said. "Before I even met him, I would have dreams. It runs in the family. I dreamed I would meet a man who looks like him, dressed in black with a guitar. And when I was thirteen I had my fortune told. My grandmother said I was going to meet a man from another country who was married. It's really worked out well for us. He's happy now. He tells me, 'You're the reason I want to keep on living.' "

Pablo says that since the trip, all the survivors are different. He feels that he's completely changed. He was never so sentimental. He used to be much more macho, but now if he watches anything sad on TV, he starts crying. Or if something reminds him of his children. When he gets nervous and cries, his woman friend tells him, "You can't keep thinking about those things. You have to look ahead. What happened has happened. I know it's sad, but you have to keep on living."

When asked what he thinks about the United States after two years, he says it's still premature to say whether he likes it better here or there. "One thing might be better here, another there. Actually I never imagined what I would run into, how hard it is to live here in some ways. I just decided, well, I'm going to go. I was fired after fifteen years with the same company, so I decided, it's time for a change, I'm going to take this as an adventure." He had heard people speak of how great it is here. "That's all people ever say when they talk about the United States. Like it's a bowl of cherries. But in some ways it's really the same as there. There you make a colon, and you have to spend a colon. Here you earn a dollar and spend a dollar. It comes out the same."

Since the desert, Pablo says he feels rededicated to God. Just when he had given up, when he lost hope and thought God had abandoned him, it was his own toothpaste-covered face that the Migra saw when they came and rescued them. It was almost dark. If they hadn't seen him, they might have gone on. By the time they were found everyone could have died. Pablo took it as a sign. That was one reason why he was crying when they came up to him.

And last of all, Flora still has a cheerful, energetic approach to her life, even though she has had to deal with some great disappointments. After she was released from the hospital, she went to jail for a night and then to the home of a very kind local family. She had originally planned to live at her uncle's house in Los Angeles, and after the trial she went there. But life was difficult. The city seemed enormous, and where they lived there were a lot of gangs and violence. The situation didn't mix well with her memories of El Salvador and the desert. Only a few weeks earlier she had been staying up nights with her mother, praying, because there was such terrible killing in the streets that they didn't know if they would be alive by morning. She couldn't stand L.A., so she moved back to the quiet of Tucson. She got a job at McDonald's, cooking pancakes and Big Macs. She could have continued to live with her Tucson family, but she wanted a place where her father could stay, if she found him. She rented a trailer in a trailer park across from Pablo and his cottage. Then she started her search.

It was one of her relatives in Los Angeles who first located her father. He gave Flora his telephone number and Flora called him. It had been five years since they had had any contact and he cried when he heard her voice. He said he couldn't believe all that had happened to her. He thanked God she was all right and told her he was coming to Tucson to take care of her. He wanted to make his life with her and share so many things. Flora was delighted. The reunion would heal the split in her family after so many years. She fixed up the trailer for him and waited. But more than a month passed and she didn't hear a word.

When she called her family in Los Angeles, they asked, "Isn't he there yet?" They checked and found out that he had gone to Phoenix instead of Tucson. She went to Phoenix to look for him. The first time she went, her adopted family drove her there and helped her search. Her relatives said that her father had become an alcoholic, so she walked through the worst slums of the Latin districts asking all the drunks if they knew him. "Oh, sure," they replied, but they didn't know where he was at the moment. The second time she went alone, on the bus. The lonely search revealed nothing. The third time she found him and brought him back to Tucson to stay with her.

It was very bad. They had both changed a great deal. They didn't share the same closeness she had hoped for all those years. And he drank constantly. She would work all day and come home to find him drunk. Finally he left and returned to Phoenix. There was a woman there he wanted to be with. Now they no longer talk, they don't visit, and they don't write. That dream has died.

But other dreams go on. Flora has a better job, sewing in a clothing factory. She gave up the trailer and got a small apartment. She has been going to Pima College in the evenings for a number of semesters, studying English at first and then typing and shorthand. She wants to be a bilingual secretary. She likes school, with its exposure to new people and new ideas. And on March 20, 1982, she married the young man she had loved for years. He seems just as warm and good-natured as she is. He's studying to be an agricultural engineer.

Last Christmas Flora sent cards to everyone at the Ajo border-patrol station, to Father Maurice, and to the hospital personnel. When I last spoke with her, she said, "If you write something about us, please tell all the people who have sent letters and cared what happened to us that we thank them very much. . . ."

Flora is happy again. Her nightmares have stopped (except around the anniversary of their time in the desert). And she recalls much of the trip in a very positive way. "We were always laughing and singing on the bus," she says. "We were happy about coming to America." She particularly remembers the last night before they started walking, when most of the women slept together on the bed of the old truck behind the restaurant in Sonoita. They were all wedged in together, sharing their warmth (Pagán, tucked into a corner with his wife, silent and comfortably forgotten), looking up at the night sky and wondering about their lives. It was a beautiful moment with a great feeling of closeness, and nothing that happened afterward has destroyed that part of the past for her. Or her faith in the future.